Sweet

POSSESSION

Cover design by:
Hang Le

Interior design and formatting by:
Christine Borgford, Type A Formatting
www.typeAformatting.com

Sweet POSSESSION

NEW YORK TIMES BESTSELLING AUTHOR
J. DANIELS

To my readers,

for all the love you have shown me.

This is for you.

Chapter
ONE

WHY DO PEOPLE EVEN BOTHER with weddings? I know, that sounds insane coming from a person who makes a living off creating decadent wedding cakes for the happy couples. The crazy-in-love future Mr. and Mrs. are what keeps Dylan's Sweet Tooth afloat, and without weddings, I wouldn't be able to afford my rent. Not to mention the fact that if it weren't for dumbass ex-boyfriend weddings, there's a chance I would've never have met Reese and I honestly can't imagine not having him in my life. But in my defense, I've never had to sit and listen to hours of debating whether cotton-blend or silk napkins are the best choice for my big day.

Until now.

Joey lets out an irritated sigh and gestures toward the direction of my mother and soon-to-be mother-in-law who are loudly arguing at my consultation table. "This shit makes me want to drink at 9:00 a.m. How many times have I suggested to you that we keep hard liquor in the back? We could totally make a drinking game out of this mess."

I tilt my head up to meet his eyes. "What, and take a shot every time one of them utters the phrase, 'this will be the wedding I've always dreamed of'? We'd be tanked before the lunch rush."

He nods, smiling over his coffee cup. "Exactly, and we'd be completely oblivious to this annoying discussion that you couldn't care less about anyway."

Joey's right. I really didn't care what type of fabric the napkins were; I really didn't care about much of anything. I've pretty much left everything in the hands of my trusted best friend who could plan a wedding wearing a blindfold. I only had a few stipulations: the cake and my dress. That's it. Napkins? Who the fuck cares about napkins?

He slides closer to me, dropping his voice to a hushed whisper although, with the noise level currently booming through the bakery, I'll definitely be the only one hearing him. "I knew your mother was a little nutty when it came to marrying you off, planning this shit since you were nineteen and all, but Reese's mother is bat-shit crazy. Did you hear her say she wanted to come out with us for your bachelorette party? Can you imagine?"

I shrug once before leaning against the counter. "I don't even know what I want to do for that. Maybe we'll just have like a spa day or something and if that's the case, who cares if she tags along?"

His mouth drops open, letting escape a loud, dramatic gasp. "Um, no. We will be going to a strip club if I have to throw you over my shoulder and pull a Reese on you myself. That's what you do for bachelorette parties. Why the hell do my two best friends not know that?"

"Excuse you. Juls' bachelorette party didn't involve any naked men, and we still had a great time. Who says we have to go to a strip club?"

"I do," he says through a tense jaw. "The only reason I let that shit slide for Juls was because I was in charge of babysitting her dumbass sister, and I knew I'd be distracted if I had a bunch of dicks in my face."

I arch my brow at him. "Isn't that a typical Saturday night for you?" We both chuckle together, and my attention is suddenly drawn to my mother who is throwing napkins into the air.

"Dylan, sweetheart, silk or cotton-blend?" she asks, tapping her foot on the hard tile.

I flick my gaze between the two mothers who are both silently pleading with me to pick their choice. If I had to guess, I'd say my mother wants the silk, but Maggie Carroll is giving off a bit of a fancy vibe right now. She's head to toe in designer clothing, which is screaming silk at the moment. *Shit. I really don't care one way or the other, but who the hell do I side with on this one?* I grimace and nervously tap on the glass display case. "Um, does it matter? They're napkins. People are going to be wiping their mouths with them."

"It matters a great deal," Maggie says, picking up two napkin swatches and carrying them over to me. "The silk is much more sophisticated. And given the location you've chosen for the reception, I think that's the one you should go for."

"But the cotton blend comes in this antique-white color that would go beautifully with the pale-gray bridesmaids dresses," my mother adds, joining Maggie's side.

Jesus. Since when does it matter if the napkins match the bridesmaid dresses?

I look back and forth between the two of them before turning toward Joey. "Thoughts?"

"Nope. I'm afraid you're on your own there, cupcake." He backs away and sips his coffee, leaving me alone in my misery.

I reach out and feel both choices between my fingers. "Um, well, I guess the cotton is most likely cheaper? So, why don't we go with that?"

Maggie gently lays her hand on top of mine. "Oh, sweetie, money is not an issue. If you want the silk napkins…"

"She just said she wants the cotton blend," my mother states with a firm tone. "Which I agree with, sweetheart. Beautiful choice."

"But, Helen, the silk would be so much more… elegant."

I drop my forehead to my hands and groan my irritation while the two of them continue to hash it out. *Who cares about napkins!* Am I completely crazy for not giving a shit about this tiny, insignificant detail? The guests could wipe their mouths on their coat sleeves for all I care.

This is how it's been for the past six months. Ever since Reese and I got engaged, our mothers have been in a battle of who can plan the better wedding, and poor Juls and I have been stuck in the middle, trying to rein in the madness. They've been so crazy about this whole thing, I've found myself contemplating the benefits of a Vegas wedding. Unfortunately, my soon-to-be husband is dead-set on marrying me in front of all our families and is having no part of that discussion. Every time I suggest he steal me away for a quickie wedding, he just shuts me up with his mouth, or his cock. And because I'm weak with lust around that man, and given the fact my head is sure to explode soon from all this momma drama, I bring it up. Often.

The front door chimes and I look up, smiling as my best friend strolls into the bakery. She takes one look at the mothers waving napkin swatches into the air and immediately goes into wedding-planner mode.

"Ohhhh, no. There will not be any changes made. Give me those." She snatches the napkin samples from the two mothers who both stare at her with shocked expressions. This is the Juls I know and love, the one who knows how to run shit. "This wedding is happening in ten days, and all decisions are final. And really, the napkin issue? Again?" She motions toward me with a crumpled-up napkin in her hand. "The bride-to-be doesn't care about the napkins. In fact, you two are the only people I know who have *ever* cared about the napkins. And I've planned over one hundred weddings. For the love of God, let it go."

My mother crosses her arms over her chest and sneers at Juls. "You know what, Julianna? One of these days, when you're planning *your* daughter's wedding, you'll care about the napkins."

"I seriously doubt that. Besides, I'm planning on having all boys."

Maggie and my mother grab their purses off the consultation table while Juls smiles in her minor victory over the two of them. The moms both walk around the counter and smother me with affection.

"We're going to go swing by the venue to take another look around," Maggie says as she releases me from a hug. "Now, don't forget to let me know about the bachelorette party. I'm all in."

"Ha!" Joey yells from the kitchen.

I smile and clear my throat loudly, hoping to cover up the end of my dear assistant's crack-up. "Tell Mr. Carroll I said hello."

My mother kisses my cheek and smiles. "I'm sure the napkins you originally picked out will suffice."

"Mom," I say in a warning tone. "There's still a chance I'll convince Reese to cancel this whole thing and get hitched in Vegas." Her eyes widen, along with Maggie's who swivels in place to gawk at me. "Don't push it."

"That's not even funny," she retorts, swatting at me with her clutch.

Once the two wedding-obsessed mothers exit the shop, Juls lets out an 'I'm glad I'm not in your shoes' chuckle and Joey reemerges from the back. I slouch back against the counter top, feeling a Vegas wedding now more than ever. "I cannot wait until all this is over with. How I've managed to survive the last six months without being heavily-medicated or drunk off my ass twenty-four hours a day is beyond me."

"Reese's mother, though she has impeccable fashion sense, is out of her mind. I am not having a fucking chaperone at your bachelorette party," Joey states with a shake of his head. Apparently, keeping my future mother in-law away from whatever I decide to do for my last night of freedom is his only concern.

Juls tosses the napkin swatches into the trashcan, which will hopefully be the last time I ever lay eyes on them. She returns to her spot on the other side of the display case. "Speaking of which, what are we doing for that, anyway? You wanna go to Clancy's like we did for mine? That was fun."

Joey slams his hand down on the counter, gaining our attention immediately. "For fuck's sake. What the hell is wrong with you two? Spa days? Clubs that have been played out? I wanna do things that I'll be ashamed to tell people about. Let me live, damn it."

"I'm sorry, but is this *your* bachelorette party? Did Billy pop the question and you've decided to keep that information from us?" Juls asks, biting back her smile. It cracks through and she winks at Joey whose mood has suddenly waned, no doubt in response to the reminder that he isn't engaged yet.

He shrugs dismissively. "Whatever. You bitches can celebrate with watered-down drinks and facials. Just don't be surprised if I bail on it."

I slide closer to him and wrap my arms around his waist, pressing my face into his shirt. Tilting my head up, I see him smiling down at me. "I'll choose something fun. You have to be there; it wouldn't be the same without you."

"She's right." Juls rounds the counter and mimics my position against Joey's back. "We'd miss you terribly, JoJo."

He grunts above us. "You're lucky I'd do anything for either one of you." Juls and I both unlock our death grips from him and stand side by side. "But I swear to Christ, there better at least be a cake shaped like a penis at this thing."

"Chocolate or vanilla?" I ask teasingly.

He smiles, bending down and removing a half-empty tray of pastries from the display case. "Chocolate. I've never had black dick."

Juls and I both chuckle as he walks toward the kitchen, giving us a scandalous eyebrow raise over his shoulder.

"So, I have a favor to ask you." Juls pulls me into the far corner behind the bakery counter, clearly wanting to put distance between this favor and Joey. *Oh, Lord.* My best friend doesn't ask me for many favors but when she does, they're usually whoppers. A certain wedding dress she made me try on months ago comes to mind. I motion for her to spill it, and she eyes me up nervously. "Umm… so, Brooke got fired from her job at that bank. Apparently, she was caught blowing one of the other tellers during work hours."

"Good Lord." That sounds about right, though. Brooke Wicks was in the running for horniest bitch in Chicago, competing solely with Joey.

"Yeah, she *needs* a job and fast; otherwise, she'll lose her apartment." My eyes widen, the realization of her favor hitting me. "And since you're so busy at the shop…"

"No fucking way."

She fists both hands at her side. "Oh, come on, Dyl. She's having trouble finding something, and she's been looking for over a month." Her face softens and she reaches out to me, pulling my hand into hers. "Please? If she loses her apartment, she has to move in with Ian and me. And that shit can't happen. I love my sister, but I can't live with her."

"What about moving back in with your parents?"

"Not an option. She and my mom would kill each other." She pauses and squeezes my hand gently. "I really want to help her out."

Damn it. This has bad news written all over it, but I have trouble saying no to Juls. She's always been there for me. Always. I groan and her eyes light up. "Fine. She can start Monday. But don't think I won't fire her just because she's your sister." She pulls me into a hug with an excited squeal. I cringe as Joey strolls through the doorway, coming from the kitchen. He grins, adorably oblivious to the information that will surely send him into a shit-fit. "I should really make you drop this bomb on him," I mumble under my breath.

"Oh, relax. It's not that big of a deal."

"Yeah, okay. We'll see about that."

We both release each other and Juls spins on her heels, walking over toward Joey and placing her hand on his shoulder. "Don't freak out."

His eyes widen with a curious fear. "If I don't get my penis cake, I'll disown both of you. Nobody comes between me and my dick-shaped sweets."

I walk up to him and brace myself for the reaction that is sure to blow the roof off this building. "Joey. JoJo. Bestest friend." He rolls his eyes as I play with the string on my apron, wrapping it around my finger. "You know how busy we've been lately with custom orders and all the spring weddings coming up? It's getting pretty crazy in here, and I think maybe it's time I hired another employee."

"That's fantastic." His body relaxes and he glances between Juls and myself. His brows set into a hard line. "Why the hell do I have a feeling I'm about to regret those words?"

"Just remember how much you love us," Juls says. "And this… addition will allow you and Dylan to spend more time together. The benefits are sure to outweigh any concern you might have."

I pause, waiting to see if he'll pick up on the clues that are obvious to me. It only takes him a few seconds; the reaction spreads through him like a wild fire.

He squeezes his eyes closed tightly, reaching up and rubbing his temples with his fingers. "Please tell me this addition is a blind monkey, because they would surely get more accomplished than who I fear you're about to say."

"Brooke could be a good addition, Joey," I state with a mild assurance.

"Are you insane? Why the fuck would you hire that mess?"

Juls shoves his arm. "Hey! She's my sister, and she's been through a lot."

"A lot of what? Dick? Dylan, this is not a good idea."

I limply shrug. I'm not at all surprised he's reacting this way; in fact, I predicted it. But, unlike Joey, I'm willing to give Brooke the benefit of the doubt. And as long as she doesn't try to molest him like the day before Juls' wedding, things shouldn't get too hostile. I gotta give the girl a chance. "She needs a job or she'll lose her apartment."

He throws his hands into the air. "Oh, I'm sorry. How is that *our* problem?"

"Joey," Juls scolds. "Don't be so rude."

"She's on a probationary period. If she messes up, I'll fire her without thinking twice about it. Right, Juls?"

She nods in my direction before turning back toward my heated assistant. "Right. So, calm the fuck down, JoJo." She makes a face at him and he issues her his smile, softening her expression. "And a lot of dick? Like you're one to talk."

The three of us start laughing, letting go of the stress of knowing Brooke Wicks will soon be gracing us with her presence. This could actually be a good thing. We are extremely busy, and having another employee means being able to spend more time in my kitchen instead of ringing up customers. So, I'm not going to let this worry me; I have enough stress with my upcoming wedding to last me a lifetime.

Juls gives us both hugs before she exits the shop to go tackle a bride. Just as a customer slips inside and makes her way up to the counter, my phone beeps in my pocket. Joey gives me a smile, indicating he's got things handled and allows me to slip into the back.

REESE: *What are you wearing?*

I giggle as I hop onto a stool.

ME: *Are you spanking it right now, handsome?*

REESE: *That depends on your answer.*

I'm definitely not wearing anything worthy of a wank session. My ripped skinny jeans and flour-covered apron have seen better days, so I let my imagination take over.

ME: *A skin-tight, pale-pink dress that stops just below my panty line. Or, it would, if I was wearing panties.*

REESE: *You are such a tease. Do you have any idea how hard my dick is for you right now? I could probably fuck you through a wall.*

Jesus.

ME: *It's a shame you'll have to handle that situation on your own. I'm* locked in consultations the rest of the day. Otherwise, I'd give you a hand. Or a mouth.

REESE: *You can handle my situation as soon as you get home. I want that pussy wet and ready for me.*

I smile, loving that dominant edge in every word he types.

ME: *Always is.*

No imagination needed there.

Chapter
TWO

AFTER LISTENING TO JOEY RANT about all the possible ways Brooke could screw my business over, six o'clock finally came and I was able to wave goodbye to him and his negativity. Reese and I split our time between my place and his, usually only staying at mine if I have to wake up early to get started on some baking. Reese has affirmed his desire to move me into his condo permanently after the wedding, but I've been dragging my feet on preparing for that. I like having my loft above the bakery. It was the first place I ever owned all by myself, containing many Joey and Juls memories I don't want to let go of. But I understand his reasoning; it wouldn't make sense to make payments on both places. So, even though it saddens me, I'll be saying goodbye to my loft in ten days.

I park Sam, my delivery van, in my usual spot next to Reese's vehicle in his parking garage. The contrast between my cupcake-covered van and his pristine Range Rover still makes me giggle, especially when Reese expresses his concern over my choice of transportation. But I let all that Sam-hate roll off my back; he's reliable and very hip, in my opinion.

I step off the elevators onto the tenth floor and stop at Reese's door, fumbling with my keys. Once I'm inside, I lock the door behind me and toss my purse and keys onto the table. I glance around at the immaculate space, noting my fiancé has been very busy cleaning today. Everything is in order and the entire place smells like something Italian. I'm starving, but not just for food, and the meal waiting for me on the stovetop will have to wait.

"Reese?"

I walk down the hallway, stopping at the bathroom door when I hear the shower running.   Swinging the door open, I'm hit in the face with a cloud of citrus and have to grip the doorframe to steady myself. *Good Lord, he's delicious. His smell alone riles me up like nothing else.* The curtain is pulled back and our eyes lock, his mouth curling up in the corner as he breaks our contact and slowly rakes over my body. His lip twitches into a smile.

"Liar. I was expecting a dress with no panties."

I lean against the doorframe, admiring my amazing view of the gorgeous man in front of me. "If I said I was wearing this—" I sweep my hand in front of my body, "—would you have appreciated it as much?"

"I appreciate you in everything you wear." His tone is low and thick, and it still has the same effect on me as the first time I heard him speak. Like he could command me to do anything. It's not just his body that leaves me pooling at his feet. That voice of his is my undoing. He shoots me a smile, opening the curtain farther. "Get your sweet ass in here."

I strip hastily, swiftly stepping into the shower with him. Inhaling deeply, I wrap my arms around his neck and relish in the glorious sight and smell of him. His arms scoop me up and pull me against him, his forehead dropping to mine. I close my eyes and let the water cascade off his body, running down my front that is pressed to his. His warm, minty breath heats my face as his hands lightly stroke my back, slowly trailing lower and lower. I open my eyes and meet his, the greenest eyes I've ever seen burning into mine with that same intensity. His intensity.

"You know, it's literally impossible to not want to fuck you every time I see you naked. Or clothed, for that matter." He cocks an eyebrow at me, and I run my tongue along my bottom lip. "You have me perpetually wound-up here."

"I know the feeling." I tilt my head up and press my lips to his jaw, slowly trailing kisses down his neck and onto his chest. He moans softly, his body vibrating the tiniest bit against my mouth as I work my way lower. His stomach tenses, the way it always does as my lips brush against his taut skin. I'm almost to my destination when his hands grip under my arms tightly, lifting me up and pressing my back firmly against the cold tiles.

"Oh! Hey, I wasn't finished." My legs wrap around his waist, his hands firmly gripping my hips the way I like. His chest heaves rapidly, pushing up against mine with his quick, forceful breaths. I feel him there, right there, and the anticipation is killing me. "Come on, do it," my raspy voice taunts him, daring him to give me what I know we both want.

"Do what, love?" His lips meet mine and his kisses are gentle, the sweet kisses he gives me when he wants to take his time. I fucking love this kind of Reese-kissing and he knows it, but in all honesty, I'll take his mouth any way I can get it. I open for him, allowing his tongue to stroke softly against mine. He delivers the perfect amount of pressure and I moan into him, firmly tangling my hands in his wild mess of hair. He moves down, tilting my head up for access. "I love you," he whispers against my neck.

Those words send me into hyper drive like they always do, ever since he first said them to me the day of Juls' wedding; a day I started off dreading and now am immensely grateful for. I'm panting, clawing down his back and I know what he needs to hear to get him where I want him. "Please, I need you. Please, Reese." I beg him because he likes it and because it's true. I do need him; I'll always need him. How I ever managed to convince myself otherwise is beyond me. I was a complete fool for ever denying my feelings for him. He's always been it for me, ever since I fell into his lap.

He tilts his head up and locks eyes with me, slowly easing forward as his breath comes out in a quick burst. "Christ, Dylan." He begins to move, sliding in and out of me easily due to my fully-aroused state. I'm certain I'm permanently wet around him and am totally fine with that; he owns my body. "Jesus. So fucking good. Every damn time."

"Oh, God, yes." I grip onto his neck with one hand and his bicep with my other, squeezing tightly and feeling his muscles contract. His hips pound against my pelvis, pushing me farther and farther up the tiled wall. I don't think I'll ever get used to his power during sex, the way he moves in me and with me, commanding my body that willingly obeys without any hesitation. Groans and grunts echo around us as he moves fluidly inside me, hitting the end of my channel. "Reese." His hands grip my hips harder and he becomes more forceful with his thrusts, my back slapping hard against the wall.

"You're almost there. Let go, love," he says against my lips.

He always knows when I'm close, and it never takes me long to get there. I'm extremely responsive to everything this man does, and he loves it. With one quick movement, he unhooks my legs and places me on the shower floor, dropping down to his knees in front of me. His mouth is on me instantly, sucking my clit as he grabs my thighs and hooks them both over his shoulders.

"Come for me, Dylan."

"Shit. Oh, God, right there." I come hard and fast, reaching down and gripping his hair with both hands. He's so unbelievably good at this, and he knows it. Moving his head rapidly between my legs, he moans softly against my clit, lapping between my folds. I'm trembling against him like I always do, seeing his eyes flick up to mine as he gently places me down on my feet. My legs are wobbly, and it takes a lot of effort to remain upright. "Jesus. How do you keep getting better at that?" I rake through his hair as he gazes up at me, giving me the slightest shrug as his answer. "My turn," I declare, seeing his eyes light up as he stretches out above me. I excitedly push him against the wall, practically bouncing on my post-orgasm feet as he watches me in amusement. "Hands or mouth?"

He arches his brows at my question, his sweet smile pulling at the corner of his lips. "Both."

I enthusiastically rub my hands together and lean in, pressing my lips against his mouth for a quick kiss, which turns into an intense make-out session the moment he grips my neck. His tongue tangles with mine, swallowing my tiny whimpers and sending a shock wave through my body.

"See how good you taste? Like fucking candy."

I shudder against him like I always do when he talks to me that way. The man is an expert in dirty talking, dirty texting, and dirty love-letter writing. Yes, I've decided all his little notes to me during our *casual bullshit* phase were love letters. I know, I was a fucking idiot to think they weren't.

I reach down and grip him in my hand, his body jerking at the contact as he drops his head against mine. My hand doesn't slide as easily as I'd like and I get an idea, a very naughty idea. Stepping back, our eyes meet as I pull my bottom lip into my mouth and slip two fingers inside me. His penetrating green eyes broaden as I moan and swipe my wetness onto his cock, repeating the action until I've gotten him well lubricated.

"Holy shit. That's so fucking hot."

"I just thought I'd share what you do to me," I reply playfully, stepping into him and stroking his length. "You make me so wet." I lick his stubble and hear him moan softly. "Just by being in the same room with me." My free hand grips his arm as his breath warms the side of my face. I'm sliding up and down, fast then faster, my grip tightening as his hands wrap around my waist. "No man has ever done that to me before." He groans deeply against me, and I know it's because of what I'm doing to him and what I've just confessed. He loves that he's the only man who's ever affected me; the only man who ever will.

His bottom lip is pulled into his mouth, indicating he's close. It's his tell; that and when he rakes his hands through his hair, signifying he's either anxious, nervous, or really fucking pissed. "I love how wet I make you. That pussy belongs to me." His breathing hitches in my hair. "Fuck, I'm gonna come."

Dropping to my knees, I wrap my lips around him and stroke him with my hand, pumping him into my mouth. He grunts loudly above me, his thighs tensing and his hands holding my head, tangling in my hair. I swallow every ounce of him, moaning against his skin and feeling him twitch. His breathing steadies above me and I glance up, seeing a very-amused grin on his gorgeous face.

"I love you," I say softly, planting a quick kiss to his cock before I stand up. His arms wrap around me and I immediately shove my face into his neck, claiming my spot.

"Me or my dick?"

I giggle against him and feel his laugh shake my body. "Your dick." He pulls me away from him, issuing me his *don't fucking push it, Dylan* look, and I crack. "You *and* your dick. I'm mad for both of you. Can't live without either one of you, actually."

Reaching up, I grab my shampoo and turn to see his hand held out for me, waiting for me to squirt it into his palm. I do it and grab his body wash, squirting it into my hand before I put it back on the shelf. I wash his body as he washes my hair, my hands roaming freely over his skin. I linger on his shoulders and upper back, giving him a rubdown as his eyes close. He loves this, me touching him this way, pulling and kneading his muscles until they loosen. His tiny moans of gratification make me smile as I move down his body and spread the lather around. He massages my scalp the way he always does, building up the suds with his hands until they begin to trickle down my face. I'm rinsed off quickly, and my body wash is grabbed.

"Hey, use yours," I demand, trying to snatch it from his grasp but remembering instantly just how quick he is, and how I don't stand a chance in taking *anything* from him. We've been down that road.

"No. I want you to smell like you."

I grumble unconvincingly, loving how he prefers the way I smell to anything else, even though I'd be much happier smelling like him. I watch as I'm thoroughly cleaned as only Reese Carroll would do. The man is meticulous about everything, concentrating on covering every inch of my skin in the soapy bubbles. He lingers on my breasts, kneading them for several minutes before he rinses them clean. His marks are on me, permanently branded onto my skin due to his daily freshening-up sessions. I moan softly as he latches onto the left one, pulling the skin into his mouth and planting a soft kiss to it after it's darkened.

"So, how bad was today?" he asks, licking the mark on my right breast before sucking on it.

I grab his head and hold him against me. "Tolerable." He narrows his eyes at me, not buying my elusiveness. I sigh, dropping my head down. "I mean, if you *really* loved me, you wouldn't want to wait ten more days to make this official. You'd whisk me away to Vegas and make me yours right now."

He stands up, pressing his lips to my forehead. "Do you need my dick in your mouth again?" I nod quickly and he laughs. "If I could arrange it, I'd have the entire world witness you becoming mine." He smirks. "Officially."

"Officially," I echo, reaching behind me and shutting off the water. For all intents and purposes, we both know I've been his since that first wedding, but until his last name becomes mine, it won't feel real to either one of us.

After securing a towel around his waist and blocking my amazing view, he wraps a towel around me and follows behind me into his bedroom. I don't bother getting dressed because he prefers me naked in bed; anything I put on my body right now would be ripped off and discarded.

No barriers.

Nothing getting in his way of me.

That's his thing.

"You hungry?" he asks after stepping into a pair of boxers.

"Aren't I always after you ravage me?"

He disappears down the hallway, returning moments later with two bowls. He hands me mine with a smile and I lean back against the headboard, lifting the bowl to my nose. "Mmm, this smells amazing. I might just keep you."

He laughs softly next to me before he begins inhaling his food. "So, there's this last-minute account Ian and I are taking on that requires some traveling this weekend. And we were talking and thought it'd be cool if everyone came with us."

"Where are you going?"

He stretches his legs out next to mine, my feet stopping at his calf. "New Orleans. We have to be there really early on Friday, so you'll have to take a separate flight." He pauses, exhaling roughly. "I need to talk to you about something." I cock my head and see his jaw twitch slightly just before he rakes his hand through his hair.

Uh oh.

"This account, it's a business Bryce is investing in. He hired us to show them how to make better use of their resources and increase profitability. The only reason why I agreed to do it is because..." he clenches his eyes tightly, swallowing loudly. His eyes refocus on mine after he takes in a calming breath. "It's just important. I need this account, and I need you to understand that."

Bryce Roberts has been flying under the radar since Reese and I got engaged but before that, he made it very clear he was interested in me. The last time I saw him was when I delivered treats to Reese's building for a business meeting. I had no idea they knew each other, but there that little shit sat, staring at me like I was one of the pastries I had made. They don't work together and apparently, hardly ever have to deal with each other, which is a good thing. Reese isn't shy when it comes to how he feels about guys hitting on me or making me feel uncomfortable, and Bryce did both.

I see the pent-up irritation on his face that he's failing miserably at hiding. Humor works best in situations like this. "Well, it sucks he's still breathing. I was hoping he had gotten mauled by a bear." My jokester smile fades when Reese remains in serious, concerned-fiancé mode. I dip my head, forcing his eyes that are burning a hole into the sheet to focus on mine. "I get it; it's an important account. I told you before, I can handle assholes like Bryce."

In fact, I'd very much like to handle Bryce. I haven't slapped anyone in months, and my hand is beginning to twitch.

He aggressively stabs his noodles, taking out his anger on the delicious dinner he's made us. "And I told *you* before, if he makes you uncomfortable in any way, I'll break his fucking neck. That doesn't just include him coming into your shop. If he so much as looks at you in a way you don't like…"

I place my hand on his arm, halting his threat. "Relax. He won't." *Unless he's dumber than I think, which is entirely possible.* I swallow my mouthful and twirl some noodles onto my fork. Time to get the subject off Bryce before my fiancé has a coronary. "I've never been to New Orleans. I'm kinda excited." I shove my forkful into my mouth and bob my head to the side, chewing animatedly. Reese laughs softly next to me, finally relaxing. "So, what do I need to do?"

He sits his empty bowl on his nightstand, sliding down in the bed and settling on his side facing me. "Just book your flight. I already rented the house for all of us to stay."

I arch my brow at him. "And what if I would've said no?"

He pinches my side and I yelp, prompting him to pull me closer so our bodies are touching. Constant contact. "I knew you'd say yes. You don't have a wedding to bake for this weekend, so you're all mine."

I smile wide. "Look at you knowing my schedule. Oooo! We can do our bachelor and bachelorette parties this weekend! In the Big Easy!" I kick the covers off and scramble out of bed, setting my half-eaten bowl of spaghetti on my nightstand.

"Where are you going?"

"To call Joey! He's going to freak out!"

I hear his faint laugh as I grab my phone from my clutch and dial Joey's number. Returning to the bedroom, Joey answers as Reese pulls me back into bed.

"If you're calling to tell me Reese's mother is in charge of making my penis cake, I'm hanging up."

I giggle and settle back down on my side, staring at a very sleepy-looking Reese. He's been working long hours lately, plus some weekends, leaving him exhausted most nights by the time I get to him. Especially if he decides I need a good dicking as soon as he sees me, which is what usually happens. He lets his eyes fall closed, keeping his one arm wrapped around my waist.

"What would you say to a weekend in New Orleans with your two best friends and our men?"

"I'd say count me the fuck in. When?"

"This weekend. It's perfect. We don't have any weddings to bake for, and Reese and Ian have to go anyway. Plus—" I pause for dramatic effect, prompting Joey to give me an impatient grunt, "—we can go all-out for my bachelorette party, Mardi Gras-style."

"Oh, fuck yes! Do you know how many gay bars they have there? Oooo, cupcake, I'm busting. This is going to be fantastic."

I listen to my easily-excitable best friend and smile at the man I love who has completely passed out next to me. Reese's breathing is slow and steady in my ear as I press my forehead against his, feeling the dampness of his hair against my skin.

"Billy's in, too, right?"

"Of course. As soon as he heard me say 'gay bar' he was in. Do I need to do anything besides buy our plane tickets?"

"Nope. The place we're staying at has already been booked. Oooo, maybe it's in the French Quarter."

"Babe, I want a window seat. A *window*." I hear Billy's muffled response in the background, prompting Joey to let out a cross grumble. "Oh, for Christ's sake. Cupcake, I gotta go handle this. You better book your flight now if you want a decent seat."

I roll over and sit up, grabbing Reese's iPad off the nightstand. "Yeah, I'm on it. I'll see you tomorrow."

Just as I hang up from Joey, my phone beeps with an incoming text message.

JULS: *NEW ORLEANS, SWEETS! Booking my flight now. There's just the one leaving late afternoon on Friday, so you'll have to close up early. Hope that's doable.*

ME: *Totally doable. I'm so excited!*

JULS: *Me, too! I may have mentioned it to Brooke.*

I slam my head back against the headboard. *Seriously? Has she gone completely mental?*

ME: *You are out of your fucking mind.*

JULS: *It'll be fun. And don't worry about JoJo. I'll handle him.*

ME: *Good. Cause I'm not.*

I place my phone down and power on the iPad, letting go of *that* stress and grinning at the image that appears on the screen. It's still the one of me, passed out after my first-ever sleepover in this bed.

I can't believe I ever fought it.

Him.

Sleepovers.

Him.

Intimacy.

HIM.

Even though I acted like a complete idiot and tried to ignore every screaming thought in my head that said what we were doing was more than I was prepared to admit, I wouldn't take it back. I will never regret the way I fell in love with Reese; I can't. Every single second of it was worth it because it led us to this. And I'd go through eighty-five more days of complete torture to have him next to me, because he's always been mine. And in ten more days, I'll officially be his.

Chapter
THREE

"**A**RE YOU SURE YOU WANNA send that bag through security? What with all the sex toys you have tucked away in there?" Juls teases as Joey puts his suitcase on the conveyor belt. Billy conceals his smile behind his hand, turning a slight shade of pink.

Joey turns his eyes up to the monitor, watching as his delicates are scanned. "I doubt National Security gives two shits that I like to use a spreader bar."

"Baby, really? Is that public knowledge?" Billy asks, grabbing his and Joey's suitcases.

I bite back my laugh and join the three of them after retrieving my luggage. "There's nothing sacred between the three of us, Billy. You should know that by now."

"Especially when it pertains to sex," Juls adds.

We all begin the walk through the terminal toward our gate. Reese and Ian left early this morning on their flight, so we'll be catching up with them later on tonight. And, by some miracle, Brooke is late and keeping Joey blissfully ignorant at the moment; it might actually be in her benefit to miss the flight entirely. Juls thought it best to let the news of her crashing our weekend getaway 'unravel organically', as she so innocently put it. *Organically?* I'm not sure how organic it's going to be watching Joey freak the fuck out in the middle of an airport. Because other than Maggie Carroll showing up and boarding our flight, Brooke Wicks is the only other person who could send my dear assistant into a shit-fit.

"This is going to be ahhhmazing," Joey sings as he puts his luggage into the overhead compartment. Juls and I have settled into our seats behind the boys and my eyes keep darting to the front of the plane, even though I'm sure I'll hear Brooke before I see her. "I hope you're all aware we will be having separate bachelor and bachelorette parties." Joey shifts his eyes between the three of us. "Baby, you're with the boys."

Juls and I both laugh as he sits down next to Billy. Then I sense it: the shift in the atmosphere, causing my back to go rigid in my seat. Juls must feel it, too, because she leans forward into the crack between the seats at that exact moment.

"JoJo, please don't do anything that could get you kicked off this flight."

He turns his head, gazing back at us with suspicion. "What? I'm not *that* inappropriate."

"Hey, bitches. Who's ready to party in the Big Easy?"

I see Brooke in my peripheral vision, not able to turn away from Joey's face, which has tensed up considerably. He doesn't even look in her direction. "You have got to be fucking kidding me," he snarls between the seats before finally whipping his head around and greeting Brooke with what I can only assume to be anything but a smile. "Who the hell invited you?"

"Joey!" Juls snaps.

Brooke's lip twitches into a conniving grin. "Will the three of us be sharing a bed? I've been told I'm an excellent little spoon." She tucks her luggage away and ruffles Joey's hair before taking her seat next to me. He grumbles under his breath, prompting Billy to reach up and fix his coifed do. "Who bottoms of the two of you, anyway?"

"Jesus, Brooke," I say, just as Billy and Joey turn around in their seats. "There are other people on this airplane."

"I hope your dildos got through airport security, since they're going to be the only thing entering that mess of a vagina this weekend." Joey points to Brooke's lap, smiling after delivering his dig.

She flips him off, moving her finger closer to his face and prompting him to lean back. "If you want to enter a competition with me to see who can get the most dick over the next two days, bring it, bitch."

"Battery operated doesn't count, Brooke. Remember that," Joey retorts.

I put my hands between them, breaking up the verbal battle. I glance to my left and lock eyes with Brooke. "It better not be like this between the two of you every day in the shop. I'm telling you right now, I'm not putting up with it. I'll have enough stress on me next week as it is."

"I can be civil," Brooke states, feigning affection toward Joey. He rolls his eyes and turns around, entering quiet conversation with Billy, which I'm sure is revolving around the hot mess sitting next to me. Brooke offers me a genuine smile. "Thank you, by the way. You're really helping me out here."

"You're welcome, but be warned. I don't care that you're my best friend's sister; I will fire you if you and Joey can't get along."

She nods her understanding, buckling her seatbelt and prompting me to do the same. The flight attendants begin their safety demonstrations in the aisle as Joey continues to animatedly gesture to Billy.

Juls leans over me and taps her sister's knee. "Do us all a favor and try not to torment him too much this weekend. Don't make me regret inviting you to this."

Brooke huffs and scowls in the direction of her sister. "Everyone needs to relax. Jesus Christ, you all act like I'm incapable of handing myself in public."

Thankfully, at that exact moment, the flight attendant stops in front of our row with the cart of beverages, preventing a rebuttal from Juls and myself. "Would anyone like anything?"

"Liquor," we all answer simultaneously. The flight attendant smiles and hands out mini-bottles of vodka which none of us waste any time in downing.

"All cell phones off, please. We're about to take off."

Everyone reaches into their pockets and messes with their phones. I notice the text message on my screen and open it with the same nervous excitement I always have when I see his name.

Reese: Eight more days, love. Get your ass here already.

Mᴇ: *Hurrying. And you can do better than eight more days. Put that brain to work, handsome.*

I power off my phone and tuck it away, relaxing against my seat. Eight more days that can't get here soon enough.

ೋ

"HOLY HELL. THIS PLACE IS fabulous."

I hear Joey's voice register somewhere in the house as I make my way upstairs toward the bedrooms. He isn't lying, though; this place *is* fabulous. My man did well. It looks like a civil war-era mansion from the outside, and the inside is very rustic and warm. The kitchen and living area are downstairs, both spacious and lovely, and the house is equipped with three bedrooms. I open the first door I come to and notice the brown, worn-leather luggage on the bed that screams Ian in every way.

"Juls, your room is the one on the right," I yell over my shoulder toward the stairs. She's probably too busy moderating downstairs to even hear me at the moment, but I give her a heads-up anyway.

I open the room across the hall and am immediately hit in the face with my favorite smell in the world. Reese has probably only spent a limited amount of time in here, considering he and Ian had to meet with the client shortly after arriving earlier today, but his scent is already saturating the space we'll share for the next two days. And I couldn't be happier about that.

I drop my suitcase next to his on the floor by the dresser and spot his iPod laying on one of the pillows on the bed. A tiny brown card is next to it. I crawl up the length of the bed and grab the iPod, setting it on my stomach as I open the familiar card.

Dylan,

64,863 seconds. (Give or take a few depending on when you read this note.)

X, Reese

P.S. Listen.

I can't help the ridiculous smile that spreads across my face; I never can. It's always been like this, and I know it'll always be like this. No matter how many notes he leaves me or deliveries he sends me, I'll never lose that wild excitement I feel at even the smallest gesture. I grab the ear buds and pop them into my ears. After turning on the iPod, I scroll to the songs, expecting to find a huge playlist because I know this is the iPod Reese takes with him when he goes to the gym. But there's only one song on it, so I conclude he must have erased all his other music specifically for this moment. I close my eyes and let the music fill my ears, concentrating on the lyrics just like I did the first time he played this song for me. I think every time Reese and I have sex, it's always some form of making love, even when it's rough and urgent. But he only reserved this song for that first time.

The bed dips by my feet, prompting me to peek one eye open as I listen to "Look After You" for the second time. Joey joins me by my side and steals one of my ear buds and the card I'm holding to my chest.

I study his face as he places the bud in his ear and reads my note. He frowns, hands the note back over, and lets his head fall on the pillow next to me. "That man of yours makes every other guy in Chicago look bad. Especially mine."

I elbow his side, seeing him smile through a silent 'ouch', and turn the song down so it's playing softly for both of us. "Billy does a ton of romantic stuff for you. He asked you to move in with him after only knowing you a little over a week, and he worships the ground your pretty feet walk on. He'd do anything for you; you know that."

"Then why hasn't he asked me to marry him?"

I open my mouth to speak but shut it almost instantly. I honestly don't know the answer to that question. I've wondered it myself, especially lately with all my wedding planning going on. Billy is perfect for Joey. He keeps him grounded but also brings out the playful side in him that I completely adore. I love seeing them together; I've never seen my dear assistant this happy before with anyone. But maybe Billy isn't the marrying type.

"Have you two talked about it? Getting married?"

He plucks the ear bud out, seemingly done with the love song that is probably fueling his irritation. I do the same and wrap them around Reese's iPod before turning on my side and facing Joey.

"Sort of. He said he could see himself getting married someday, but he didn't name drop and say with me."

"Well, maybe he's waiting for you to ask him."

Joey snaps his head toward me and raises his eyebrows. "Are you insane? I'm not proposing; that's his job. He can at least give me one fucking grand gesture."

My bedroom door pushes open and Billy fills the doorway, looking apprehensive. He rolls his eyes and grimaces in our direction, keeping one hand on the door while the other pinches the top of his nose. "Baby, Brooke wants to know if she can share our room."

"Ha!"

I chuckle at Joey's outburst before turning my attention back to Billy.

"There are only three bedrooms. It really doesn't bother me if you don't mind."

Billy's face is filled with a softness I only ever see him use with Joey. Though I'm not sure he knows what exactly he's in for by agreeing to this sleeping arrangement; he's barely had to spend any amount of time with Brooke.

Joey sits up, bracing himself on his elbows. "Oh, I do mind. There's no way in Hell I'm sharing a bed with her. I believe I saw a couch downstairs she can plant her ass on when it comes time to sleep."

"Well, do you want to go tell her? I think she is already starting to unpack in our room."

"Of course she is." Joey swings his long, muscular legs off the bed and walks toward the door, passing Billy after planting a brief kiss to his lips. "Brooke. You're out of your fucking mind if you think I'm sharing a room with you." I hear her muffled response, followed by Joey's dramatic rebuttal, which causes both Billy and me to laugh.

He turns to me and smiles. "You ready for next weekend? Tying down the unattainable bachelor of Chicago and all is a pretty big deal."

"Ha ha. Speaking of bachelors—" I scoot off the bed and walk over to him, "—can I ask you something?" He closes the door and leans against it, waiting for my question with a welcoming expression. I put my hand on his shoulder. "You wouldn't hurt Joey, would you?"

He tilts his head with a frown, seemingly thrown off by my question. His eyes dart to my hand that's resting on his shoulder before flicking back to me. "Dylan, I'm well aware of your capabilities when it comes to bitch-slapping somebody, but even if I wasn't, I'd never hurt Joey."

I squeeze his shoulder before dropping my hand to my side. "Okay. I'm just looking out for him."

"I know. You and Juls are crazy-protective over my baby. One of these days I'll be married to all three of you." He notices my quiet enthusiasm and puts a finger to his lips. "Not a word."

I nod eagerly. "That's so exciting," I whisper.

He opens the door and peeks his head out into the hallway, glancing in both directions. "All's quiet. Think they killed each other?"

My phone begins to ring in my pocket. I slip it out as I reply, "It's possible. You might want to go check."

Billy gives me a wink before he walks out of the bedroom, closing the door behind him. I answer the call as I walk back over to the bed.

"Hi, handsome."

"Hi, love. Are you here?"

"Yup. Just got in about an hour ago. When will I see you? It's already almost eight o'clock." I fall back onto my pillow, rolling over and placing the note he left me next to his iPod. "I need my Reese fix."

He laughs softly. "Are the two orgasms I gave you last night not keeping you satisfied?"

"No way. I'm greedy when it comes to that mouth of yours."

"Just my mouth?" I can practically hear his smile through the phone. Playful Reese is one of my favorites.

He probably could keep me satisfied with just his mouth if he wanted to. But I've had the rest of him, and I'm not giving that up for anything. "You know I'm addicted to all of you," I reply before my grin breaks into a yawn. I'm suddenly not wanting to leave this bed at all, especially after Reese does get here.

"You better be. Tired?"

"Very. Long day. Even longer flight." I reach up behind me and pile my hair on top of my head so the coolness of the pillow touches my skin. "Brooke and Joey are already going at it."

I hear Ian's voice in the background. "All right," Reese directs away from the phone. "I gotta go. We should be getting out of here in a few hours, though."

I yawn again. "Mmm, okay. Miss your face."

"Miss yours."

I hang up the call and get out of bed, picking up my suitcase and plopping it down in my place. Grabbing the University of Chicago T-shirt Reese gave me months ago, which, besides a garter and stockings, is the only thing he willingly allows me to wear to bed, I strip quickly and slip it over my head. Our bedroom has its own private bath, which I'm grateful for; sharing a bathroom with two gay guys and two other girls would be a nightmare, I'm sure. Joey alone has more hair care products than I do. After I remove my makeup and brush my teeth, I climb back into bed just as someone knocks on my door.

"Come in."

Juls pops her head in with a smile. "Hey. The guys should be here in a couple of hours."

"Yeah, I just talked to Reese. I'm exhausted. I'm just gonna turn in for the night."

"Good idea," she says through a mischievous grin. "You'll need your energy for tomorrow." She closes the door after giving me a quick wink, and I pull the covers up around me.

Tomorrow.

My bachelorette party.

Juls and Joey have been whispering all over the shop the past two days, secretly planning my last hoorah. I know I'm going to be dragged to some strip club against my will. Joey is insistent on male nudity happening, that I know for sure. In all honestly, I'd much rather just go dancing at a club like Juls did for hers. I don't need to celebrate my remaining days as a single woman with greased-up men grinding on a stage. I'm dick-set for life. I don't need to look at other options.

Goddamn it, Billy. Propose to your boy already so he can worry about his own bachelorette party.

Chapter
FOUR

FEEL HIM, HIS MOUTH, his hands, his everything on me and I'm immediately pulled from my dream. Slowly opening my eyes, I see Reese on top of me, trailing kisses below my breasts and running his hands up my thighs. His wild hair is perfectly disheveled, sticking out every which way and brushing softly against my skin. He quickly removes my T-shirt and panties and tosses them off the bed.

"Mmm. I love waking up like this." I feel his lips curl up against me as he trails lower. Nibbling at my hip bones, his teeth graze along my skin and I squirm underneath him. I glance to my right, seeing the time on the alarm clock. "Did you just get here?"

"Yeah." His lips brush along my ribs while his hands mold over my breasts. "I know it's late. And if you're too tired…"

Yeah, right. Like I would ever object to this.

Reaching down, I grip his shoulders and pull him up to me, bringing his face to mine. "I don't care what time it is; you always have my permission to wake me up." I lift my head and brush my lips softly against his, tasting his minty flavor. "Thank you for my note and my song. Let's go get married right now."

He laughs against my mouth, the gentle pressure turning urgent. I'm silenced, as I always am when he kisses me this way, and I really couldn't care less. Opening for him, we move our tongues against each other's, stroking and savoring as my fingers tangle in his hair. His hands move all over my body, touching and caressing every inch of me with his calloused palms. I moan softly as he teases my breasts, pulling and pinching my nipples in the way I like. My need for him builds quickly, and I reach down between us and grip his length in my hand. "Hard day?" I ask playfully.

He groans deeply before he answers. "Hardest. I hate being away from you."

"We're always apart on Fridays for work." I slowly stroke his length, feeling him thicken even more in my hand.

"I know. This just felt different."

My heart constricts at his words, knowing exactly how he feels. Even though we're used to some distance, this did feel different somehow. Maybe it's because he's so close to becoming officially mine, or maybe it's because I've been stressed to the max lately. Either way, I'm not a fan of being away from this man; where he goes, I go.

"Reese," I whisper across his lips, hearing his breath hitch at the sound of his name.

"I need you," he proclaims, thrusting forward and entering me in one quick push. I gasp with him, pulling my legs up and wrapping them firmly around his hips. He moves fast and hard, plunging deep then deeper into me. My eyes are locked onto his as he holds himself above me, lunging forward in his perfect rhythm. He whispers his sweet words to me between each drive.

"It's like Heaven being in you. Tell me you're mine, Dylan."

"I'm yours. I always have been."

"Fucking right."

I arch my back and press my chest against his, needing the contact. Needing every part of him touching me. I can never get close enough to this man. I want him on me at all times; I crave it. I love the way our bodies fit together, so perfectly and so in tune with each other's. He drops his head and latches onto my right breast, flicking against my nipple before sucking on it. I groan loudly, loving the way his mouth feels against every part of my body. My eyes go to the inside of his right arm, seeing the words I scrolled on him all those months ago. The fact that he got it tattooed still blows my mind, and every time I look at it, my heart swells. I lean up and press my lips against the words, my words I marked him with. Trailing my tongue across my script, his thrusts pick up, as he slams harder into me. Hearing his loud grunts ring out above me, I glance up and see him pull his bottom lip in and bite it.

"Make me come, Reese."

Dropping his hand between us, he picks up his movements and brushes against my clit, in the way only he does. He knows exactly what to do with my body, and he does it better than anyone ever could. Not that I have any desire to test that theory; this is the only man I'll ever want. I'm falling fast, clenching around him and softly chanting his name.

"Dylan," he growls, crashing his mouth down on mine. I pull his tongue into my mouth and suck on it slowly, swallowing his moans as he gives me his release. Our lips brush against each other's, tasting and teasing as we both come down from our high. He lifts his head toward the direction of the nightstand.

"Seven days," he says before looking back down at me. "You know this is hard for me, right? To be this damn close to having the whole world know you're officially mine."

I slide along his cheekbone with my fingers, studying his face. "I thought I was the only one struggling out of the two of us. You're always so quick to silence my quickie-wedding suggestions."

He shakes his head slightly, leaning into my palm that's resting flat against his cheek. And then I see it: the shift in his eyes, the possessive, hungry glare he does so well. "It fucking kills me to wait, but I want this to be perfect for you. I don't ever want you to regret the way you gave yourself to me, and I'll have no problem moving that preacher along. That ceremony will be brief."

I laugh softly before planting a kiss on his jaw. "I love you," I murmur against his skin.

He drops his forehead to mine and closes his eyes. "I love you."

He always says it like that when I say it first. It's never *I love you, too*. Never. It's as if he's stating it as a fact, not giving me an automated response to my declaration. The way Reese says 'I love you', I feel it more than I hear it.

He lets his weight press me firmly into the mattress as he collapses down on top of me, tucking his head next to mine. "Seven days," he whispers, and I barely make it out. It's as if those words are just for him, the reassurance he gives himself.

I kiss his shoulder and hold him against me, not wanting him to move. I could wake up with the worst cramp in the morning, but this closeness would be worth it. I press my lips to his ear. "We got this. Seven days is nothing."

And with those final words, I feel his body relax.

❧

I FEEL THE BED MOVE and hear the soft creaking sound of the mattress. Peeking one eye open, I see the back of Reese as he sits on the end of the bed, facing the bathroom. He's shirtless, his broad back covered in tiny water droplets. His hair is wet and fuckably messy and his scent is overwhelming me, blanketing me and causing me to purr as I stretch. At the sound of my noise, he turns his head and lets his eyes roam freely over my body, which is barely covered in the white sheet.

"You are impossibly beautiful. Do you know that?"

I hold my hands out, reaching for him. He drops the towel he is holding and crawls toward me in a pair of shorts, settling on his side and pulling me against his chest.

"You showered without me," I state as I press soft kisses to his chest.

"I had to. Ian and I went for a run."

I lean back to look into his face. "You're that disciplined to work out on vacation?" My eyes take in his hard body, and I realize the absurdity of that question. "Never mind. Look at you. The term 'rest day' is not a part of your vocabulary." A knock on the door prompts Reese to grab the sheet and cover me up to my neck.

"Hold on," he yells over his shoulder.

He shifts quickly and straddles my waist, moving his hands along the side of my body and tucking me in burrito style. I squirm underneath him. "Reese, I could've just grabbed a T-shirt."

He smirks at me before turning toward the door. "All right, you can come in."

The door opens and Joey pops his head through. He smiles at the sight of the two of us on the bed. "Well, look who's finally awake."

Finally awake? I quickly turn toward the alarm clock. "Oh, my God. It's after twelve o'clock already?" I gaze up at Reese. "You tried to wake me, didn't you?"

"Of course I did. Multiple times."

I shake my head at myself with a grimace; I'm in New Orleans, and I'm spending my time here in bed. Of course, if Reese promised to stay with me, I'd never leave this bed. What girl would?

"The party bus is leaving at three o'clock. And no boys allowed," Joey says with a smile. He looks almost devious in my doorway, no doubt thinking of everything he and Juls have planned for the evening. "And I have two rules for you, cupcake: wear the sexiest outfit you have in that suitcase, and hand over the cell phone."

"What? No way. I'm not giving you my phone." Reese shifts above me and grabs my phone off the nightstand before getting out of bed. "What are you doing?"

"He took my phone, too. Let him have it; I don't need a phone to get to you."

I watch him hand my cell over and Joey takes it with a smile. "Thank you. And don't even think about *getting to her.*"

I don't see Reese's reaction to what Joey's just said, but I do see Joey's reaction to the look he is getting from Reese, and that look makes my dear assistant straighten up in the doorway. I hide my giggle underneath the sheet as Joey exhales loudly.

"If I see your gorgeous face at any of the places we go to tonight, you and I will be having words."

"Joey," Reese says, placing one hand on the doorframe and gripping the edge of the door with the other. Even though he and Joey are roughly the same height, Reese seems to tower over any opponent with his body language alone. "Nothing stands in my way of Dylan. Not even you."

Joey sighs heavily and glances in my direction. "Three o'clock, cupcake."

"Got it."

The door closes and I immediately flail my arms and legs, breaking free of the cocoon I've been wrapped in. I slide off the bed and grab my T-shirt, pulling it over my head. When I brush my wild bed-hair out of my eyes, I see Reese staring at me in the way only he does, like he's committing me to memory. I sit on the edge of the bed and tap the spot next to me. He smiles, sitting down and placing his hand on my thigh.

"So, what are your plans for tonight? Naked girls? Lap dances?" I ask as I twirl my engagement ring around my finger.

His forehead creases with concern. "Do you think I have any desire to see another naked woman when I have this waiting for me?" He tugs at my T-shirt, exposing my bare hip. His finger trails along my skin. "I love this spot right here. Do you know why?" I watch as his finger glides over my hipbone toward the taut skin of my inner thigh. When he turns his head up and locks onto my eyes, I shake my head. The corner of his mouth curls up into a smile. "When I kiss you here, you shake against my lips. You always have." His finger trails lower, dipping between my legs. I gasp when he feels how wet his words have made me. "Mine."

"Yours," I answer breathlessly. I let my head fall against his shoulder. "I need to start getting ready. Joey will freak out if I make us late to wherever the hell we're going."

He kisses the corner of my mouth before sliding his hand out and sucking on his finger. "I need to get ready, too. But you will be sitting on my face later."

"Promise?" I tease, standing and making my way to the bathroom. I turn when I don't get a response just in time to see him drop his shorts, displaying his massive erection. I stumble a bit. "Wow. I mean, we have a little time, right?"

He arches his brow. "Get in there before I pin you against the wall. You know I hate rushing when it comes to you." I pull my shirt over my head, flashing him and pairing it with my best flirtatious smile. He shakes his head. "Go, love."

"Yes, Mr. Carroll."

❧

BY THE TIME I REEMERGE from the bathroom, ready to get this night over with, Reese has already dressed and left the room. I walk over to my suitcase and grab the black high heels I packed. They are dangerously high, buckle around my ankle, and scream sex kitten. I might actually kill myself wearing these tonight, but when the hell else am I going to wear them? Besides to bed with Reese, which will definitely be happening very soon. I strap them on and walk over to the floor-length mirror hanging on the wall. My blonde hair is falling over my bare shoulders. My makeup is looking on point and very sexy, thanks to my false eyelashes, and my dress is short, black, and practically a second skin. It's probably a good thing Reese has left the room already because I seriously doubt he'd let me walk out of here in this. He took it upon himself months ago to categorize the majority of my wardrobe as *for his eyes only*, leaving me with only a few dresses deemed fit for public outings, according to his standards. And none of those dresses would do tonight. This *is* my bachelorette party; I'm supposed to look sinful. Besides, he can rip this off my body later and do whatever the hell he wants with it. And by it, I mean my dress *and* my body.

"Holy shit," Joey practically squeals as I walk very carefully down the stairs. Juls and Brooke are standing by the doorway, both in tight dresses themselves, and Joey is looking exceptional in a dress shirt and khakis. "Thank Christ the guys left already. There's no way in Hell Reese would approve of that dress, which you look amazing in."

I smile widely. "Thanks. You don't look so bad yourself."

"You look incredible, sweets," Juls adds as I come to a stop at the last step. She points at my feet with her perfectly manicured finger. "I need to borrow those shoes immediately. *They* are fabulous."

"The limo's here!" Brooke chirps, swinging the door open. "Let's get this party started."

I hold my clutch with one hand as Joey takes my other, looping it through his arm. "Are you ready to get down and dirty, cupcake?"

I smile at him, concealing my apprehension. "As ready as I'll ever be."

Chapter
FIVE

"I CAN'T BELIEVE YOU GOT a limo for this. Did the boys leave in one, as well?" I ask, climbing into the back of the stretch-Hummer-style limo that could easily fit twenty people. The last time I was in a limousine was prom, and it was nowhere near as nice as this one. The cool leather of the seats chills my legs as I slide over to the bench seat.

"No. They aren't fabulous like we are. They all left in a cab," Joey answers as he settles into the seat to my right. Juls slides in next to him and smiles at me, pulling the hem of her dress down on her bare thighs.

Brooke opens one of the cabinets and grabs a bottle of champagne and several flutes. "Let's make a toast."

"Should you be pouring that? Didn't you pre-game it at the house with a few of the minis from the fridge?" Joey asks, scooting closer to Brooke.

Brooke glares at him. "Shut up, you queen. I'm perfectly capable of pouring under tipsy conditions." She fills the glasses, handing them out to the three of us. Joey takes his with a disapproving look before dropping it to give me his winning smile. "Who wants to do the honors?" Brooke asks.

"Me. I have to practice for Saturday anyway." Juls holds her glass in front of her, prompting the rest of us to do the same. She beams at me sweetly. "To my very best friend, Dylan, who deserves all the happiness in the world. We all love you very much, sweets." Her lip quivers a bit and she looks down, hiding her teary eyes. She wipes her finger across her cheek. "Sorry. I'm just so happy for you."

Joey sniffles next to her and squeezes her knee.

"You guys are lame. Is this how it's going to be all night?" Brooke asks. She tips her glass back when no one responds and downs the contents. I smile over at my two best friends, motioning to them for us to do the same. Brooke collects our empty glasses before reaching up and rubbing the back of her neck. "That stupid couch was not meant to be slept on. I'm getting a bed tonight."

"Not mine," Joey informs her. He looks out the window as the limo begins to slow down. "Oooo, we're here!"

My nerves hit me in one big rush, not knowing what to expect when I step out of the vehicle. I try to look out the window, but Brooke blocks my view as she stands and smoothes her dress. *Shit. I really don't want to go to some seedy strip club where you're most likely to catch an STD just from breathing the air. But I can't bail, not when we're already here.*

Juls places her hand on the door, looking back in my direction. "You ready, sweets?"

I nod and force my most convincing smile. Juls and Joey file out of the limo, followed by Brooke. I scoot myself along the bench seat and take Joey's offered hand that's held out for me, mentally preparing myself for what I'm about to endure. And then, I step out of the limo.

I am expecting neon lights and loud music pumping from a building.

I am expecting drunk patrons stumbling along the street and the smell of booze and cigarettes.

But I am not expecting this.

The limo has dropped us off outside a very ritzy establishment, the words 'Bella Donna Day Spa' scrolled in fancy script above the doorway. I turn toward my two best friends who are smiling at me. "We're having a spa day?"

"This is what you wanted, isn't it?" Juls asks.

The tenseness in my shoulders has disappeared completely. I reach for Juls' hand and she places hers in mine, squeezing it gently.

Joey wraps his arm around my shoulder. "Did you really think I'd make your bachelorette party all about me? What kind of friend would I be if I did that?"

"But you told me to dress sexy."

He runs his eyes up and down my body. "And you knocked it out of the park. Don't worry, we'll put that dress to use when we go dancing after this."

I lay my head on his shoulder as he directs me to the door, following behind Juls and Brooke. "Thank you, Joey."

He kisses the top of my head. "Come on, cupcake. Let's enjoy some massages."

৽৶

I REALLY HAVE THE TWO best friends in the world.

Juls and Joey set me up with a two-hour hot stone massage, which worked every single knot from my back that had begun to set in due to wedding-planning stress. Juls, Joey, and Brooke all received massages themselves while I passed out during my session. If I had my phone with me, I would've informed Reese that my masseuse had amazing fingers. Very feminine, amazing fingers. I'd never let him think another man had his hands on me. I'm very aware of his views on that, even if it is in a spa setting.

After that, the four of us drank wine while we got manicures and pedicures. Brooke even seemed happy about the festivities, not once complaining she wasn't getting her rocks off somewhere. Once we were all relaxed and buzzing from the wine, we were served a fancy lunch in the private bridal room: tiny cucumber and chicken salad sandwiches, assorted fruits and cheeses, and of course, more wine. Thank God for the food because I would've needed carrying out of there if I didn't have something to absorb the alcohol that seemed to be free flowing.

Feeling full and borderline-tipsy after my relaxing afternoon, I can barely keep my eyes open as we make our way to our next stop. Juls and Brooke are talking quietly as I lean my head on Joey's shoulder.

"What do you think the boys are doing right now?"

He sighs. "Well, if it were a different bunch of men, I'd say they were getting panties thrown at them. But Reese only desires your panties, and Ian is so whipped it's almost laughable." Juls overhears this and flips Joey off as she continues to giggle with Brooke. "And Billy…" Joey's voice trails off as he reaches up and fixes the collar of his shirt.

I lean up and kiss his stubbly jaw. "He loves you. You know that, right?"

He nods, dropping his worried façade. "I know. I'm just in a funk. Once you're hitched, I'll be the only single girl left at the party." I swat at his leg and he laughs just as the limo comes to a stop. He peers down at me. "You ready to work that outfit at the hottest club in the Big Easy, cupcake?"

Dancing with my two best friends… and Brooke? I glance around at the three smiling faces. "Hell yes, I am. Let's do this."

Joey leads the way past the bouncer and into the Raging Rhino. The dance floor is packed with people, and the music is bumping through the speakers. This place is massive and a serious step up from the clubs we've been to in Chicago, and I always considered Clancy's to be on the fancy side. It's two floors, the bottom one containing a bar that stretches the length of the dance floor. The top level is roped off and a security guard is standing at the bottom of the stairs, granting access to certain individuals. Brooke squeals excitedly behind me as Juls turns her head and leans close to Joey and me.

"I say we dance first then hit up the bar," she yells over the music. Joey and I both nod in agreement, making our way toward the middle of the dance floor.

By some miracle, I'm able to dance without any problem in my sky-high heels, and I do just that with Joey, Juls, and Brooke dancing next to me. Even though there are tons of people around us, the dance floor is so large we all have plenty of room to move. Joey uses that to his advantage and spins around in a way only he does. I hold my hair off my neck and move my body to some remixed version of "Sexy Back" by Justin Timberlake. It becomes a competition, the three of us all trying to out-dance the other for what feels like hours. My feet at one point become numb, and I don't care in the least that I'll probably have blisters; I'm having too much fun to care. As one song blends in to another, I glance around and realize Brooke is missing.

I wave my hands out in front of me, getting the attention of Juls and Joey. "Where's Brooke?"

They both glance around, Juls spinning in a circle and looking over the heads of the other dancers. She shrugs when she turns back to both of us. "Bathroom, maybe?"

"Who cares where she is? Ooooo, this is my jam!" Joey squeals.

"Single Ladies" by Beyoncé comes on, and Joey begins to do the entire dance routine from memory, probably better than Mrs. Carter herself, and that's saying a lot. Juls and I buckle over in laughter as he nails it, not caring what the hell anyone thinks of him. Because it's Joey we're talking about; the man has zero shame and I love him for it.

Not wanting to interrupt my best friend's dance number, I wait 'til after the song is over to demand a break. I grab his arm, motioning to Juls, and give them the universal hand gesture for 'let's go get a drink'. They both nod, Joey reaching up and wiping the sweat off his forehead and Juls resituating her dress, which shifted on her body.

We all walk up to the bar, and Joey motions for one of the four bartenders. "Helloooooo. Seriously? How can you ignore this?" Juls and I chuckle as he frantically waves his hand out, desperately trying to get someone's attention. Just then, Brooke comes stumbling up to the group, rubbing her left eye.

"Does anyone have any Visine?" she asks, dropping her hand down and blinking rapidly.

"Where have you been?" Juls asks. "And why the hell do you need Visine?"

She rolls her one eye that isn't being rubbed. "I got semen in my eye."

I don't know what the hell I was expecting her to say, but it definitely wasn't that. And given Juls' and Joey's reaction, they weren't expecting it either. I slap my hand over my mouth to contain my hysteria while Juls throws her head back, unashamedly laughing her ass off. Joey covers his face with his hands, his shoulders shaking with his laughter.

Brooke's face turns bright red as she rubs her eye with the heel of her hand. "Oh, like none of you have ever had a face shot go wrong. This really fucking burns. I've been flushing it out for the past hour."

"Oh, my God, Brooke," I barely get out through my chuckles. "Why did you let him shoot it on your face?"

She stares at me like I've just asked her the most ridiculous question. "I'm not swallowing a stranger's load. It was either that or on my dress, and this shit was expensive." She takes note of the laughter around her and huffs loudly. "It was an executive decision I'm seriously regretting. Someone Google whether or not it's possible to get permanent damage from this." The three of us are too busy roaring with laughter to be able to Google anything. Brooke surveys us with annoyance. "Asses. Next time you get cum in your eye, you're on your own."

"Finally," Joey says through a giggle as one of the bartenders walk up to where we're standing. He's holding a bright pink cocktail and places it on the table in front of us. "Uh, I didn't order yet. Although, that looks delicious."

"It's for her." The bartender motions at me with his head. "From the guy at the end of the bar."

The four of us all turn toward where he has directed, the laughter fading out as we all seemingly focus on the same individual.

Fucking motherfucker.

Bryce is staring at me with that same smug smirk, which is apparently a permanent fixture on his face. He's as eerie looking as I remember, with those yellow eyes that seem to glow in the bar, like a stalking reptile.

"What is that fucker doing here?" Joey asks, moving closer to me. I register his question but can't seem to find the words. I'm too busy coming up with ways to lay this asshole out.

"Damn. He's hot. Who is that guy?"

The three of us all turn to see a very horny-looking, one-eyed Brooke.

"Really, Brooke? You just gave some stranger head and you're patrolling for more ass? Maybe you should pace yourself," Joey says before returning his gaze back to Bryce. Brooke simply shrugs her response as he continues. "He must have a death wish to be in the same building as you. Reese is going to freak out."

"Is that Bryce?" Juls asks. I nod and see her eyes widen. "Shit. You were right, sweets; he is creepy looking."

Creepy seems to downplay it. The man makes my skin crawl, and this is only the third time I'm seeing him. I step up to the bar and grab the drink off the counter. There's a possibility that what I'm about to do will get me kicked out of this pristine club, but right now, I don't care. I've had an amazing time with my friends and if it ends now, I'm fine with that.

"Dylan! Hold up!"

I hear Joey's voice behind me as I move between the patrons. Bryce keeps his chilling smile on me as I inch closer, either not knowing or not caring how his gesture is being received. In fact, if anything, his stupid face seems to break into an even-bigger grin as I step next to him.

"Dylan, it's been too damn long since I laid my eyes on that tight body of yours. Remind me to thank your fiancé for bringing you along on this little trip," he spews through his venomous grin. His eyes slowly rake over my body, giving extra attention to my breasts. "Damn, girl, that dress belongs on my bedroom floor. Wanna get out of here and make that happen?"

I waste no time in drenching his face in my bright-pink cocktail, placing my now-empty glass down on the bar and gaining the attention of everyone around us. "Go fuck yourself, Bryce. Even if I wasn't with Reese, I would never go anywhere with you. The dickhead vibe you got going on doesn't really do anything for me. Nor do your lame-as-shit pick-up lines." I feel movement at my back as Juls, Joey, and a stunned-looking Brooke flank my side.

Bryce wipes the drink from his eyes, not dropping his smile even the slightest. "I heard you had a bit of a temper. Does Reese like that? Do you fuck him angry?"

"Oh, no, you did not just say that," Joey spits, stepping closer to Bryce.

I hold my arm out and stop him from getting in Bryce's face. "Don't, Joey. He isn't worth getting arrested over." Because that's exactly what would happen. Bryce is such a punk, he'd press charges instead of manning up and actually fighting back.

Joey looks down at me, nostrils flaring. "He's not going to talk to you like that. Let me handle this."

"Oh, but I'd much rather Dylan handle me, Joey." Bryce leans against the bar, his white polo shirt now stained light pink. "You want that, don't you, baby? You want to handle me?"

"Fuck you, asshole. I really hope we're all around to see you get your ass beat," Juls says, grabbing mine and Joey's elbows and tugging us back. Bryce's smile touches his eyes, making them practically twinkle at the sentiment. "Come on. Let's go."

"Just for the record: up close, you're not hot," Brooke adds behind us. I turn and see her flip him off over her shoulder.

I place my hand on Joey's back, making sure he's moving with me as we both follow Juls away from the bar and toward the entrance. "Goddamn it," I utter to myself. Nothing would've pleased me more than to slap the snot out of that jerk. Well, except for maybe throwing my first punch. But I couldn't do that. I couldn't do anything.

We all pile into the limo and as soon as we get situated, Brooke opens the liquor cabinet. "I don't know about you three, but I need to get trashed."

A collective "yeah" fills the inside of the limo. *Alcohol after that encounter? Yes. Absolutely.* I find the button that lowers the window dividing us and the driver, dropping it down. I meet the man's eyes in the rear view mirror.

"Would you mind driving around for a while before you take us back to the house?" I ask him.

"Not at all, Miss."

"I cannot wait until Reese finds out about this. That prick is going to get the ass-beating of the century," Joey says, taking a champagne bottle from Brooke. She hands Juls and me ours after opening them.

"Reese isn't finding out about his," I inform him after taking a swig. I glance between the three pairs of eyes on me, all filled with concern. "I mean it. This account he and Ian have with Bryce is important enough for Reese to put aside his hate for that asshole and actually work with him. If we say anything, he'll drop the account for sure, and most likely go to prison for murder. He doesn't need to know. Nothing happened."

Juls taps her free hand nervously on her knee. "Shit. That account is huge. Ian said it's the biggest one their company has taken on. They're going to make an insane amount of money off it."

"Who gives a shit about the money?" Joey asks with a clipped tone. "That prick seriously crossed the line, and Reese needs to know about it."

"Joey, please, let it go." My voice is firm and final. I can't have Reese finding out about this; he will surely go homicidal on Bryce's ass. And it really wasn't that big a deal, so there's no reason to involve him. Nothing happened.

"Fine. Whatever." Joey tips his bottle back, taking several loud chugs. He wipes his mouth with the back of his hand when he finishes. "How many bottles are in there, Brooke?"

Brooke opens the cabinet and ducks her head inside. "A lot. It's fully stocked."

"Good," he says.

"Good," Juls echoes.

"Fucking great," Brooke adds.

I take a massive drink, letting the alcohol burn away the memory of those sinister, yellow eyes.

Each and every bottle that the limo came stocked with is emptied, and the mood inside the vehicle elevates with each sip taken. There's dancing, laughing, and Brooke, who cracks us up with her recount of the face shot heard round the world. When we're all fully tipsy, giggling loudly in the back and falling all over each other, the limo comes to a stop.

"Oh, my God. This was so much fun," I choke out, wiping underneath my eyes. I am way past the point of tipsy, as is everyone else in the vehicle.

"Brooke, you are fabulous. Any time you want to come out with us, feel free," Joey slurs out. "That cum-shot story won me over."

She smiles up at him, pushing her curly brown hair out of her face. "Even though my eye is still slightly blurry, that guy can come at me any time. He was smoking hot." Slapping her hand over her mouth, she spits out a laugh. "Psst! Get it? *Come* at me!"

Hysterical laughter fills the limo as the door opens, prompting Brooke and Juls to climb off the floor they had slid onto sometime during our joy ride.

"If you still want a bed, Brooke, you can share ours," Joey says as he crawls along the seat to the open door. "But I'm sleeping in the middle.

Nobody touches my baby."

Brooke's mouth drops open. "Really? We get to snuggle?"

Juls and I both gawk at each other in complete shock. Joey must be out-of-his-mind drunk to have offered that. I smile at Juls and motion for her to let this one play out. The morning after should be quite interesting to say the least.

We all file out, everyone's laughter fading into the air as they step out of the car. I steady myself on my feet, grabbing Joey's arm for stability, and lift my head toward the front door of our house. Ian and Billy are both sitting on the stairs, grinning amusingly in the direction of the four of us. But I don't linger on them. I can't, because Reese's frame is filling the doorway; his very tense frame. As my eyes focus on his face, the hard lines, the tight jaw, and those eyes of his that are heavy with disapproval, I'm quickly reminded of my wardrobe selection for the evening and the reaction I knew I'd get. What were my thoughts earlier? *This is my bachelorette party. I'm supposed to look sinful.*

Dylan Sparks. You asked for it.

Chapter
SIX

"UH OH," I WHISPER, HEARING Juls' and Joey's muffled laughs next to me. My eyes widen as Reese makes his way down the stairs, walking between Ian and Billy who both stand. I step to my left and slide behind my very tall assistant, concealing my inappropriate outfit. Like that will do me any good. One, he's already seen it, and two, it's Reese; nothing stands in his way of me.

Joey steps aside and looks over at me with raised eyebrows. "Are you nuts? He'll chuck me across the street to get to you."

I open my mouth to argue but close it when I realize he's probably right.

"You four look like you've had a nice time. I think Brooke wins for most drunk," Ian says with a teasing tone, crooking his finger and motioning for Juls to come to him. Juls immediately begins walking as Brooke moves past her and practically trips up the stairs, laughing in the process.

Joey leans over and kisses the top of my head. "Good luck, cupcake." He moves away from me and grabs Billy's hand. Billy winks at me over his shoulder before leaning in and kissing Joey.

"Oh, thanks a lot. Way to stick with your fellow woman," I yell out, seeing everyone turn and laugh at me as Reese stops inches away. I can practically feel the irritation boiling off him, radiating in waves directly onto me. I customarily tug the hem of my dress down, knowing full well it won't do me any good now, and then I look at him, all 6 foot 3 inches of him. He's so hot when he's angry that I momentarily consider wearing dresses like this daily, consequences be damned. This look is worth it. I'm certain there is no other man who can command attention the way Reese does, especially when he's pissed. I glance up at him from underneath my lashes, connecting briefly with his eyes before dropping my gaze and letting it take in his casual-yet-ridiculously-sexy polo shirt and khakis. "Hi. You look nice."

Understatement of the century. Reese has probably never looked *nice* a day in his life.

He steps into me, flattening my body against the limo and letting me know that even though he's about to freak the hell out on me for my dress selection, because that's what he does, he can't deny the way I affect him. I let out a soft gasp as he presses his lips to my temple. "What the fuck are you wearing, Dylan?"

"Uh, a dress. You never labeled this one."

"That's because I never fucking saw it," he growls. "Did you really think I'd be okay with you wearing this out tonight? This shit barely covers you."

I wrap my arms around his waist and pull him against me tighter. Harder. Wanting to feel the desire that is betraying his anger right now. It really is the only thing saving me from a Reese-style flip-out. Besides, I'd much rather get fucked in the traditional sense as opposed to verbally. If I can get my hands on an advantage here, I'm taking it.

I tilt my head up, my drunken smile spreading across my face. "I think you're *very* okay with me wearing this right now, handsome. Your massive and very-loved boner is giving you away. And just so you know, I'm not attached to this dress, so feel free to rip it apart." I slide my hand down between us, stroking him through his pants.

He grabs my hand and halts me, pinning it against my body. "No playing for you tonight, love. Not after this stunt." He bends down and lifts me, throwing me over his shoulder while keeping one hand on my ass; no doubt to make sure it remains covered.

"Reese! I'm going to throw up." The ground beneath me begins to spin as he carries me up the stairs and into the house. I bring one hand up and cover my eyes. "I'm serious. Can you not go all caveman on me right now? Drunk Dylan is getting dizzy."

He shifts me in his arms, bringing me down and cradling me against his chest. I immediately stick my face in his neck and inhale, wrapping my arms around him as we begin the climb up the second set of stairs. I feel his lips on my forehead. "Must you always challenge me? You know it makes me crazy."

"Mmm. I love you, too." I press kisses to his neck, feeling the vibration of his growl against my lips. "Do you like my shoes?" I ask, kicking my feet in the air as he pushes the door to our bedroom open. I tilt my head up and see his eyes darken, feeling his intensity hit me like a bullet.

"Very. I want them digging into my back while I fuck the breath out of you."

Holy Hell. Yes. Tonight. Please.

He drops me on my feet at the foot of the bed, keeping his arms wrapped around my back. I drop my head against his chest with a soft thump.

"How much did you have to drink?"

"Not sure. A few bottles, maybe," I reply, keeping my head down. *Definitely a few bottles.* I hear his gruff exhale, prompting me to raise my head. "Relax, Mr. Sassypants. I was only slightly tipsy shaking my ass at the club." I cover my mouth with my hand, muffling my giggle. *Mr. Sassypants. Good one.*

"That gives me no comfort, Dylan."

I drop my hand and wrap it around his waist. "Well, what did you guys do tonight? I'm sure you weren't angels."

Keeping me in his arms, he turns us so the back of my legs hit the bed. "We went out to dinner and then came back here."

I turn my head up to him. "That's it? What kind of a bachelor party is that?"

"I didn't care about having a bachelor party; you know that. Now, stop talking and get on the bed."

Oh, hello, bossy Reese.

I bite my lip to contain my smile, doing as I'm told and stretching out on my back. "Are you going to fuck me now?"

He leans over me, grabbing the hem of my dress with both hands. "No," he sternly replies as he tugs my dress in separate directions, ripping it up the middle.

"No?"

His hands move higher underneath the material, brushing against my upper thigh. His eyes lock onto mine. "No," he repeats, pulling again and splitting my dress even higher. My garter and panties are revealed to him in the process. His eyes appreciate the sight with an endearing caress while his lips remain in a hard line.

"What do you mean 'no'? You said you wanted me digging into you with my shoes." Bending my knee back, I press the sole of my heeled foot against his crotch and apply the tiniest bit of pressure. Keeping one hand on my dress, his other grabs my ankle and he gives me a warning look. I shoot him one back, my tipsy state giving me the courage I need. "I want to get fucked. By you." In case clarification is needed.

He pushes my foot down and grabs the two halves of my dress, locking eyes with me as he yanks the remaining material apart, exposing me completely. I lay underneath him, practically naked, and I see the struggle in his eyes to stay angry with me. But he manages. "You're not coming tonight, Dylan. Not after going out in public in this shit." He pulls the shredded material out from underneath me and tosses it onto the floor. "And don't even think about trying to handle that situation on your own. If I hear one moan or sexy little whimper out of you, I'll spend the rest of the night withholding your orgasm."

My eyes widen at his threat. *Shit. That sucks. He's crazy-good at that.* I cross my arms over my chest, blocking his undeserved view as he brings my foot in front of him, his fingers working the strap around my ankle. "Whatever. If I don't get off, then you don't get off either. You'll be suffering as much as I will."

He drops my shoe onto the floor and arches his brow at me. "Is that right?"

"Yes," I state with a clipped tone. My other shoe gets tossed over his shoulder, but I don't care where because all my attention is drawn down to his hands as he works his cock free and begins stroking it. I gasp and reach out for it, my mouth watering at the sight. "Oh, my God. Let me do that."

"No." He lets his khakis slide down to mid-thigh as he stares at my body, his hand working his glorious cock. I've never seen Reese jerk off before, and I'm kicking myself for never requesting that he do it in front of me. This is insanely hot, probably one of the hottest things to witness. His upper body is flexed completely, every muscle bulging out at me, screaming for my hands. And then there's his cock.

That. Cock.

So desperately hard and making my pussy ache with a stark need, because it belongs there. He strokes it leisurely, letting this moment last as his breathing becomes irregular. *Sweet Jesus*. I begin to pant right along with him.

I sit up, putting my face at the perfect height. "Fuck my mouth."

He pushes me back down and continues pulling his cock. "No."

"What? Why?"

"Because you get off on that. And I told you, you're not coming tonight."

Goddamn it. Why do I have to enjoy sucking him off so much?

Because it's awesome.

I grunt my irritation, slipping a hand between my legs. He grabs my wrist with his free hand and pins it against my body, angling himself over me. "I told you no," he grates out through clenched teeth, his lips curling back and revealing them to me. "You knew I wouldn't approve of that dress, so why did you wear it?"

My eyes stay glued to the hand around his cock, ignoring everything else around me. I see the veins in his arms jut out as he gives me the biggest tease of my life.

"Dylan."

"Huh?" I croak, reaching up and placing my hand to my chest. It's heaving, forcefully pushing against my palm. He slows his stroking, prompting me to look into his eyes. "I wanted you to rip it."

His eyes widen, sparkling with curiosity.

I swallow the uncomfortable lump that's lodged itself in my throat before explaining myself. "I... I think it's really hot when you get all crazy over what I wear. You like showing me who has control, but I see you struggling with it when you see me in outfits like that. I like knowing I can do that to you. You're not easily unraveled."

He releases my wrist and grips my hip, digging into my skin as he slides me closer to him. He's hovering above me, close enough to touch, but he won't let me. His face relaxes slightly. "Your body belongs to me. When you wear shit like that and I'm not around, other men think they have a shot at what's mine. They don't. And I'm half-tempted to go to that club and kill every motherfucker in there who looked at you."

I place my hand on his chest, lightly applying pressure. "Hey. It was just a stupid dress. Are you going to act like this on Saturday and go on a killing spree at the Whitmore? The bride gets a lot of attention on her big day."

One eyebrow raises. "Are you planning on wearing something like that?" I smile sweetly and shake my head, my eyes dropping to watch him return to his task. "You want to see me lose control?"

"Yes," I answer breathlessly.

His eyes roll closed and he starts stroking faster, gripping tighter, breathing heavier. I can only lie back and watch, completely fascinated and way the hell turned on. "Fuck," he pants, eyes flashing open. "You unravel me every second, love. Every time I look at you." He groans loudly, finding his release and shooting it onto my stomach. His nostrils flare as his eyes slowly reach my face. "My eyes only. Remember that."

I nod, unable to form a verbal response. My mouth is too dry for words at the moment.

He straightens up and lets his pants and boxers fall to the floor, stepping out of them. His shirt is removed next and I watch in complete awe as he walks toward the bathroom, his glorious, bare ass tempting me to give my clit the attention it's screaming for. "Don't even think about it."

His voice cuts into my lustful thoughts and I stop myself from responding with a lie. Because that's exactly what it would be. I was thinking about it; it's hard not to at the moment. He returns with a small towel and proceeds to wipe me clean.

"Reese?"

"Yeah?" He chucks the towel across the room, returning his eyes to mine. And there it is, that endearing look he seems to reserve just for me. The look that makes my heart swell against my ribs. No tension in his face, no tight lips or creased brow, just him. The man I'm going to marry.

I turn and glance at the alarm clock. I was originally going to threaten to withhold his orgasm someday, but that look of his totally gets to me. Like it always does. "Six days."

His eyes flick quickly to his left, verifying what I've just told him. A light smile touches his lips as he climbs onto the bed, sitting with his back against the headboard. He taps his lap, eyes soft and no longer laced with anything besides affection. I can't resist that look. And I want my spot. Crawling into his lap, I lay my cheek against his chest and nuzzle away. His arms wrap around me, pulling me closer before he bunches the covers around my waist. My favorite smell in the world fills me, intoxicating me further, and I feel my body relax into his as my sexual frustrations slip away.

"So, Juls said this account with Bryce was worth a lot of money. Is that why you're doing it?"

I feel his fingers play with the ends of my hair as it falls down my back. "No. I'd never work with somebody who made you uncomfortable because I want to get paid. It's just really important, that's all."

I lean back, not feeling satisfied with his cryptic answer. "Why?"

We stare at each other for several seconds before he speaks. "Do you trust me?" My back stiffens and he notices, prompting him to grab my hips and pull me closer. "Do you?"

"Yes."

"Then trust me when I say it's important. I can't talk to you about it; not yet, anyway. But I will. I promise I'll tell you everything when it's all said and done."

I don't understand how any part of Reese's job can be secretive; he's an accountant, not in the mob. But I do trust him. Completely. So I'm not going to question this. "Promise me something?"

He smiles cunningly. "Depends on what it is."

I grab his face and lean in, brushing my lips against his. "Don't do anything that would keep you from marrying me. I will be a very angry bride if you spend our wedding day in jail."

He laughs against my mouth. "Nothing could keep me away, love."
I drop my head back down and close my eyes.
Nothing could keep me away either.

Chapter SEVEN

I'M NEVER DRINKING AGAIN.

My head is pounding, my stomach is rolling, and my face is plastered to the cold tile of the bathroom floor.

This is not a good look for me. Nor is it one I wear often.

I've puked most of the night, the wave of nausea hitting me hard sometime after I passed out on Reese's chest and sending me barreling head-first toward the toilet. But miraculously, I'm a quiet puker, so my well-rested fiancé was kept blissfully unaware about my nightly vomit-fest. That is, until he caught me praying to the porcelain God this morning, which is where I've spent most of my time while he packs for both of us. I'm dressed now, so at least progress has been made.

I feel his hand on my hip as I stay in my permanent fetal position. "Here, love. I brought you some water and two Advils. Have you thrown up recently?"

I shake my head, keeping my eyes closed.

"Do you think you're going to throw up any more?"

I shake my head again. I haven't thrown up in a least an hour, but I also haven't tried moving either. I hear the soft clink of a glass and then feel his arms wrap me up as he lifts me off the floor, effortlessly as usual. I lay my head against his chest until he shifts me in his arms. I feel the bathroom countertop underneath my thighs as he sets me down on it and settles between my legs.

He picks up the glass of water and holds it out to me with the two pills in his other hand. "Take these. It'll help. And we'll get you some ginger ale on the plane for your stomach."

I swallow the pills and drink close to half the glass before setting it down next to me. My head drops forward and my shoulders slouch. "I hate having you see me like this."

He laughs quietly. "Like what?

I tuck my hair behind my ear and groan, keeping my eyes on my legs. "Like a train wreck. This isn't like me; I can usually hold my alcohol. I don't think I've gotten sick since the singing-telegram tequila incident." My stomach churns at the word tequila. That hateful bitch and I can't be in the same room together. I bring my fingers up to my face and begin massaging my temples. "What time do we have to leave?"

"Soon. The cabs will be here in thirty minutes." His hands run down my bare arms, gently applying pressure. "Can I do anything else? Do you need anything?"

I shake my head before dropping it against his chest. "Just you."

He presses a kiss to my hair. "You got me."

The sound of our bedroom door opening alerts us both, and Ian emerges in the bathroom doorway. He surveys my pathetic condition as he leans against the doorframe, crossing his arms and his ankles. "What the hell did you and Juls drink last night? She's been throwing up since 3:00 a.m."

I shrug, barely moving my shoulders an inch. All my strength seems to have left me. "Just champagne. We had some wine at the spa, but not enough to make us sick." I grab onto Reese and slide off the countertop. "Let me go see her."

I pull my hair into a messy bun as I walk through our bedroom and into the hallway. My head still feels like it's in a vise, but my stomach seems to have settled. I see the suitcases lined up outside the rooms, ready to be taken out. Four suitcases. Reese, Ian, Juls, me. *Where are the others?* Joey's door is still closed and I panic that he and Billy might oversleep and miss the flight. Without knocking, or thinking, I open his door and barge in like I own the damn place.

Three heads pop up in the bed. Three very startled heads. And one of those heads becomes very alarmed being sandwiched between the other two.

"Brooke! What in the fuck are you doing in here?" Joey grabs the covers and pulls them up into his lap, covering him and Billy.

"Relax, baby. You invited her," Billy says, before lying back on his pillow.

Joey looms over him. "I sure as shit didn't. Did you?"

Billy grimaces before rolling over, pulling the covers over his head.

Brooke rubs her eyes and smiles. "You invited me, Joey. You also called me fabulous, I think, and said I'm welcome to join you guys anytime you go out." She slips out of bed, revealing herself in a man's T-shirt that barely covers the line of her panties. She flattens her palm against her forehead, frowning. "Oh, hello, hangover."

"I would never invite you to share a bed with us. And get the hell out of my T-shirt. That's one of my favorites."

"Calm down, JoJo. You most certainly did ask her to share your bed. Drunk Joey is a major fan of Brooke," Juls' voice comes from behind me. I spin around a bit too quickly and have to steady myself with a hand on the wall. And then I look at her. She's dressed in skinny jeans and a blouse, her hair pulled back into a bun and her makeup looking fresh. Even if she has been throwing up since 3:00 a.m., she doesn't look it. Julianna Thomas has never looked anything less than chic a day in her life. She grins at me. "Sweets, can I talk to you?"

I nod, turning back around. "Cabs will be here in thirty minutes. You guys better get moving." All three bodies scramble out and around the bed while Joey quietly grunts his disapproval of the situation. I follow Juls out of the bedroom, down the hallway, and down the flight of stairs.

"What's up? And why don't you look like shit? I know I do," I say as we make our way into the kitchen. She holds a cup of coffee out to me, and I take it with an appreciating moan.

"I think I'm pregnant."

I inhale the biggest, hottest mouthful of coffee known to mankind when I hear her statement. The scalding beverage slides down my throat, searing my tissue as I cough it up and hang my head over the sink. Mouth open, I let it run out down my chin and into the deep basin. "Owwwahhhhhh."

Her hand touches my shoulder. "Oh, shit. Are you okay? Do you want some water or milk or something?"

I wave her off, wiping my chin with the nearby hand towel. "No. But maybe next time wait 'til after I've put my coffee down before you say something like that." I let my mouth hang open, inhaling the cool air that fills the kitchen while my mind processes her words to me. I feel my slightly-sore lips curl up. "You think you're pregnant? I didn't even know you guys were talking about that yet."

She hesitates slightly before nodding with quick drops of her head. "Well, Ian wants babies yesterday. I always thought I'd wait until I was in my thirties, but it's all he talks about. And the more he talks about it, the more I think about it." She plays with the buttons on her blouse, looking over my shoulder in the direction of the stairs. I turn and see Ian and Reese walking down the stairs with our suitcases, both of them smiling in our direction before they walk out the door. I return my attention back to Juls as she begins twisting the diamond stud in her ear. "My doctor told me it can sometimes take a while for birth control to get out of your system completely. Years for some women. So I stopped taking the pill a few months ago and didn't tell Ian."

I step closer to her, the excitement building in my gut. "Are you late?"

"My periods are irregular. I really haven't had one since I stopped taking the pill. But, my boobs are really sensitive and there's no way the amount of champagne I drank last night could've made me that sick. I can usually handle way more than that and not have my head stuck in a toilet."

My thoughts begin to scramble as I lean back against the counter and stare at the floor. I can usually handle way more than that, too. I was pretty tipsy last night, but I wasn't *that* drunk. Not to the point of it warranting the dry-heaving session I endured for several hours; at least I don't think. And my periods are so damn sporadic I never know when to expect them. But I got my shot a few months ago, so I should be covered. There's no way I could be...

"Sweets, are you okay?"

Juls' voice cuts into my thoughts. I twist the towel around my one hand, making it look like something a boxer might wrap his punching hand with. "Huh? Uh, yeah. I just—" I look up at her, "—are you going to tell Ian?"

She shakes her head. "Not until I take a test first. You know how he is. He'll tell everyone on that damn plane he's going to be a daddy if I say anything to him now. And I'd hate to get his hopes up."

I chuckle. Ian would do something like that. That man is crazy when it comes to Juls. I smile at the idea of my very best friend driving a minivan full of little black-haired Ian lookalikes. She'll have no trouble balancing her wedding planner business with soccer practice and PTA meetings. She's amazing at everything and makes it look effortless. And then another image fills my mind: me, working in the kitchen of my bakery while tiny little feet run circles around my worktop. I can see the wild mess of brown hair just above the counter height and little grubby hands reaching for a taste of whatever it is I'm making. And that image makes my eyes suddenly misty.

Juls grabs my hand, squeezing it gently. "Hey, what's wrong? No crying during your wedding week."

I reach up and wipe underneath my eyes, turning my body toward her. "I want to take a test, too. Do you think we could do it together?"

Her eyes go wild with excitement and then instantly water over. She wraps her arms around me. "Oh, my God. Yes, of course. Have you talked to Reese about having kids yet?"

"No, not yet. But it's weird. I got sick too."

She leans away from me and frowns. "That is weird. Although, it could just be nerves. You have been stressed out to the max lately." Her eyes glance over my shoulder and she immediately shakes off any trace of baby emotion on her face. "We'll keep this between us until we know for sure," she whispers.

I nod, spinning around and seeing Brooke pull her luggage down the stairs, followed by Joey and Billy who are arguing. Once they reach the bottom, Joey hands Billy his suitcase and makes his way over toward us with distinct annoyance. Billy and Brooke walk outside, leaving the three of us alone in the kitchen.

"Any chance your sister can ride with the luggage? I'm in no mood for another plane ride with her."

Juls steps into him and pokes her finger at his chest. "Buck up, JoJo. And drop the attitude. Poor Billy doesn't deserve to put up with your moodiness because you're on your man period." She stalks away from him like she's just delivered an epic blow, swaying her hips and letting her heels click loudly on the marble floor.

Joey huffs dramatically. "My 'man period'? What the hell has gotten into her?"

Hormones.

Reese walks through the front door, grabbing the last suitcase Brooke apparently left for whomever to pick up for her. My eyes narrow in on his perfectly-messed-up hair, and I can't hide the smile that will most likely blind anyone who looks at it.

Mini-Reese's running around my shop. How crazy cute would that be?

He raises his head and locks eyes with me, shifting the suitcase into his left hand and holding his right out for me to take. "Cabs are here. Are you two ready?"

I'm ready. To go back to Chicago. To take a test and find out if I'm simply losing my edge when it comes to my drinking ability. To be one day closer to marrying the only man I've ever pictured having tiny lookalikes with.

I could be pregnant right now. There could be a tiny peanut inside me, pissed the hell off that I chose to drag him to my bachelorette party. I flatten my hand against my stomach as I move toward Reese, holding out my other hand for him to take.

His brow furrows. "Is your stomach still upset? I can ask the driver to stop on the way to the airport to get you something for it."

I shake my head, patting my stomach before dropping my hand down. "No. I'm okay."

You hear that, peanut? If you're in there, I'm definitely okay.

e&

"YOU WANT THE WINDOW SEAT, love? Is doesn't matter to me."

I glance up at Reese, bringing my attention away from my belly. He secures my carry-on in the overhead compartment above our row before turning his eyes to me. I smile and press a kiss to his stubbly jaw before I move between the seats, feeling his hand smack my ass. "Thanks, handsome. Juls hogged it on the way here," I say with a teasing tone, loud enough for her to hear.

She scrunches her face at me in the row ahead of us.

"I'm going to use the bathroom before we take off," Brooke says, getting out of her seat in front of me and proceeding toward the back of the plane.

Joey stands from his seat across the aisle from us and claims Brooke's, kneeling so he's facing me. He motions for me to come closer, grabbing Juls' attention in the process. "So, what happened with the dress? Did it survive the night?" he asks in a hushed whisper.

I glance over my shoulder at Reese, making sure he's unaware of Joey's questioning which apparently can't wait 'til we land in Chicago. His head is tilted down as he glances at his phone, completely focused. I scoot to the edge of my seat. "No, it was destroyed in a very Reese-like manner."

"Hot." Joey wiggles his brows playfully at me. "I bet you got laid hard, didn't you?"

Juls slaps his arm. "Shouldn't we be asking you that, Mister Three-some?"

"That did not happen. I'm gayer than gay, and so is Billy. We just snuggled."

"Oh?" I ask, teasingly. "You snuggled with Brooke?"

He looks from me to Juls and then back to me. "Yes. In my drunken stupor, I snuggled with a girl. Now, if you both don't mind, I'd like to hear about someone getting laid last night because I sure as shit didn't."

Juls rolls her eyes as I scoot closer to both of them. Frowning, I shake my head before I reply. "No one got laid in my bedroom. I wasn't allowed any relief and was forced to watch Reese jerk himself off. It was hot and frustrating. And hot. Did I mention hot?"

Joey and Juls' both stare at me, mouths gaped open. Ian turns his head and glares over the seat. "What did you just say?"

Oh, shit.

I sit back quickly, glaring at Juls and Joey with panicked eyes. Juls turns and plants her butt down in her seat while Joey stands and excuses himself across the aisle.

Reese places his hand on my leg. "Everything okay?"

"Hmm mmm." I slide my hand underneath his, interlocking our fingers. "Do you want to have kids?" The words cascade out of my mouth like the scalding coffee did earlier, surprising us both in the process. *Shit, Dylan. Way to just blurt it out.* I drop my head against the seat, feeling my hand tighten against his and my breathing become slightly restricted.

He tilts his head, leaning closer to me. "With you? I've thought about it."

"Yeah?"

He nods, his lip twitching in the corner. "Yeah." Before I can pry anymore, he brings his free hand across his body and places it flat against my stomach. I stop breathing all together as I watch his eyes go to my belly. "I want to mark this, too." I feel his palm slide across my shirt, applying the tiniest amount of pressure. He's studying his hand on my belly like he always studies me, with pronounced focus. Like nothing could pull him out of his moment.

"Shit. He couldn't stay here," Juls grumbles in front of us.

My eyes lift and land on Bryce as he walks down the middle aisle. I immediately tense and Reese feels it. The hand on my belly is removed, and he brings our conjoined hands to his lap. I take my eyes off Bryce and watch as Reese sits back in his seat, his chest rising with a deep inhale. He's radiating with an unspoken threat, and I know Bryce feels it. I can see the apprehension in his eyes as he approaches our row. He tries to hide it, but it's there. And it should be; Reese could easily snap this asshole in half.

He doesn't say anything to us, but I see the shift in his expression, the moment he grows balls as he walks up to our row. All uneasiness fades and I immediately recognize the Bryce who came into my shop that day. The one who stared at me as I kissed Reese goodbye outside the conference meeting. The one who bought me the drink last night.

The fucker who thinks he actually has a shot.

"I'm sorry," Reese says to me as Bryce moves past our row to the back of the plane. I look at him with confusion and he shakes his head with a heavy sigh. "I didn't know he was going to be on this flight. I thought he was staying here for a few more days."

"It's okay."

"It's not. I don't like him around you."

I place my free hand on his forearm. "Reese, it's fine. Really." My voice is full of conviction, and I see it working on his suddenly-geared-up state. He brings my hand to his lips and kisses it just as Brooke walks past him and stops in front of Ian.

"That guy is a total douche-canoe." Her eyes meet mine as I hold my breath.

Don't say it. Please, God, don't say it.

"Seriously, Dylan. Good on you for throwing your drink in his face last night."

Fuuccckkkkkk.

"Sit your ass down," Juls growls, reaching out for her sister and yanking her into the row. Brooke yelps as she tumbles over Ian, claiming her seat next to Juls.

I clamp my eyes shut, preparing myself for what could quite possibly ground this airplane. I don't need to look at Reese to know that he is fuming right now. I can sense it in the air.

"Dylan, what the fuck is she talking about?"

Maybe if I jump out the emergency exit, he won't follow me. That might be my best option here. Or I could punch myself in the face and pray for unconsciousness.

"Dylan, answer me."

His voice is so commanding, my body submits without a fight. I'm immediately turned toward him and grabbing both his hands, pulling them into my lap. "He was at the club we went to last night. We didn't know he was there until he bought me a drink and when that happened, I threw it in his face. He ran his mouth a little and then we left. That's all that happened, I swear."

His chest rises several times, heaving with fury. "He saw you in that dress." He pulls his hands out of mine and settles back into his seat. He's rigid, every muscle flexed as he struggles to keep himself seated. I know he wants to run to the back of the plane. I know he wants to beat the shit out of Bryce. And I know, by the way he isn't touching me, that I'm in deep shit for keeping this information from him.

Goddamn that dress. It's really screwing me left and right.

Chapter
EIGHT

THE TWO-AND-A-HALF-hour plane ride home was the longest of my life. I'm not sure why I complained about the one to New Orleans. I would much rather listen to Joey and Brooke banter endlessly as opposed to complete silence from my fiancé, the man who is never quiet with me. Juls kept giving me sympathetic looks over the seat, while Brooke kept mouthing 'I'm sorry' throughout the eerily quiet flight. But even though he was pissed, even though he was angrier than he's ever been with me, he was still my Reese.

He got me a ginger ale from the flight attendant without me asking for it. He carried my luggage with his as we walked from the terminal to his Range Rover. And he opened every door for me. I knew he wasn't purposely trying to make me feel even worse about keeping information from him, but that's definitely what ended up happening.

I hear the TV turn on in the living room as I plop myself down on the edge of his bed. I feel drained, mentally and emotionally. We've been home for nineteen minutes, not that I'm counting, and he still hasn't said one word to me.

I hate this.

Reese's words mean more to me than a lot of things. It was what I missed the most when we were apart for eighty-five days, and I could give him space right now and let him talk to me when he's ready, but I don't want space from Reese. I never will. If he doesn't want to talk to me in the traditional sense, maybe I can coax a few written words from him. I grab my phone out of the suitcase I haven't bothered unpacking yet and sit back down on the bed, folding my legs underneath me.

ME: *Do you know the exact moment I knew I loved you?*

I press send and hear the alert on his phone go off in the distance. I can't see if he's reading it and typing a response, reading it and deciding I don't deserve a response, or ignoring me completely. I go with option two. I'm not sure I deserve much of anything right now.

ME: *It was on your birthday. Do you remember what we did?*

I'm typing the answer for him when my phone beeps.

REESE: *How could I forget? I never thought I'd get you in my bed.*

I blink and send the tears down my cheeks, sniffing loudly. Loud enough to possibly alert him of my crying. But it's hard not to cry when he's given me his words. I've only been deprived of them for a little over three hours, but it felt like longer. Much longer. As I type my response, movement in the doorway catches my attention.

I'm in his arms before I can speak, before I can tell him I'm sorry, before I can wipe the tears from my face. I'm so drawn to him that even if I wanted to remain on the bed, there's not a chance in Hell I could. Not when I've fucked up and I need him to *feel* how sorry I am. My body trembles as he lifts me off the ground and holds me against him. He moans into my hair, and I cling to him like I'm desperate. Like I've been deprived for years of his contact. Like it could be taken away from me at any minute. And that's exactly how he holds me.

It kills me.

I cry harder, grip him tighter, bury my face so far into his neck it becomes borderline painful. I don't register that he's carried me through-out his condo until he crouches down and sits on the couch with me in his arms. I scoot closer until I'm practically in his skin. Until it's hard to determine where he ends and I begin. He keeps one arm on my legs while the other stays wrapped around my upper body.

I brush my lips against his neck, fisting his shirt in my hands. "I'm so sorry, Reese. Please talk to me. Yell, scream, I don't care. Just give me something. I can't stand not hearing your voice."

His breath warms the side of my face as he tilts his head down. "I wanted you on that trip with me because I can't stand being away from you. I'm selfish when it comes to you, Dylan. I always will be. I knew there was a possibility you would have to see Bryce. I knew he made you uncomfortable, but I took that risk and asked you to come with me anyway." He shifts me in his lap so we're face to face. "And then when I saw how you reacted to him on the plane, it killed me. I put you there. I made you feel that way. He saw you in that dress because of me. He stared at you, thinking the same thing I thought when I saw you in it. Because. Of. Me. I didn't put you first, and I should have. I don't deserve to know when you fell in love with me. I don't deserve to hear *your* voice."

My heart thunders in my chest as I absorb his words, words I wasn't expecting to hear. I had prepared myself for a Reese-style flip-out, but not this. How can this man think I wouldn't follow him anywhere? That any of this is his fault?

"No." I grab his face with my hands, brushing along the stubble on his jaw. "I wanted to be with you just as much as you wanted me there. Even if you wouldn't have asked me to go, I would've snuck in your suitcase or booked a flight without you knowing. I can't stand to be away from you either, so don't you dare act like this addiction is one-sided. I'm just as obsessed and selfish as you are."

Did I mention how much I hate to lose at anything? The competitive streak in me is fully engaged right now and if Reese thinks he's got me beat on this, he's dead wrong. In a battle of who loves who more, I'm taking the prize on this one.

I turn my body completely, straddling his lap and dropping my hands to his shoulders. "Now you listen to me, Carroll. I'm the one who should be feeling like shit here. Me. Not you. I'm the one who's constantly challenging you with outfits and my incessant need to push your buttons. And I'll always be like that. You're marrying someone who will most likely drive you crazy for the rest of your life. Why?"

Why? Shit. Why the hell did I ask that? Good job, Dylan. Let's make the man you love question the biggest decision of his life.

He opens his mouth to speak but I quickly slap my hand over it.

"Ignore that. We're getting off topic." I feel his laugh against my hand before dropping it to my lap, allowing the slightest smile to touch my lips. "I should've told you I saw Bryce at the club last night. I didn't because I was afraid of what you would do to him. And I also didn't want anything to mess up that account."

"What happened?" The sorrowed look he had moments ago has completely vanished, replaced with a look I'd never want to go up against. He seems to grow in size as he waits for me to recount my evening; that, or I'm suddenly cowering down. Could be a bit of both. "Dylan, do I need to call Brooke and ask her to tell me?"

I narrow my eyes at him and pout. "No. You don't." I exhale loudly, grabbing his hands and moving them to my breasts.

He frowns, looking at his hands. "What are you doing?"

"I'm using what I have to my advantage. You need to stay calm, and keeping your hands on my body is like a mild sedative for you."

"Not for my cock," he grunts. "And don't try to distract me. I want to know right now what happened last night. Every fucking detail."

I slide my hands to his wrists, lightly holding him. He doesn't make an attempt to move, so I decide to continue. "None of us knew Bryce was at that club until we went to the bar. The bartender gave me a drink and told me Bryce had bought it for me, which really pissed me the hell off. I mean, really. The nerve of that asshole. Like I would ever accept a drink from him."

"Dylan... focus."

"Right. Sorry." I clear my throat and think back to last night. "I went over to him with it and he opened his big stupid mouth, saying it's been too long since he's seen me and my dress belonged on his floor." Reese clenches his teeth and tries to drop his hands but I keep them on me. "I threw my drink in his face and he acted like he liked it, which pissed me off even more. Then he said something about me having a temper and asked if I fuck you angry. Joey tried to step in but I told him to drop it. Juls cussed him out. Brooke did, too. We left right after that."

Reese closes his eyes, keeping his hands on my breasts. I see his nostrils flare, and the veins in his neck become taut like tight coils. He takes five deep, calming breaths and I move my hands to his chest, flattening them out. His heart hammers against my palm as he slides his hands down and grips my hips tightly. "You should've slapped the shit out of him for saying that to you."

I lift my gaze off his chest and see his eyes beaming at me. "Your eyes are so green right now." I hold his face, studying the brightness. I've never seen anything like the color of Reese's eyes. Close to emerald, but not quite. "And you're right, I should've. But I couldn't because he's a little bitch who would either like it or call the cops on me. Bryce isn't a man, and he'd never take a slap like one."

"He won't be taking a slap from me."

And this is what I was worried about. "Reese, you can't. What about the account? And if you hit him, he could have you arrested."

He grabs my wrists, pulling my hands off his face. "I'm going to hurt him, Dylan. It's going to happen." He pauses, blinking heavily. "This shit better work," he all but whispers, dropping his gaze away from mine.

"Please," I beg through a strained voice, ignoring his last comment and only focusing on his threat. "Please, don't do anything. Beating the shit out of him isn't worth losing your job or going to jail over." My lip begins to tremble and the tears come again. "Please, Reese. I can't have anything happen to you." *We can't have anything happen to you.* I drop my head to his shoulder, feeling his arms wrap around me as I place a protective hand over my belly. Something *would* happen. This gut feeling I have isn't going away.

"Shhh. I don't want you to worry about this, okay? Dylan, I'm a smart guy. You need to trust me. I'm not going to do anything that's going to get me put in jail. Hey, look at me."

I keep my head down. "No. I'm ugly-crying right now."

He laughs into my hair before forcing my head back, tucking my hair behind my ears. "You don't ugly anything." I see his eyes drop down to my stomach. My hand is still there and he places his on top of mine and studies it for several seconds. I hear my breathing quicken as his brows furrow. And then he looks back up at me, lips partying slightly, and I see it. The moment it hits him. His free hand cups my face. "Love, are you…"

I place a finger to his lips and smile. "I don't know. I was thinking maybe I could be. It would explain why I got so sick this morning. Juls put the thought into my head. She thinks she's pregnant, too." He shifts me off his lap and gets to his feet, stepping into his shoes. "What are you doing?"

"I'm going to the store to get you a test. You're taking one tonight."

I sit on my knees and stare up at him. "What? No, I'm not. I'm taking one with Juls. We made a pact."

He glares at me. "Fuck that. I'm not going to be able to fall asleep tonight unless I know." He places a kiss to the top of my head. "I'll be back." He goes to walk toward the door but halts mid-step. Turning around, he bends down and places a kiss to my belly.

I giggle. "Reese. You could just be kissing the pretzels I ate on the plane."

He hits me with a wink before grabbing his keys off the counter and walking out the door.

❧

"HOW MANY DID YOU BUY?" I hover my finger over the boxes Reese has just dumped onto the bed, counting them out. All my Bryce anxieties vanished the moment Reese assured me he'd be smart about things. And now the only thing I'm concerned with is how much money my fiancé just spent at the local drug store. "Fifteen, sixteen, seventeen? You bought seventeen pregnancy tests? These things are like twenty bucks a piece."

He looks over at me curiously. "How the hell do you know?"

I wave him off. "Please. Every girl knows how much these things cost." I pick up the one that has a smiling mother-to-be on the front. "Well, I guess this one looks good." I take the box with me out of his bedroom and step into the hallway bath. Turning around, I see him at the door. "Um, what are you doing?"

He shakes his head, seemingly in a trance. "I don't know. Should I come in with you?"

I scrunch up my face. "You want to watch me pee?"

"No, I guess not."

I lean into him and kiss his cheek. "Relax. I'll be out in a second."

Closing the door behind me, I begin to open the box and hear a faint whooshing sound. I place my ear to the door. "Reese?"

"Yeah?" he answers immediately.

"Are you sitting outside the door?" I hear movement and smile, followed by a faint "no" in the distance a few seconds later. I pull out the instructions and read them over quickly, trying to calm the anxiousness building rapidly within me.

He's pacing in front of the bed, hands raking through his hair and down his face in a continual pattern. He looks up just as I step into the room. "Well?"

"Three minutes."

He sighs heavily, gripping the back of his neck with one hand. I sit on the edge of the bed and watch him burn a hole into the carpet. Back and forth, each step more purposeful than the last. His hair is a right mess and he's chewing nervously on his bottom lip. I see his eyes routinely go to the clock on the nightstand. I'm not even taking note of the time. I know he'll let me know when the three minutes are up. He glances once more at the clock and stops, turning toward me.

"Ready?" I ask, holding my hand out to him. He hesitates before forcing a nod and grabbing my hand. I stop at the doorway to the bathroom and look up into his glazed-over eyes. I've never seen Reese nervous before but right now, he's definitely nervous. I'm trying to keep my apprehension hidden, but it's there. "Can you check? I'd rather you tell me."

He drops all hint of uneasiness and steps into the bathroom, placing one hand on either side of the test and hovering over it. He leans in closer, studying it before grabbing the instructions I left out on the counter. I watch him for what feels like hours, his eyes going from the test to the instructions and back again. I see his shoulders sag, and my stomach drops. He places the test down and walks over to me, grabbing both my hands.

He shakes his head. "It's negative. Two lines mean you're pregnant, right?"

I nod, swallowing the huge lump that formed at hearing the results.

"There's only one line." I drop my head against his chest, and he immediately picks me up and carries me down the hallway. "I'm sorry, love. Are you sad?"

I nod as he places me down on the bed. He settles on top of me as I lay back on the pillow. "I really thought I was pregnant, but I guess I'm just losing my edge when it comes to drinking. How depressing is that?" I look up at him and run my fingers through his hair, taming the wild mess. "Are *you* sad?"

He shrugs once, his finger tracing my jaw. "A little. But I think I'd be really fucking worried if you were pregnant and went out drinking like that last night. Did you stop taking your birth control?"

I shake my head and bring my hands down to his shoulders. "I got my last shot almost three months ago. If you wanted to start trying now, I just wouldn't get it again."

He smiles, dropping his head and kissing my lips. His tongue trails along my bottom one before he nips it. I whimper and he moans softly. "I want to start trying. Right now." He sits back between my legs and removes his shirt. "How effective is that shot?"

I furrow my brows, confused by his questioning. "Umm, like 98% I think. Why?" He sits me up and pulls at the hem of my tank top, his boastful smile growing. "Oh, you think your super sperm can get through my defenses, huh? Is that it?"

He tosses my shirt and crawls on top of me, pressing his lips to my stomach. "Nothing stands in my way, love. Modern medicine included." His fingers work at my jeans, unbuttoning and unzipping them. "And I'm always up for a challenge. Fuck that 98%."

I giggle as he slides my jeans and panties off. "Reese?"

"Yeah?" He keeps his head down as he unbuttons his shorts. When I don't answer immediately, he lifts his gaze to me and his smile fades.

I bite the inside of my cheek, straining to keep the serious face I have on. "You know we can't have sex when I'm pregnant, right?"

Oh, I'm devious.

He freezes after dropping his shorts and boxers. "I can't fuck you for nine months? Are you serious?"

"Yeah. It's not good for the baby. You could poke it and stuff."

He strokes his jaw, dropping his gaze to the floor. "Why haven't I heard about this?" he asks himself. He drops his hand, slapping his thigh and lifts his head. "Well, can we do other stuff during that time? There's no way in hell I'm going to be able to keep my hands off you for that long. Not happening. We'd have to live separately."

My body begins to shake with my silent laughter as I cover my face with my hands. I feel the bed dip and slide my hands down, seeing his curious expression above me. I smile wide and continue laughing. "I'm sorry. That was too easy. You should've seen your face."

He looms over top of me, dark and dangerous, and my laughter quickly fades out. "Oh, you're going to pay for that one, Sparks."

I reach up and grab his face, bringing his lips to mine. "Bring it on, Carroll."

He totally brings it.

Chapter
NINE

REESE WASN'T KIDDING WHEN HE said he was up for a challenge. I'm pretty sure some orgasm-giving record was broken last night by him. Every time I came, it seemed to drive his need to do it again and again. He was relentless, fucking me until he didn't have anything left to give me. Literally. I'm fairly certain the man is out of viable baby-makers today. And he didn't need time to recharge between sessions, either. While I was panting on the bed, the couch, and in the shower, trying to catch my breath and needing a moment to regroup, he was bouncing on his feet like a boxer, amped and ready for the next round. I've never seen him so geared-up for sex before, so I gotta give it to the man. When he sets his mind on something, he definitely goes for it.

Hard.

My vagina is screaming for an ice pack as I make my way down Fayette Street and toward the bakery to meet Joey for our daily run. Running always helps me keep my sanity, and I'm going to need it with the week I have prepared. Not only is my wedding in five days, but Brooke is also starting today, and besides that, I'm feeling bloated and terrified of the possibility of not squeezing into my lace masterpiece of a dress tonight at my final fitting. I'm not even sure alterations can be made this close to the big day. And it has to fit. I'm wearing that dress. It's *the* dress. The one Juls made me try on all those months ago when we were shopping for her wedding gown. The one I desperately tried to not picture myself walking down the aisle toward Reese in. The one I was always meant to wear. So my injured vagina can hate me all she wants, but I'm pushing myself during this run.

After parking Sam behind Joey's Civic, I round the corner and see my dear assistant bouncing around on his feet in front of the bakery. He turns his head, smiling when he sees me, and flattens his palm against the glass window as he stretches his hamstrings.

"Morning, cupcake. You look freshly-fucked."

I wince at his sentiment, mimicking his position and grabbing my ankle behind my back. "That's an understatement. I think Reese broke my vaj."

He switches legs, raising an eyebrow. "I just pictured the weirdest image." He seems to picture it again, blinking several times as he stares off past me. I laugh, prompting him to bring his focus back to me as he bends at the waist and reaches for his toes.

"So, I'm going to assume he isn't still pissed at you for keeping the whole Bryce incident from him?"

I grab my other ankle, stretching out my sore muscle. My vagina isn't the only thing recovering from my marathon sex.

"Actually, he was more mad at himself than anything. He hates that he put me in that position in the first place, which is ridiculous. Like there isn't a possibility of me running into that massive dickhead here. I'm actually surprised he hasn't come into the shop since the last time."

Joey straightens quickly, averting his gaze toward the busy street. I notice his shifty behavior and drop my leg, stepping sideways and forcing him to look at me.

"Joey, Bryce hasn't set foot in my shop since his initial creepy visit, right?"

He drops his head from side to side, stretching out his neck. "He may have stopped in a few times while you were in the back or on a delivery. I dealt with it."

Oh, that piece of shit. "What? Why didn't you tell me?"

He motions with his head for us to start running, setting the pace as we make our way down the sidewalk. "Because I dealt with it. The last time was weeks ago, and I told him to stay the hell away from you. He hasn't been back since."

I jump over the jagged part of the sidewalk I'm sure to trip over one of these days. "I want to know if he comes in again, Joey. I'm not putting up with this." That jerk has another thing coming if he thinks I'm okay with him coming into my shop. I don't care if it's for treats or not. He can get his baked goods elsewhere. He probably wouldn't even eat my decadent creations anyway. He'd probably just use them to taunt children or something; lure them into his creepy van with cookies and non-existent puppies.

I'm not sure when Bryce became a pedophile in my mind, but right now, that's how I'm picturing him.

Joey huffs loudly as we make our way up the hill. "Can you get a restraining order on somebody for just being a creeper? My cousin tried to get one a few years ago on this guy who kept asking her out but the cops said because he hadn't threatened her in any way, she couldn't get one."

I shake my head and push myself harder, picking up speed. "I don't know. Slapping that asshead with a restraining order isn't exactly the kind of violence I have in mind. I was thinking more along the lines of shoving his dumb ass into oncoming traffic."

"Preach," Joey says through a laugh. He turns around, jogging backwards as I slow down a bit. "Let's talk about something else. You're getting all worked up, and this week needs to be relaxing for you." He spins back around and blows out a loud breath. "What time is the fitting tonight?"

I smile over at him, letting go of the anger causing me to clench my teeth. "6:30 p.m. Are you coming?"

"Of course. The Man of Honor wouldn't miss it for anything."

We both chuckle at the title I gave Joey when I asked him to be in my wedding six months ago. I couldn't pick between him and Juls for the highly-coveted Maid of Honor spot. They are both so special to me, so I decided to make Juls my Matron, since she's married, and Joey my Man. It works out perfectly, and Joey couldn't be happier about it. He even tossed around the idea of getting it sequined on the back of his tux for the big day. I wouldn't expect anything less.

"I can't wait to see you in that dress. You're going to look fabulous."

I take off running, hearing him yelp behind me. He catches up and gives me a flustered look. "If I'm going to look fabulous, I need to burn off the booze we drank this weekend." I nudge against him and he laughs. "Come on. I'll race ya around the block."

AFTER MY FIVE-MILE RUN, WHICH leaves my legs feeling like over-cooked noodles, I dash upstairs and hop into my shower. Another reason why I love keeping the loft above my bakery is for this very reason; I don't have to go back to the condo to get ready for my day after my daily runs. The space still looks the same, seeing as the only thing I moved out of here was half my wardrobe. I actually wouldn't mind it if Reese agreed to just move in here after the wedding. I know it's a small space, but I don't need much. Of course, if we are to have kids, I'm not sure a one-bedroom loft will cut it. Especially if we have a lot of kids, which is what I'm leaning toward. I want a bakery filled with mini-Reeses'. Tons of green-eyed, messy-haired cuties who can taste test my creations all day. And if last night was any inclination as to how he feels about the subject, I'm thinking he won't be disagreeing to that idea.

I hear my cell phone ring as I wrap a towel around my chest, prompting me to dart out of the bathroom and grab it off my bed before I miss the call. I don't even register the name on my screen before I answer.

"Hello?"

"Hello, sweetheart. And how is my bride-to-be?"

My mom's voice has me falling backwards onto the bed with an exhaustive grunt. *Damn it to Hell.* I should've looked at the name on the screen, or let this call go to voicemail entirely. There's only one reason why she's calling me. One topic she wants to discuss. I hear the sound of papers ruffling and know she's got her trusted notepad ready, full of last-minute changes she's about to suggest or insist I make. Because with five days until my wedding, we have all the time in the world to change shit around.

I rub my free hand down the side of my face, bracing myself for this phone call that will surely end in her throwing that same notepad across the room.

"I'm good, Mom. How are you?"

"I'm wonderful, dear. Listen, I swung by this quaint little Italian restaurant yesterday in Printer's Row, and it would be the perfect venue for the rehearsal dinner. And I already checked to make sure they're available."

I feel my frustration level quickly rising. "Mom, Reese and I don't want a rehearsal dinner. I've told you this already. We want to run through the ceremony and go out afterwards with our friends."

My mother gasps as if she's just now hearing this information for the first time, which is definitely not the case. "Dylan, every wedding has an actual sit-down rehearsal dinner. You can't skip that detail. It's crucial."

"Crucial? You make it sound as important as our wedding vows."

"It is," she insists with a firm tone.

I grumble and roll over, rubbing my face into the comforter. The faint smell of citrus calms me down a bit, but not enough to agree to this absurdity. "Mom, this is what Reese and I want. It's *our* wedding. I'm sorry if you don't agree with our decision, but it's final. No dinner. If people get hungry, they can go hit up a drive-thru."

"Oh, that's just ridiculous, Dylan. A drive-thru? How tacky is that." The sound of her exhaling loudly fills my ear, followed by the crinkling of paper. "Fine. No dinner. I suppose I'll have to pack some snacks for your father to munch on during the actual rehearsal. You know how he gets when he goes without a meal."

I chuckle into the comforter just as the sound of my loft door opening catches my attention. I roll over quickly, keeping the phone against my ear as Reese emerges behind the door. He closes it and I hold my hand out, palm up, silently asking him what he's doing here. It's almost six o'clock and he's usually at the office by now. He smiles his response before he walks toward me. He's dressed in his usual work attire, a dress shirt, tie, and khakis, and it gets me like it always does. The man does office-wear like no other.

"Hey, Mom, I gotta go. I'll see you tonight at the fitting, right?"

More papers rustling comes through the phone before she answers, prompting me to roll my eyes. "Of course. I'd never miss it. Maggie and I will meet you there at 6:30 p.m. Goodbye, sweetheart."

"Bye, Mom."

I press end and drop the phone onto the bed before lifting my gaze to Reese. "Handsome, what are you doing here? Don't you have numbers to crunch?"

He steps around my screen that divides my one large room into two and stops just in front of me. "I do. But I couldn't stop thinking about something."

"Oh? My sparkling personality?"

He laughs, reaching out and opening my towel. His eyes linger on my breasts for several seconds before he lifts his gaze to meet mine. "Do you think one of the times last night took?"

I watch his eyes shift back down and trail lower. "Um, I don't know. Maybe. You definitely gave it your all. Is that really what you can't stop thinking about?" *Cause your body language is screaming something else entirely.* Of course, Reese always looks at me like this. I'm certain that even if we were in church, he'd be able to melt the panties off me right in front of Jesus.

He nods, keeping his eyes on my body. "I want that so bad. I've never wanted that, Dylan. You don't understand. I've never thought about having kids before. Hell, I've never thought about getting married before." He leans into me, forcing me to lie back onto the bed. I reach for his tie, wrapping it around my hand as he holds himself above me. "But when I look at you, it's all I can think about. Marriage. Kids. Everything. I want it all with you. And I don't want to wait."

Oh, Reese. I raise my eyebrows, loosening my grip on his tie. "To marry me or to have kids?"

"To have kids. I'm dealing with the other thing." He leans down and kisses the corner of my mouth, once and then once again before slowly moving down my body. "Don't make me wait, love. I need to see you like that."

I moan as he brushes his lips against my rib cage. "Like what?" I know what. I just want to hear him say it. Because what the hell is hotter than the man you love wanting you to carry his child? Nothing. Especially coming from this man.

"With my baby inside you."

I reach down and thread my fingers through his hair. "Are you going to be late for work so you can make that happen right now? Because I'm all for another round of baby-making sex with you if that's where this is headed." *Suck it up, vagina. You can be sore tomorrow.*

"No, that's not exactly why I'm here. Close, though." He drops to his knees and drapes my legs over his shoulders. His hands grip my hips and he slides me closer to the edge of the bed, his lip curling up into a sly grin. "I'm going to be late for work because on top of not being able to stop thinking about last night, I also can't stop thinking about the taste of your pussy. And I was too busy yesterday fucking you all over the condo to get any of it. So lie back, keep your legs open, and give me what's mine."

"Jesus. I love when you order me around like that. Seriously, please do that all the time. Just not like to do your laundry or anything." He swipes up my length with his tongue, prompting me to fist the comforter. "Oh, God." His fingers dig into my hips as he flicks against my clit in a pulsing rhythm. At the feel of his teeth on my swollen spot, I arch off the bed and dig my heels into his back. "Reese. Jesus Christ."

"Mmm. You like that. You want it rough?"

I push his head down to silence him. I'm shaking, my thighs convulsing against his cheeks as he ravages me like it's his first time tasting me. Of course, he always goes at me like this, like he'll never get enough of me. He alternates between my clit and my pussy, stroking and sucking until he begins to fuck me with his tongue. I can't take it. I'm begging him to stop, to keep going, to do whatever the hell he wants. I'm a blubbering idiot right now because that's what his mouth does to me; it wipes all coherent thoughts from my head. And when I feel his finger dip into me briefly before trailing my wetness down to my backside, I lose my mind completely.

"Yes. Oh, God, please. Right there. Right fucking there."

He buries his face between my legs, humming against me while he presses his finger against my ass. This move of his, one I never thought I'd be into until he was the man doing it, this move makes me see fucking stars when I'm coming. He doesn't do it all the time, but when he does surprise me with this stellar addition to his orgasm-taking routine, my body vibrates for hours afterwards.

"Goddamn, you're beautiful when you come. Did that feel as good as it looked?"

"Hmm," I reply, unable to form a proper response as I slowly come down. My lifeless body hangs limp on the bed and over his shoulders as he plants gentle kisses to the inside of my thigh. I look down the length of my body and catch his smile. "Anytime you want to be late for work to do that, please, go for it."

He stands, licking his lips and holding his hands out to me. "I need to get going. Thanks for my fix." He pulls me to my feet, the towel covering me falling to the floor.

"You stole my line," I say against his mouth as he kisses me sweetly. "You good? No hand or mouth action required?"

He reaches down and adjusts himself in his khakis with a wince. "Actually, I think I need some recovery time after last night. Ask me again in eight hours."

I giggle as I bend over and grab my towel, securing it underneath my arms. "Don't forget, I have my fitting tonight so I won't be home until late."

He eyes me up suspiciously. "Do you really think you need to re-mind me about anything involving you?" Grabbing the back of my neck, he pulls me into him and plants a kiss to my forehead. "Bye, love." He releases me, turning and walking toward the door.

I enjoy my spectacular view, nodding in appreciation. The man's ass is a thing of wonder. Muscle upon muscle; it's insane, even through his pants. I don't know what exercises he does to work that perfectly-sculpted entity, but it's working.

I'm brought out of my fantasy when he opens the door. Lifting my gaze, I see he's caught me in my obsessive gawking. I'm not ashamed, not in the slightest. I smile the biggest, cheesiest grin I can muster and he laughs. "Bye, handsome. Five days."

He shakes his head, turning back around. I don't miss the smile on his face as he disappears behind the door, my words no doubt playing on loop in his mind.

Because they definitely are in mine.

Five days.

Chapter
TEN

AFTER STEPPING INTO SOME JEANS and one of my favorite tees I left behind, I slip into my ballet flats and head back into my bathroom. I yawn as I pull my hair up into a messy bun, tugging a few stray pieces out and tucking them behind my ears. After the all-nighter marathon sex, my five-mile run, and the orgasm that just rocked my body, I'm suddenly feeling ready for a nap instead of the day that's ahead of me. I apply the usual minimal makeup I wear daily and walk back into my living space, grabbing my phone off my bed. It's almost time for the shop to open and I have a massive amount of baking to do, considering I didn't get any done this weekend. And if I don't get started on it now, we're sure to run out of treats by lunch time.

As I pull out my mixer and set it on my worktop, the doorbell dings and seconds later, Joey comes rushing into the back.

"Extra-large, double shot of caramel for my favorite cupcake," he sings, depositing my piping-hot cup of coffee on the wood and pulling up a stool to watch me. He's dressed in one of his favorite baby-blue polo shirts that brings out the color in his eyes, his blond hair still damp from his shower.

"Oh, man, I seriously love you." I grab it and immediately take a sip, moaning as the hot liquid coats my throat. "Brooke's supposed to be here any minute and I've got a shit-load of baking to do, so unfortunately, you're going to be in charge of showing her the ropes."

He keeps all grumbles to himself, taking a sip of his coffee. "Whatever. As long as she doesn't try to grope me, I'm sure I can tolerate her for eight hours."

The doorbell dings and we both glance up, seeing Juls emerge in the doorway. She's chicly dressed in a tight, black dress with sky-high heels, her hair wrapped in an elegant twist. "Morning, lovies." She glances around the kitchen and her smile disappears. "Where the hell is Brooke?" Joey and I both shrug as I open my bags of flour, pouring a generous amount into my mixing bowl. "Oh, for Christ's sake. I'm going to kill her." She pulls her phone out of her purse and stalks out into the main bakery, leaving Joey and me alone with our amused expressions. A flustered Julianna Thomas is not something we're used to seeing.

"Ten bucks says she's late," Joey says confidently.

I cock my head and turn on my mixer, wiping my brow with the back of my hand. "Ten bucks says you'll snuggle with her again if the moment arises."

He narrows his eyes at me as Juls reemerges moments later.

"It went straight to voicemail. I'm sure she's on her way."

I start throwing the ingredients for my banana nut muffins together into my mixing bowl, feeling Juls' eyes on me. I glance up. "What?"

She pouts and moves closer to me, placing her hand on my arm. "I'm sorry. I know we agreed to wait to take a test together, but I slipped up last night and blurted out to Ian I thought I might be pregnant. As soon as I said it, he rushed out and bought me a test. There was no stopping him. I'll still take one with you, though."

"Umm, excuse me?" Joey asks, tapping the counter top impatiently with his fingers. "What the hell are you talking about?"

I turn the mixer off and smile at Juls, ignoring Joey's comment. "I took one, too. I'm sorry. The same thing happened with Reese. He was dead-set on me taking one last night. Mine was negative."

"Mine wasn't."

My mouth drops open as Joey squeals next to Juls. "What? You're pregnant?" There is no hint of sadness or jealousy in my voice. Even though I was disappointed last night in my test results, the news my best friend just dropped on us fills me with the same excitement I felt at the possibility of being pregnant myself.

She nods her response, putting her hands up to her face and covering her crimson cheeks. Joey and I both engulf her in a giant hug, and she wraps an arm around each of us. "I took several just to make sure. I thought Ian was going to make some sort of public service announcement last night. He's beyond excited."

"Oh, my God. Juls, this is amazing," I blink and send the tears down my face. "You're going to be such a kick-ass mommy."

"Helloooo," Joey interjects, stepping between the two of us and dropping his enthusiasm. "Both of you cock whores thought you were pregnant and didn't tell me? What the fuck? I thought we were besties."

I shove him off with my hand. "We are. We just didn't want you to get all excited for nothing."

Juls turns her attention to me and grabs my hands, her smile fading and replaced with a look of concern. "I'm sorry you're not pregnant, sweets. I know you were excited about the possibility."

Of course Juls would think about me when she should be jumping up and down like a maniac. She always puts others before herself. And she probably thinks I'm sensitive to this topic, but I'm not. I couldn't be happier for her.

I squeeze her hands gently and smile. "It's okay. Reese is in full-on 'get me pregnant' mode, so I'm sure it'll happen soon enough."

"Oh, shit," Joey mumbles, gaining mine and Juls' attention. His eyes widen and he grabs his coffee cup off the worktop before elaborating. "Reese is going to be crazy when you get pregnant. I can't imagine him being any more possessive over you than he already is, and you're not carrying his baby yet. He's nuts when it comes to you. Unreasonably nuts at times." He pauses, glancing around the kitchen. "Mmm. Do we have any cashews back here?"

"Over on the shelf," I scoff, dropping Juls' hands and turning around to grab my muffin tins. "And he's not *that* possessive over me."

"Yeah, right," Joey says at the same time as Juls' "yeah, okay."

Joey chuckles softly, popping a few cashews into his mouth as I place my tins onto the worktop. "Face it, cupcake. That gorgeous man is going to put you on lock-down when he knocks you up. And when that time comes, your wardrobe won't be the only thing he dictates."

I restart my mixer, licking the splash of batter off my finger. "I like possessive Reese. It's hot."

"It'll be real hot when he gives you a food list you have to eat from. Or when he asks you to stop working."

I snap my head up at Joey. "I'm not quitting my job. Reese would never ask me to do that. He knows how important my business is to me." Juls reaches over and stops the mixer, dipping her finger into the bowl. I swat her hand away. "Raw egg, prego. Back up."

She grunts and retracts her hand. "Damn it."

I shake my head, walking over to the racks and pulling out the container of muffins I made before closing on Friday. Grabbing a banana nut one, I hold it out to Juls and she excitedly takes it. "And it's not like I do manual labor. With Brooke starting, hopefully sometime today, I'll be able to plant my butt on a stool and bake away back here. I won't even have to be on my feet that much when I'm pregnant."

Juls bites into the top of her muffin, leaning her body against Joey who has reclaimed his stool. "She's right, JoJo. It's totally doable. And Reese may be possessive over her, which I agree is mad hot, but he'd never ask Dylan to give up working. This is her love." She glances down at her watch, straightening up. "I gotta get going. I'm meeting with the caterers this morning to make sure the menu is finalized. Text me when Brooke arrives." She plants a kiss to the top of Joey's head and blows me one before turning on her killer heels and heading for the door.

"If she arrives," Joey murmurs, winking at me before he heads up front.

❦

I KNOCK OUT SEVERAL DOZEN cookies, cupcakes, and pastries, which helps keep my mind mostly off all things wedding. But not entirely. One, I am crazy excited about it and two, my mother calls three times in a forty-five-minute time period. I let her rant in my ear while I baked, ignoring her last-minute suggestions, because these aren't tiny, doable suggestions. These are major. Like why in the world aren't we having a full-blown Catholic service in the middle of our ceremony. Why? Because a Catholic wedding ceremony is anything but brief. I sat through one of those a few years ago and almost fell asleep. And there is no way in Hell Reese will wait that long to give me his last name; she should know that. He's going to have a hard enough time as it is waiting the thirty-five minutes it should take us to run through everything. In fact, I'm predicting his hair will look a right mess by the time the preacher pronounces us man and wife.

And I can't wait to see that.

Joey occasionally pops his head into the back while I bake to see if I need help, and to remind me that Brooke still hasn't shown up. I'm all about giving the girl a chance, but I am not the type of boss who tolerates lateness well. An occasional few-minute slip-up? Fine. But not a few hours, and definitely not on your first day.

As I'm cleaning off the worktop, having finally finished all the baking I'm planning on doing for the day, the shop door opens and Joey's voice comes booming from the front.

"Well, look who finally decided to show up."

I move quickly through the doorway, stopping at the sight of Brooke's nervous expression. "Oh, my God, Dylan. I'm so sorry. I swear to God…"

I hold up my hand and cut her off midsentence. "If you're late again, you're fired. This is serious, Brooke. And you could've at least called me." Stepping behind the counter, I grab the new employee paperwork I'd set out for her to fill out two hours ago. "Here, go in the back and fill this out."

She eagerly reaches for the paperwork and rounds the counter, wrapping me up in a massive hug. "I forgot to set my alarm. And I forgot to plug my phone in to charge. I'm so sorry. It won't happen again."

"Good," I reply.

Stepping back, she holds onto my arms and smiles warmly at me. "I do have one question though." I tilt my head and wait patiently, hearing Joey's soft grunt of disapproval from behind her. "Any wiggle room on the pay?"

"Ha!" Joey squawks.

Her eyes widen at my stern look. "Get your ass in the back and fill these out before I change my mind."

"Right. Sorry." She turns and brushes past Joey, earning herself an evil look.

"Fucking disaster. Seriously, let's keep her in the back away from the customers. Lord knows she'll probably only drive away all the business." He reaches into the display case and pulls out two muffins, offering me one. I take it and begin peeling off the wrapper.

"Give her a chance, will you? I can remember you being late, on occasion. For example, last week when Billy refused to untie you from your bedpost."

Joey wiggles his brows at me as he tosses his wrapper into the trashcan. "That lateness was totally worth it. As were the rope burns on my wrists."

I roll my eyes at him just as the front door dings open. A young woman, probably close to my age, comes barreling through the doors, eyes reddened and misty. She walks up to the counter, tucking her clutch under her arm.

I smile, setting my muffin down on the counter. "Good morning. How can we help you?"

She lets out a shaky breath, looking around the bakery quickly before meeting my eyes. "I don't know if you can help me. I know this is terribly last minute, but you're my only hope at this point."

Joey steps up next to me. "Are you okay? Would you like a glass of water or something?"

She shakes her head and offers him a weak smile. "Oh, no, thank you." She flicks her stare back to me. "You make wedding cakes, right?"

"She makes kick-ass wedding cakes," Joey corrects, motioning toward me. "Not only do they turn out looking fabulous, but they taste amazing. Trust me. I've eaten my fair share."

The young woman's face seems to relax a bit but not completely. "I'm getting married, and the bakery I had originally lined up to make my wedding cake closed down. They didn't even tell me. I went there this morning to make my final payment and the place is boarded up."

A sickening feeling rumbles in my gut. I can't imagine having that happen to me. "Jesus. That's awful. When is the wedding?" I ask.

She winces. "Saturday. Like I said, I know this is last minute. I've been to every other bakery in town and you're my last option." She looks down at her feet. "I'm sorry. I'm not trying to put any pressure on you. It's just… I don't know what else to do. I need to have a cake. I'll pay you extra. Double if I have to."

I reach my hand out and place it on her shoulder, prompting her to lift her gaze. "You don't have to pay me double. I'd love to make your wedding cake."

"Really?" Her soft voice is filled with a cautious hope.

Joey loops his hand through my elbow and pulls me back, dropping his lips to my ear. "Are you crazy? You'll have enough to do on Saturday getting ready for your *own* wedding. How will you have time for this?"

"You're getting married on Saturday, too?" the woman asks. Her excitement seems to fade as she glances between Joey and me. "Maybe he's right. You'll be so busy that day. It's okay if you can't do it."

I shrug off Joey and smile at her. "I won't be that busy. And besides, your cake will be done the night before. I'll just need to add the finishing touches to it that morning." I step closer to the counter. "But I probably won't have time to deliver it. Would it be a problem if someone stopped by here that morning to pick it up?"

Her eyes widen as she fidgets with the clutch under her arm. "No. Not at all. Thank you so much. You have no idea how much this means to me."

I smile and point to my consultation table. "Why don't you have a seat over there and you can tell me all about what kind of cake you want for your big day."

The sorrowed mood she entered the shop with has completely vanished, replaced with that typical bride-to-be joy I love seeing. As she makes her way toward the table, I turn and see Joey shaking his head at me.

"What?" I ask quietly.

His lip curls up in the corner as he crosses his arms over his broad chest, his muffin still in his hand. "You. You'd be late to your own wedding if it meant making some stranger's day perfect. Not many people would do that."

I reach underneath the counter and grab my design binder. "You'd do it, too, Joey Holt. I know you would."

"Not for just anybody. You or Juls? Yes. But you, cupcake, you'd do it for somebody you don't even know. And that's what makes you amazing."

I straighten up and blink heavily, feeling the tears well up in my eyes. "That's what you should say."

His brow furrows in confusion. "Huh?"

I walk up to him and shift my binder to one side of my body so I can wrap my free arm around his waist. I lay the side of my face against his chest. "On Saturday. I know you're worried about giving your Man of Honor speech. It doesn't have to be long. You should just say that." I let go of him and see his glowing smile.

"Oh, I'm going to rock that speech. Don't you worry. Now, while you do your bride thing, is there anything you'd like me to do?" I don't say a word. I simply grin at him and shift my eyes toward the kitchen. He closes his eyes tightly while reaching up and pinching the top of his nose. "Of course. You're lucky I love you."

"I am," I reply, rounding the counter and taking my seat at the table. I lay my book out and open it up, turning it so the excited young woman practically bouncing in her seat can look at my portfolio. "Here you go. This is some of what I can do, but I'm not limited to this. Take a look, see if there's anything you like. I can modify just about anything in there. And the cake and icing flavor choices are listed in the back."

She smiles wide and slides the book closer to her, her eyes shifting between each picture.

Joey's right. I would do this for anybody. Because the look on her face right now, the blissful glow radiating from her, this look is totally worth it. It's what makes my job so rewarding. The long hours. The late nights of baking. The sometimes overly-picky clients. I love my job because I get to see this look. And even if I am a few minutes late to my own wedding, it won't matter.

Nothing will ruin that day.

Chapter
ELEVEN

"**T**RY AND SUCK IN A little more," the woman says behind me as she struggles to zip and button my dress.

If I suck in anymore, I might actually crack a rib. *Thanks a lot, five-mile run. You obviously were pointless.* I shift on my feet and brace myself against the mirror with my hands while I take in shallow breaths. "I am sucked in. How close is it to fastening?" She pulls the material taut and I gasp, dropping a hand down to my diaphragm.

"There. Have you been eating a lot?"

"No," I barely manage to get out. "Jesus Christ. I can't have it be this tight for Saturday. I'll pass out before the ceremony starts." I spin around and see five pairs of eyes on me. Two amused sets, courtesy of my best friends, two motherly pairs full of anxiety, and the distraught-looking set belonging to the seamstress. My mother's jaw is tight, her face full of discontentment. "I swear to God, Mom. I haven't been eating a lot."

"Did you have a lot to drink lately? Like in the past week?" the seamstress asks, stepping forward and grabbing onto sections of my train.

I don't reply right away, and my mother decides to cut in. "Oh, for Christ's sake, Dylan. Don't you know not to drink alcohol at least a week before your final fitting? That's common sense."

"To who? And it was my bachelorette party. Of course there was drinking." I look down at the hands tugging the side of my dress. "Can't you take it out a little?"

She sighs, flattening her hand against the material and smoothing it down the front. "I could. But if it's just tight from drinking, I wouldn't alter it. As long as you don't drink anymore this week and stick with a low-carb diet, it should fit perfectly on Saturday."

Well, fuck me.

I grimace at the seamstress. "But I love carbs. And I'm a baker. I taste-test all my stuff."

"I'll take that burden off your hands," Joey offers, stepping up and putting his hands on his hips. His gaze trails up my dress to my face. "I must say, it does look seriously hot on you skin-tight. Fashion before comfort, cupcake."

"It's too tight. She can barely breathe in it," Juls states. She smiles up at me. "But you do look amazing. I'll never forget when you tried this on for me the first time."

I shake my head at her, playing over the memory of that day in my head. "Only you can get me to try on a wedding dress when I'm not even engaged."

She reaches out and squeezes my hand lovingly. "I think we both knew Reese was going to be seeing you in this dress."

I blush, putting my other hand on top of hers. *Yup. I definitely knew.*

"I must say, I absolutely love this dress, Dylan." Mrs. Carroll walks up to stand in front of the pedestal I'm on. She motions with her hand for me to twirl around and I humor her. "You look stunning in it. I love all this lace and the pearls on the back. And this train. My goodness. Absolutely gorgeous." She moves around me and grabs the train of my dress, fanning it out in front of me. "My son is going to lose his mind when he sees you in this."

"And his sperm count," Joey snickers under his breath. I glare down at him and he clears his throat as Juls elbows him in the side. "Well, it looks like I'll be the only one partying Friday night at The Tavern. Fine by me. And just in case this needs to be said, I'm retired from Brooke babysitting duty."

My mother steps up next to Maggie and looks at Joey critically.

"Joseph, I will not have anyone showing up to this thing Saturday hung over, so keep that in mind, please. This will be a classy event."

"Of course it will be. I'll be there," Joey retorts. "Nothing screams class like the sight of me in a tux."

I spin around on my pedestal and look at myself in the mirror while the four of them talk amongst themselves. Even though my dress is uncomfortably tight right now, it still looks just as amazing as it did the first time I stepped into it. Lace upon lace, it's so elegant I feel almost undeserving of wearing it. But no other dress is worthy of Reese. This has always been the one he was meant to rip off me. So, even though my love affair with carbs has been my longest and second-most-satisfying relationship, it will have to be sacrificed. Because there is no way in Hell I am not wearing this dress in five days. Maggie says her son will surely lose his mind on Saturday at the sight of me in this.

And that's exactly the reaction I'm going for.

‿

AFTER PEELING OFF MY DRESS and being reminded what foods and beverages to avoid for the next five days, I say goodbye to everyone and make my way out to Sam. Reese and I will be staying at the loft every night this week, which I'm grateful for. I want to have as much time there as possible since I'll be moving out this weekend. Juls, Joey, and I will be having our last sleepover together on Friday night there while the boys all stay at Ian's condo. That took some major convincing on my part; Reese doesn't like being away from me, not even for one night. But I begged, telling him it'll be sweeter if we go a little bit without seeing each other before the wedding. He was still reluctant until I told him I didn't want him seeing our wedding cake beforehand. That got him to agree to it. He appreciates my work more than any other person and knows I want him to be surprised. And now I'll have two wedding cakes to tackle on Friday night after the rehearsal, so he might as well hang out with the guys and have some fun.

As I walk up to the driver's side of my trusted delivery van, I notice something red on the windshield. A stand on my toes and reach my hand across the glass, grabbing the single red rose tucked underneath my windshield wiper. I study it curiously and smile. Roses are definitely not Reese's style. Nor is any flower. He's way more original when it comes to sweet gestures. But even though this isn't his typical way of showing me he's thinking of me, or that he loves me, it still warms my heart.

The sound of a car slowing down next to me catches my attention. Turning, I see Joey's red Civic come to a stop and the passenger window rolling down. He lowers his head to see me. "What's up, cupcake? Everything okay?" I hold out the flower in front of me and see Joey's face contort into a snarl. "Goddamn it, Billy. One fucking gesture would be nice. I'm a major fan of flowers."

I try to contain my laughter but fail at the sight of his irritated face. "So not like Reese, though. Maybe Billy put it there for me." I grab my door handle and duck my head down, winking at my assistant. "I'll see you in the morning."

He speeds off down the street, no doubt on his way to give Billy an earful as I hop up into Sam. After placing my rose on the passenger seat, I buckle up and pull away from the curb. It's late, already after 8:00 p.m., and I know as soon as I put my head on my pillow, I'm going to pass out.

Once I enter the security code, setting the alarm for the front door of the shop, I grab a small glass off one of the back racks in my kitchen work area. I fill it with water and place the rose in it, putting it in the middle of my worktop. Taking the steps two at a time, I make my way up the stairs and swing the door open.

There are boxes everywhere. On my bed. On the floor. On the kitchen counter. Way too many boxes for the amount of stuff I have. I close the door behind me and peek around my screen, seeing more boxes filling the space around my bed. "Jesus."

The bathroom door swings open and Reese emerges, a cloud of steam surrounding him. He's dressed in only his boxers with a towel draped over his shoulder. I moan softly at his appearance. The man could seriously rock a shampoo commercial.

He rubs the towel over this head. "Hi. Did you just get here?"

I nod, glancing around the space and motioning with my hand around the room. "Where did all the boxes come from?"

"A guy at work brought them in for me when I told him we were moving you this week. I've gotten a lot of stuff packed away already." He places his towel on the counter, the crease in his brow becoming prominent as he surveys my expression. "Are you okay?"

I move over to the bed and sit down, kicking my shoes off. "Yeah. I'm just tired." I pull my knees up to my chest and rest my chin on top, staring at one of the boxes Reese has labeled 'miscellaneous'. *I'm not ready to pack. Not yet. But I get it. It makes sense to start.*

I feel the bed dip behind me and hear the soft creak of the mattress. "Come up here."

I turn, seeing him sitting with his back against my headboard. Letting go of my knees, I crawl toward him and straddle his lap. His hands run up my thighs, stopping on my hips. I let my eyes wander over his face, admiring his features before settling on his eyes that are studying me. Always watching. "Hi."

His lip twitches. "Hi, yourself. What are you thinking about?"

I trace the muscles of his arm with my finger, trailing up toward his shoulder. "That I'm not ready to say goodbye to this place." I see his smile fade and shift closer, feeling his hands wrap around my waist. I drop my forehead so it's resting against his, my fingers interlocking behind his neck. "It's not because I don't want to live with you. Please, don't think that."

He licks his lips before exhaling roughly. "I don't. I wish we could live here. I know how important this space is to you. But with us trying to start a family now, I don't see how it would work. We're going to need more than one bedroom." I nod against him, feeling his fingers trace along the exposed skin of my back where my tank top has ridden up. "Dylan, I'll pay for you to keep this place if it'll make you happy. You can use it as storage or for whatever you want. Do you want me to do that?"

"No. It wouldn't make sense to pay for a space we really wouldn't use anymore. It's fine. I guess I just wasn't prepared to see the boxes yet."

He frowns. "I'm sorry. I knew this would be hard for you so I figured I would do the packing. I'll do it all, I don't care."

I run my finger along his jaw, feeling the day-old stubble tickle my skin. "You're too sweet to me. How much did you get done?"

"About half. I found your yearbooks."

I drop my head and cover my eyes with my hand. "Oh, God. Please tell me you didn't." *Why the hell did I keep those?* I know everyone goes through an awkward stage, but something tells me the man I'm currently straddling never went through such a thing. And I definitely did.

He laughs, grabbing my hand and pulling it away from my face. His fingers tilt my chin up to meet his stare. "I did. You were fucking hot at sixteen."

Relief washes over me. *Thank God. My high school years were good to me.* I arch my brow playfully, licking the corner of my mouth as I make a mental note to burn all my middle school yearbooks. "Oh? Would you have liked sixteen-year-old, virginal, Dylan?"

"I would've gone to jail if I touched you. But I definitely would've thought about it."

Christ, that's crazy-hot to think about.

I slide my hands along his bare chest, feeling his chiseled body tense against my palms. "Mmm. I would've thought about you touching me, too." I glance up at him from underneath my lashes, seeing his green eyes blazing. "At night. When I was alone in my bedroom." I lean in closer, pressing my lips to his ear. "I would've thought about it a lot," I whisper.

He growls, moving his hands underneath my tank top and rubbing along the skin of my back. "Would you have gotten yourself off thinking about me and what I'd do to you?"

I nod against his cheek, grinding my hips into him. "Every night. I masturbated a lot back then. I was the horniest teenager."

"Shit," he grunts, grabbing my hips and directing the tempo. I hear his breath hitch as he tilts his pelvis up, his length rubbing against me in the most delicious way possible. "I don't know if I would've been able to keep myself from you. I can't now. I would've done anything to touch you. To taste you. Jail would've been worth it if I got to watch you come apart in my arms."

"Reese," I moan, rocking my hips faster against him. "This feels… oh, God, this feels so good." *Who would've thought a little grinding with clothes on would feel this spectacular?* Of course, the dirty-talking man underneath me doesn't hurt.

"I would've made you come like this. Rubbing my cock against you.

Letting you feel how fucking hard I am for you." His fingers unbutton my jeans and tug at the zipper. "Take these off. It'll feel better."

I quickly discard my jeans onto the floor and am pulled back into his lap. His rough hands grab my ass, pulling me closer so we're chest to chest. "Now, where were we?" I ask, as he rocks me against him, putting us back into that erotic rhythm.

"You were about to come."

"Was not," I reply, dropping my head to his shoulder as he rubs his cock against my clit. *Wow. If he keeps this up, I definitely will be coming. A lot.* I moan loudly, digging my nails into his shoulders. "Why are we still wearing underwear?"

He turns his head and presses his lips to my temple as a groan rumbles in his throat. "Because I'm pretending I've just snuck into six-teen-year-old Dylan's bedroom. This is how I'd get you off. I don't need you naked to make you come."

I moan again, tilting my head up and locking on to his eyes. "I've never done this before."

His breathing becomes labored as he grips my hips harder. "You've never done what? Dry-humped?"

"No," I reply through a gasp. I lean back and see him take in what I've just confessed. A smirk forms on his lips. "You like that, don't you? You like knowing you're the first guy to do this to me."

"No, I don't like it," he answers, his jaw clenching. "I fucking love it. You want me to make you come, love? Just like this?" I nod, closing my eyes as the slow burn in my gut becomes almost unbearable. "Look at me. You know I have to see you."

I obey and open my eyes, bringing my gaze down to his mouth. That mouth that drives me completely wild with his words and the way he uses it. I brace my hands on his shoulders as he begins thrusting his hips up to meet each grind. Each pulse against my clit sends me into a frenzy. "I'm so close. Please, tell me you're close."

"Fuck. I'm right there," he grunts out through gritted teeth. He digs into my hips to the point of it being painful as I feel him shudder underneath me. "Holy fuck. Now, Dylan."

I take over, moving against him as if he was inside me and we aren't just fooling around like horny teenagers. And then it hits me, the orgasm racing through my body like the blood rushing in my veins. I arch my back and shout his name, riding out my climax. I'm panting, barely able to take in a deep breath as I drop my head down and see the sexiest grin on the man who's just snuck into my bedroom. I bite my lip playfully. "Holy shit. I'm kinda crushing on the twenty-two-year-old version of you."

His amused smile spreads to his eyes, softening them as he drops his head back against the headboard. His slightly-tanned chest heaves with two deep breaths. "Next time I sneak into your room, you'll be grinding that pussy against my face."

Sweet Lord. I clench my thighs against his, feeling like I could come again just from that declaration. "Did you love going down on girls back then, too?" I ask, shifting off his lap. I know he hates these types of questions, but I ask anyway. I can't help that I'm curious with everything involving Reese.

He stands and slips off his boxers, bunching them up in his hand and wiping himself off. He shakes his head before replying. "I would've loved going down on *you*. It's the way you react to me, Dylan. The way you taste. That's why I love doing it." He tosses his boxers into the hamper, looking back at me. "Good answer?"

I nod and reach out for him. "Great answer. Come back to bed."

"Hungry. You want some Chinese? I got those egg rolls you like."

I grunt and plop down sideways onto the bed, resting my head on my hand. "Can't. I'm on a strict no-good-food diet until Saturday. I can't even taste-test my treats."

"What? Why?"

I watch his bare ass walk into the kitchen, appreciating the angle I'm currently in that's giving me this amazing view. I sigh before responding. "Because my dress was a little snug on me tonight. The seamstress said it's probably because of the booze over the weekend." I tug at the hem of my tank top, covering my hip. "That goddamn champagne is ruining my life. I'm never drinking that stuff again." I glance up as he returns to the bed, carrying a bowl and munching on an egg roll. "You suck. Guys can eat whatever they want and not have to worry about buttoning a lace bodice."

He shrugs before sitting down on the bed and leaning back against the headboard. "I don't know why you have to worry about it. That dress isn't going to be on you long."

I sit up and leer at him. "It'll be on me long enough. I can't have it gaped open in the back. Everyone will see my present to you."

His eyes fill with curious wonder. "Your present to me? And what would that be?"

I roll off the bed and pull my tank top off. "Not telling. It's a wedding day surprise." I toss it into the hamper and walk to the bathroom to take care of my nightly routine. After washing my face and brushing my teeth, I reemerge and find Reese putting his dish in the sink. "You ready for bed?" I ask.

"Yeah. I'm fucking beat." He rounds the counter and brushes past me, slapping me on the ass before he steps into the bathroom.

I crawl under the covers, laying on the side I always occupy and facing my one and only window. I'll never forget the first night Reese slept in this bed with me. It was the night of Juls and Ian's wedding. The night that is permanently branded into my memory.

The night that will always mean more to me than he'll ever know.

Chapter
TWELVE

Seven months ago

"**W**HERE DO YOU WANT ME, love?" Reese asks, backing up the stairs that lead up to my loft.

This is it. The moment I've been dreaming about, thinking about constantly. We've only been official for two-and-a-half hours, but getting him in my bed has been the only thing on my mind. I wanted to leave Juls and Ian's wedding reception early, but I didn't. I held out. I do have some willpower; not much, but some. And having any willpower around this man is an extremely difficult task, trust me. If he hadn't fucked me in the bathroom two-and-a-half hours ago, I definitely wouldn't have made it, but he did. So we stayed. And now, he's mine. He's had me in his bed, and I'd be damned if I was going to go another second without having him in mine.

"My bed. Now." *I push against his heaving chest, feeling his heart beating rapidly against my palm. He's still deliciously decked-out in his tux and it's killing me. He's killing me. The look he's giving me right now, the way his body towers over mine, his intoxicating citrus scent. It's fucking killing me. I've never been this turned on before, I'm sure of it. My panties are still in his pants pocket and right now, I could probably use them. I can feel my wetness pooling between my legs. I lick my lips, biting down on the bottom one as the back of his long legs hit my bed. With one tiny push, he falls back and I'm on him.*

"Mmm, my girl is impatient," *he says, smiling up at me as I straddle* his waist. *"You can take your time, you know. I'm not going anywhere."* Take my time? Nonsense. His hands tug at the hem of my dress and with one quick motion, it's pulled over my head and discarded somewhere. Anywhere. Who the fuck cares where my dress is because right now, the only thing I care about is him.

"Fuck taking my time." My fingers frantically rip open his dress shirt, the tiny white buttons flying out in every direction. *"You can take your time with me, after I fuck you."*

He was just inside me a few hours ago, but the anticipation of having him again in my bed is enough to make me loopy. But, that's what happens when you stupidly decide that beds are off-limits during your casual bullshit phase. What the hell was I even thinking? I mean, yes I was trying to not fall in love with this man, which was inevitable. I convinced myself that beds were too intimate and it would be best if we didn't go there. Seriously the worst idea of my life. I've paid the price severely for that horrible judgment call, having spent the last eighty-five days wallowing in my bed which didn't contain any memories of him. But, that bullshit is all in the past and gazing down at him right now, I can't believe I ever initiated the no-bed rule. His body belongs in my bed.

I stare down at him and take in the perfection beneath me. Hair a mess and green eyes wild with lust. My hands run up his chest, feeling every inch of him as he slides further up the bed. I lean down and trail my tongue over the lines of his muscles, every cut and every dip. He moans against my lips as I trail higher, kissing and licking his neck. I close my eyes as his hands run up my thighs, stopping and playing with the clips of my garter. His thumb runs over my aching clit and dips in my wetness.

"God, you're so fucking wet. Is this killing you? Not having my cock in you right now?"

Oh, the dirty talking. Reese is a master at everything dirty, and he knows it. I bring my mouth down against his, rough and needy as I whimper against his lips. He pulls my bottom lip into his mouth and sucks on it as my hands find his belt. It's hard to concentrate, especially when he's doing that thing I love with his tongue. You know, the thing he does really fucking well when his head's between my legs. Yeah, that thing. Except he's doing it to my mouth, and I'm panting, moaning, stroking my tongue against his as his belt is finally removed. I work his zipper and slide his pants down, gripping his length in my hand. He tenses and throws his head back.

"Christ, I need you. You're right. Fuck taking our time."

In one quick motion, he's on top of me and I'm being pressed into the mattress.

My mattress.

My fucking bed.

Fuck, this is Heaven.

His mouth is on my neck, licking and kissing as my eyes roll back into my head. His warm, minty breath blows across my skin, goose bumps immediately forming on the surface. I open my eyes and lock onto his, deep-green pools of emerald burning into mine with that intensity. His intensity. My hands grip his shoulders as he positions himself there. Right there. Christ, I'm so horny I might actually combust before he enters me.

"Reese, please. Get in me already."

He laughs softly and hovers there, running his length up and down my slick pussy. "Tell me what you want, Dylan. I wanna hear you say it."

I moan loudly as he presses against my clit. But I don't talk; no, I'll let him ask me again. Because I know he will.

"Dylan." He drops his head, pressing his forehead against mine. His neck rolls with a deep swallow. "Fucking say it."

I close my eyes and tilt my head up, bringing our lips together. "Just you," I whisper. "I never stopped thinking about you. Not for one second." I open my eyes and see him studying my face as if he hasn't seen it in years. He's caressing me with his sight, delicately memorizing every inch of me. My hands grab his face, my thumbs lightly stroking his cheeks. We've been apart for eighty-five days.

"Eighty-five days. Did you…" I stop talking and see his eyes read what I was going to say. But I can't say it. Because even though he had every right to be with other women, I suddenly realize I don't want to picture it.

"No." His hand brushes my hair off my forehead, tucking it behind my ear. "I tried, though. I wanted to forget you, because it was fucking killing me. Images of you, in my mind. They were constant." His Adam's apple rolls in his throat and he lets out a shaky breath, still holding himself at my entrance. "I went out a few times to pick up someone, but I'd end up leaving almost immediately after I got there. And then I'd just go home and give in to it. I'd let myself think of you. Or I'd go for a really long run, which only made me think of you even more."

My eyes rake over his sculpted upper body, looking even leaner than it had a little over two months ago. His muscles are even more defined, the edges more rigid. "Have you been running a lot?"

He nods and swallows again. "Yeah. You have, too. You've lost weight."

I shake my head. "No, I just haven't really been eating. My appetite usually disappears when I'm an emotional wreck." I run my hands down his neck to his shoulders, feeling his muscles flex under my touch. "What did you think about?"

He smiles the tiniest bit and eases forward, entering me slowly. I moan quietly and arch off the bed, my chest brushing against his. "That, right there. The sounds you make when I'm moving in you." He begins thrusting in a slow rhythm, taking his time while he watches me below him. "The way you arch into me." His hand brushes down my face and onto my chest. "Like you need to be touching me with every part of you." His hand moves lower and grabs my leg, pinning it in front of him. "How fucking beautiful you look when you come. I couldn't get you out of my head. You were always there. Every look you gave me, every moment I held you. I couldn't let go of it." He stops moving and runs his finger along my lower lip. "I could be without you for the rest of my life and I'd never want anyone else."

I blink heavily, sending a tear down the side of my face. When I reopen my eyes, I see the pain in his, the memory of those eighty-five days and how it affected him. I reach up, laying my hand against his cheek. "You'll never be without me again. I'm yours. I always have been. Even when we were apart."

"So, you didn't..."

I shake my head, seeing the tension that set in his features when he started to ask that question slowly release. "I could never be with anyone else. Not after you."

He drops his head and kisses me like he needs my air to breathe. It's urgent. Hungry. And I feel that kiss throughout my entire body, reigniting my ache for him. "I need you to move," I whisper against his mouth.

He bends my knee and pushes it against my chest as he starts thrusting into me again. His eyes stay glued to mine, capturing my gaze, daring me to look away. I can't. Even if I want to. I missed this look of his. The look I know he only reserves for me. The look that could make me do anything.

"You know what else I thought about?" he asks.

"What?" I reach above me and search for something to grab, wrapping my hands around my bed post. His slow thrusts are hitting every nerve ending

in my body. The heavy drag of his cock as it fills me, pulsing against that spot only he has ever been able to find. I'm coming apart below him, and he doesn't seem to be anywhere near done with me. "Reese, please."

He growls through a moan. "That. How you beg me, over and over again. Like I'd ever deny you." His hands grip the sheet next to my head as his thrusts become more forceful but still slow. I tilt my pelvis, bringing my hips up to meet him and giving him deeper entry. "I'm so fucking lost in you, Dylan. I always have been."

"Fuck, Reese." My orgasm rips through me, burning in my core and spreading out quickly. I'm clenching around him, my hands raking down his back and clawing at his skin. I'm sure I'm drawing blood but I don't care, and he doesn't seem to either. He lunges deeper, deeper again and continues the sweet torture. "I want you to come."

"Not yet. Give me another, love." His hands run down my sides and grip my hips as he thrusts hard, then harder into me. His eyes are locked onto mine, holding me, keeping me with him. "Too damn long. I've been without you and it nearly killed me."

"Me, too. I... holy shit." Bracing myself with my hands over my head, I feel my second orgasm building in my gut.

Again? Already? Of course, look who's above me right now. Why the hell do I question this man's skill level?

His grunts ring out around us, filling my loft. His forehead is creased and the sweat is building just below his hairline. A drop hits my chest and rolls between my breasts. I arch off the bed, pushing against him, needing the contact. Needing every inch of him touching me. I can't get him close enough, not after eighty-five days, not ever. And then it happens. That second orgasm spreads through my body and I'm clinging to him, rocking against him as he pounds into me.

"That's it. Christ, I love watching you like this."

I'm shaking, trembling as I come down. And then I'm quickly flipped onto my knees, Reese bracing himself behind me. The movement's so fast, I don't have time to think before he enters me again. "Reese, I don't know if I..."

"You will. You know I can do this to you all night."

Oh, God. Death by orgasm. Is it possible to have three orgasms back to back like this and actually be able to function afterwards? Shit, who the hell cares? This is Reese Carroll we're talking about. Plus, how sweet would it be to die this way? *Screaming his name in ecstasy. Falling to a slow, post-climatic death. Absolutely. I'll take that.*

I bow my back and push into him, dropping to my elbows as his hands wrap around my waist. I feel his breath on my back, quick bursts of air. His lips kiss the skin there, trailing lower to my hips. He's pounding into me, giving me every bit of him and I'm taking it. He's so deep this way, his hips crashing against mine as I grip the sheets. My knuckles are stark white as I desperately try not to collapse under his power. I can feel him tense against my body, knowing he's close and I'm right there with him. "I need you to come with me. Please. I don't want to come again without you."

"You need it, love?" he questions as he fucks me relentlessly.

"Yes. Please. Let me feel you."

He hammers into me at rapid speed as I stretch my hands out above me. "Fuck. Get there, Dylan."

"Touch me."

His hand snakes around my body and drops to my clit, two fingers working me. Sliding against me. Pulsing, pulsing, until my orgasm surges through me. I grab his wrist and stop him, throwing my head back. "Now. Coming," I say breathlessly, barely able to speak.

Both hands tighten against my hips and pull me back to meet his thrusts. He groans his release as I'm rocked to the point of being delirious. I collapse on my belly, pulling him down with me. He rolls to his back and shifts my weight for me so I'm lying on his chest. We lie there in silence, my head resting on him as we steady our breathing. And then my emotions hit me in one big rush. The fact that he's here with me, when I never thought I'd be with him like this. In my bed. Me in his arms. It's overwhelming.

"I can't be without you again," I say, so low I'm not sure if he'll hear it. But I needed to say it, if only for myself, because there is no way in Hell I'd survive being apart from this man again. I'd do anything to avoid feeling that pain, the agony that ripped me apart for eighty-five days and left me a shell of the woman he fell in love with. I wrap my arm tighter around his body. "I don't care if this is all we ever are. I don't need anything besides this. But I'll always need it."

His hand is on my chin, tilting my head up to meet his gaze. That stare of his causes me to stop breathing as he studies me. Always watching. It's so extreme, full of unspoken words as he remains silent. I take the opportunity to admire his

*features, the features I've missed so much. Soft eyes. Full, slightly-chapped lips
with my favorite slit running down the middle. Smile lines that wreck me. Mild
stubble that I reach up and run my finger across. He shifts to his side, pulling
me even closer so we're chest to chest, my body completely flattened against his.
His lips meet my forehead and he holds them there, humming softly against my
skin. I feel my body completely relax next to his. All the stress, all the tension,
all the sadness and misery of the past eighty-five days dissolves instantly as he
wraps himself around my body. I'm completely smothered, completely cocooned
in his long limbs, wild mess of hair, and hot breath.*

He's in my bed. In my fucking bed. And I never want him to leave it.

"Hey. Are you okay?"

Reese's voice cuts into my thoughts, causing me to roll over. He pulls
me against his body so we're lying just like we were in my memory. I smile,
wrapping my arms around him and pressing my lips against his chest.

"I'm more than okay. I have you in my bed." A low laugh rumbles
in his throat as I dig into the muscles in his back with my fingers. "Do
you remember the first night you were in it?"

"Yes," he answers without hesitation. "Do you remember what you
said to me before we fell asleep?"

I glance up at him, momentarily stunned he remembers, and nod
once. "That I couldn't be without you again."

His eyes focus on my mouth as he brushes my hair off my shoulder.
"That. And you said you didn't care if that was all we ever were. That
you didn't need anything else." He pauses, his eyes reaching mine. "I
almost asked you to marry me right then."

My heart thunders in my chest. "Really?"

"Really." He leans forward and captures my mouth in a tender kiss,
his tongue lightly brushing against my lips, seeking entry. I give it to him
and moan softly into his mouth. He pulls back after several seconds,
blinking heavily before locking onto my eyes. "I knew then, Dylan. I
knew way before then you were it for me. And I would've never let that
be all we ever were." He kisses my cheek, my jaw, and the side of my
mouth. "You were always meant to be mine. Even before I knew it."

I kiss his jaw before tucking my face underneath his head and relishing in his scent. "Damn straight."

He wraps me against him, pressing his mouth to my hair. "You're so romantic, love."

I chuckle, feeling his body shake with laughter as he holds me. "You're hard to compete with. Shall I try?"

"If you want."

I nuzzle closer. "Will you marry me?"

He laughs, dropping a kiss to the top of my head. "Hell yes, I will."

And for some reason, hearing his answer does something to me. Even though I said yes to him six months ago, it does something to me. "I was yours when I was sixteen."

I feel his reaction to what I've just said. The way his grip on me tightens. The pause in his breathing and the shuddering exhale that follows. "Damn straight," he finally replies after several seconds of silence.

And I smile as I'm pulled closer. Never close enough.

Chapter
THIRTEEN

TUESDAY IN THE SHOP WENT by without a glitch. Brooke showed up on time, surprisingly, and was proving herself to be a good addition to Dylan's Sweet Tooth. She was great with customers, her bubbly personality winning over several of our regulars, and she and Joey were even getting along. For the most part. They were by no means besties, but they were at least tolerating each other and keeping their bickering to a minimum.

I stayed in the back all day, whipping up two special orders getting picked up on Wednesday. One was for Mr. and Mrs. Crisp who were celebrating their anniversary this week. They were my longest-standing customers, stopping in practically every morning for two of my famous banana nut muffins. I adored them and insisted on not charging for their cake. They've given me so much business over the last three and a half years, and this is my way of thanking them. Of course, the two of them argued with me until they were blue in the face about it, but I refused to take their money. I wanted to do this for them. Sixty-five years of marriage was definitely something to celebrate, and I felt honored to be a part of that.

Staying away from the foods I was told to avoid was becoming increasingly difficult. I'm sure there is no baker in the history of bakers who has gone on this strict of a diet before. I've never deprived myself of food; I'm not one of those girls. I eat. A lot. And this low-carb shit was seriously getting to me by mid-day on Wednesday. Not only did I not taste-test the German chocolate cake with extra coconut in the frosting I made yesterday, but I also steered clear of the red velvet cupcakes I whipped up for the other special order. And I don't say 'no' to cupcakes. Ever. They are my go-to treat, the thing I'd request as my last meal if I were on death row. The one dessert I'd cut a bitch for, and they were off-limits. I was eating like a damn rabbit and hating every second of it. I've never been on a diet a day in my life and for the first time in the three-and-a-half years of owning my bakery, I was finding myself wishing I would've picked a different career path.

I'm pushing the pieces of lettuce around in my to-go container, hungry but not hungry enough to swallow another bite of this garbage while my dear assistant scarfs down a cheesesteak sub next to me. I've been giving him dirty looks since he returned with our lunches fifteen minutes ago, and he's been doing his best to avoid my judging stare.

"I should fire you for eating that shit in front of me. As my Man of Honor, you should be suffering right along with me." I shove my container away down the counter and flick my disapproving stare between his sub and his face. "Give me a bite of that."

"Hell, no." He turns his body so his back is to me, keeping his sandwich out of my reach. "You only have three more days and if you don't fit into that dress, you'll be pissed at me for giving you a bite." Spinning around, he holds up his empty hands and chews animatedly. "This is so disgusting. You'd hate it," he says through tight lips, his voice thick with sarcasm.

I scowl at his obvious lie as the shop door dings, gaining mine and Joey's attention. Freddy comes walking into the bakery, the familiar white box in his hands. My chest tightens at the sight of it.

"Freddy! Perfect timing. This one is in a mood and could use something from her man." Joey nudges me with his shoulder and steps up to the counter.

I pout at him playfully before I reach out for the white box Fred has placed on the counter. "Pick something out from the display case, Fred.

You know the drill." He bends down, his eyes lighting up as he surveys his choices. I quickly sign the clipboard as Joey pulls out a chocolate cupcake, slipping it into a bag and handing it to Fred.

Fucking cupcakes. I should just give him the whole tray and get them out of my sight.

"Thanks, Ms. Dylan. Enjoy your delivery," he says cheerfully, taking his clipboard and his cupcake before exiting the shop.

I pull the white ribbon, lifting the sides of the box and flipping the lid. Joey moves closer to me as I pick out the dark brown card, opening it and feeling that same nervous energy I always get when I'm about to read one of Reese's notes.

Dylan,
Don't give me a hard time about this. This is long overdue.
X, Reese

Confusion sets in as I place the card next to the box and begin sifting through the tissue paper. I'm digging, looking for whatever he's placed in here that weighs close to nothing.

"Where is it?" Joey asks as he hovers at my shoulder.

I continue moving the paper around. "I don't know. Maybe he forgot... holy shit." I reach in and lift out a set of car keys, letting them dangle in the air below my fingers. "Oh, my God, Joey." Turning toward him, I see his shocked expression as his jaw hits the floor.

"Holy shit is right." He snatches the keys away from me, turning them over in his palm. A dramatic squeal escapes his lips as he points to the emblem on the key. "A BMW? He bought you a BMW?" His eyes look past my shoulder, widening even further before he grabs my hand and drags me around the counter.

I'm in a state of shock as he opens the bakery door and pulls me outside onto the pavement. And then I really lose my shit all together. Parked right in front of the bakery is my gift from Reese. A brand new, insanely-shiny, highly-underserved, white BMW.

Joey hits the unlock button on the keys and opens the passenger door. He ducks his head inside while I stay completely frozen in place a few feet behind him.

He bought me a car. A really expensive car. Probably more expensive than the one he drives.

Joey straightens up and motions for me to join him. It takes great effort to move from my spot on the sidewalk, but I manage and step up next to him, ducking my head down to look inside the vehicle.

"Leather interior, sunroof, and you have a built-in navigation system. Please, for the love of Christ, let me borrow this sometime."

I reach inside and run my hand along the leather seat. "This is crazy. I can't believe he bought me a car."

"I can. That man outdoes himself every time Freddy steps inside the shop. I'd only be shocked if *I* was the one getting a brand new vehicle." We both stand and he shakes his head at my car. "Remind me to tell Reese he needs to give Billy tips on how to be an amazing boyfriend."

"Poor Billy." I nudge him and he laughs against me. "He has to put up with your moody ass and what does he get out of it?"

Joey grins wickedly at me and we both chuckle. He doesn't need to say what Billy gets out of it, because I'm sure the entire population of Chicago knows full well the elaborate workings of my lovely assistant's sex life. He isn't shy about that information and will tell just about anybody.

I close the car door and take the keys from Joey. "I need to go see him. Do you think you could man the shop for me?"

He smiles giddily. "Hell, yes I..." he stops midsentence as Brooke comes hustling down the sidewalk, department store bags in her hands. Joey turns and leans his body against the car, crossing his arms over his chest. "Seriously, Brooke? When I say you can take a lunch break, it doesn't mean a fucking two-hour shopping spree."

She sneers in his direction, coming to a stop in front of us. "Relax, bitch. You're getting premature wrinkles."

Joey immediately turns, dropping down to examine his face in my side-view mirror. "That's not even funny," he growls.

She places her bags at her feet, flipping her car keys in her hand. "You're just jealous because I've got a hot date tonight and *you* don't."

"I've got a hot date *every* night, and one I don't have to pay for," he snarls, straightening up and spinning back around. "What do you charge for your company these days?"

Brooke's jaw tightens, her nostrils flaring with rage. "You know what? Now you're not getting the shirt I bought for you!"

"Brooke, knock it... wait, what?" I look down at the bags at her feet.

"What? Did you say you bought me a shirt?" Joey asks with genuine curiosity, stepping closer to her.

She shrugs, averting her gaze. "It's not that big a deal." She reaches into her Macy's bag and pulls out a light blue T-shirt, holding it against her chest. "It was on sale, and I thought it would look nice on you. You look good in blue."

I smile at her thoughtfulness, watching as Joey takes another step closer to Brooke. She holds the shirt out to him and he takes it with an astonished expression. She looks at me and grins. "Anyway, I'm sorry I took so long. It won't happen again." And before Joey can give her a thank you or react in any way to her gift, she picks up her bags and walks into the shop.

"Damn. This shirt is fucking fabulous. I kind of feel bad for the boyfriend comment," Joey says.

"You should. That was really nice of her."

He shoots me a challenging look, but it's short lived. Brooke did well and Joey knows it. And the smile he tries to hide as he folds the shirt against his chest isn't missed. Once he's done, he smoothes out his skin once more in the mirror behind him, tucking the shirt underneath his arm. "Do you think I have wrinkles?" *Oh, Lord.*

"Don't be ridiculous. Your skin is flawless."

He grins. "You know why, don't you?"

I immediately hold up my hand to stop him from talking. "Please, spare me the 'semen is the fountain of youth' conversation. I find it hard to believe that mine and Juls' swallowing habits are directly related to the number of crow's feet we end up getting." I shake my head at the memory of that discussion a few years ago. Joey really is a piece of work, trying to convince us to up our blow-job game to ward off any fine lines.

"You good?" I ask. I need to go get ready for my visit with Reese, knowing full well his lunch break is the best time to get him alone.

He smiles. "I'm great. Go properly thank that man before I do it for you." He arches his brow, the wicked gleam in his eyes beaming at me.

I chuckle at his comment as we both walk back into the shop. Practically sprinting up the stairs, I run straight for my lingerie drawer with only one thought in mind. Naughty Dylan is about to come out to play, and she's not going to hold anything back either. *Reese Carroll, you have no idea what you're in for.*

∞

THIS IS CRAZY. SERIOUSLY, COMPLETELY insane. I'm riding the elevators of the Walker & Associates building, my knees shaking against each other under my oversized trench coat. Glancing down at myself, I tighten the belt around my waist and bite the inside of my cheek. I've never done anything like this before or even remotely close to this. I mean sure, I've shown up to Reese's work multiple times and given him an office quickie, but I'm always dressed appropriately when I do it. Never, and I mean never, have I pulled a stunt like what I'm about to do. I try to shake off my nervousness as the doors ping open. Stepping out onto the twelfth floor, I begin the stroll toward his reception area.

I need motivation, so I think of the delivery he sent me as I walk down the long hallway. *A brand new car definitely deserves this type of a thank you.* A brand new car that drives like a fucking dream.

Sorry, Sam.

I spot Dave, my favorite receptionist who Reese re-hired. After firing him for being 'too cheery', I convinced Reese to give him another chance, which he didn't fight me on. And since I've spent a considerable amount of time in this office over the past eight months, Dave and I have become fast friends. His crooked smile lights up his face as I point toward Reese's door, silently asking if he's available. He nods and, like he always does, motions for me to walk right in. Glancing down one last time to make sure I'm covered, I swing open the door and step into his massive office.

He looks completely focused, eyes on his computer screen and pen stuck in his mouth. *Lucky pen.* With the sound of my entrance, he glances up slowly, his eyes locking onto mine as I close and lock the door behind me. All my nervousness is left in the hallway, and before I can give him the chance to speak, move, or even breathe, I open my coat and drop it to the floor. And that's not the only thing that drops. His pen falls out of his mouth as his eyes slowly take in my attire.

I've chosen a matching red lacy bra and panties, garter, stockings, and my black stilettos I wore the night of my bachelorette party. My bra and panties are insanely see-through, barely even classifying as underwear, and when I say red, I mean fire-engine red. I'm standing in his office, screaming at him in this outfit like a siren. My skin is flushed from the sheer contact of this ensemble. This is has to be the craziest thing I've ever done and by the way Reese is looking at me right now, it's totally worth it.

He leans back in his chair, his eyes staying glued to my body as he rakes both hands through his hair. "Jesus fucking Christ." His eyes meet mine briefly before he drops them to my chest. "I can see right through that."

"You don't like it?" I ask playfully, seeing his tongue dart out and lick my favorite slit that runs down his bottom lip. *Oh, yes, my tongue will be doing that in just a minute.* "I've come to thank you for your gift."

"I'm not gonna last long," he replies quickly, his hands firmly gripping the arms of his chair. "I'm telling you right now, whatever you've planned," his Adam's apple rolls in his throat, "I'm not gonna last with you wearing that."

"That might be the best compliment you've ever given me." My smile busts my face open, and I can practically feel his erection from where I stand. With the heated look he's giving me right now, I'm positive I won't last long either. *Please, like I ever do with this man's skill level.* I place my hands on my hips and stand up straight, ready to start my fun.

"Now, there are two rules you must follow in order for this to play out in your favor." I bend down and grab my coat, placing it on the chair after I retrieve my cell phone out of it.

"And what would these rules be?"

I can feel his penetrating stare as I scroll to my playlist. After finding my selection, I stride over to his desk and walk behind it. "Rule number one," I place my phone down next to his computer, "you're not allowed to touch me at all during the song."

"Fuck that," he states firmly, crossing his arms over his broad chest.

At the sheer sight of him behind his massive desk, I'm almost tempted to agree with him and say fuck rule number one. He's magnificently dressed in his work attire, which never ceases to have the same effect on me as the first day I saw him in it. His hair is fuckably messy, his deep emerald eyes are piercing into mine and continually raking over my body, and his lips are wet and ready for me.

I lean forward, giving him a better view of my cleavage and seeing him notice it instantly. "You touch me, and I leave. *And* I'll do it without my coat on." *Yeah, right.* I'm praying he doesn't call my bluff on this one, because there's no way in Hell I would walk outta here without being covered up.

His eyebrow arches. "How long is this song?"

"Four minutes and thirty three seconds."

"No fucking way. I'll give you two minutes and then I'm touching every part of you." He reaches out and runs his hand up my thigh, playing with the clips on my garter. I tremble at the contact. "What's the second rule?"

I smile slyly and stand up, seeing his body tense as I reach for him. "You only get to feel me." His expression shifts quickly to confusion as I loosen his tie, pulling it out from underneath his collar and walking behind him. "And if you take your blindfold off, I'll be withholding *your* orgasm."

"I can't touch you *or* look at you? Not happening." I'm quickly grabbed and pulled into his lap, his mouth firmly pressing against mine. "Nothing stands in my way of you." He kisses me brutally, his tongue invading my mouth with firm strokes. "Nothing."

I pull back, which is an extremely difficult task, and grip his shoulders tightly. "Let me do this." He starts to shake his head when I grab it, holding it in place. I drop my forehead to his and exhale softly. "Please. I love that you hate the idea of not being able to touch me or look at me, but I swear I'll make it worth it." His minty breath warms my face and I feel his muscles relax beneath me. "Let me properly thank you."

After several seconds of him contemplating my offer, he places the tie back in my hand, giving me the okay to follow through with this. Leaning closer to me, he presses his lips to my hair. "Make it count."

I shudder against him and bite my lip. *Come on, Dylan. Focus.*

"Two minutes." He pulls out his phone and sets his timer as I move behind him, draping the tie across his eyes.

After securing it, I move around him, making sure to brush against his body as I reach for my phone and cue up the song. Leaning down, I brush my lips against his ear. "Are you ready, Mr. Carroll?" I whisper, hearing him inhale sharply at my words. The song starts playing and I watch him to gauge his reaction, seeing him smile immediately at my selection.

"Two minutes," he repeats, and I'm with him on this one. There's no way I'm making it four minutes and thirty three seconds without begging him to touch me. No fucking way.

"Two minutes," I echo softly, feeling my skin flush at the thought of his hands on me.

Two fucking minutes that, I'm sure, will feel like an eternity.

Chapter
FOURTEEN

"DO I WANNA KNOW?" BEGINS playing throughout the office, the erotic tempo pulsing through the air. The bass is pumping through my body, slow and steady as I close my eyes and feel the music. It really is an insanely hot song, one that carries the perfect rhythm for fucking, or dancing. And in this case, the dancing comes first. This song holds so much history for us, and when I had decided this was going to be my response to his delivery, this song was the only song I thought of. I press the start timer on his phone and turn away from him, gripping his strong thighs with my hands. Spreading them open, I lower myself down and firmly brush my backside against his crotch along with the tempo. I repeat the motion several times, rubbing into his erection and feeling it twitch against me. He is already hard, no doubt from the sight of me in this lingerie he's never seen before, but with each movement, he gets stiffer.

"Shit, Dylan," he pants, his voice strained and fragile.

I've never heard him say my name like that. So delicately. Helpless even. I'm making him weak. Doing this to him, rubbing against his body with my own and not allowing him to touch me or see me is slowly pulling him apart. I sway my hips, continually brushing against the massive hard-on straining at the zipper of his khakis. I can see the outline of his cock, the heaviness of it and its perfect length tempting me. *Take me out, Dylan. You know you wanna touch me.* It's insanely difficult to ignore, but I can handle two minutes. Leaning back against his chest, I feel his hot, panting breath on my bare shoulder as I grind to the music.

"Mmm, you're so hard for me."

"I'm always hard for you. Let me see you."

I groan softly, gripping his thighs and dipping my body between them. "Not yet."

He moans, lifting his pelvis to meet my movements. His hands are holding tightly to the arms of his chair, his knuckles stark-white. Low, rumbling groans escape his slightly parted lips as I press my body against his. I feel him shake against me with each breath he takes, straining to stay still and keep his hands off me. My body glides against him, swaying and pushing against his with a teasing pressure.

"If I come in my pants, it's your own damn fault."

I giggle, shaking it off instantly because I need to stay focused. I've never given a lap dance before and was actually worried walking in here that I wouldn't be capable of pulling it off. But apparently, according to the reaction I'm getting from my sexy-as-fuck fiancé, I'm more than capable. I slide against his clothing, feeling him tremble slightly from the contact.

"You're doing so well, Mr. Carroll. Only one more minute."

Spinning around, I straddle one of his legs and lean in close. I hear his deep inhale as I brush my breasts against his face, letting him linger between them for several long seconds. His breath warms my chest, tickling between my breasts and instantly heating the area. He moans softly against my skin, his lips vibrating as he plants a gentle kiss to my breast before I pull back. I'll allow that one touch, considering how good he's being. I run my hands through his hair as I move to the beat, pulling on it slightly before I move down. Roaming over his broad shoulders, I squeeze gently and rub my hands down his heaving chest. His muscles contract beneath my touch, his torso pushing roughly into my palms. Aching for more. Begging for me to touch every inch of him. I'm insanely aroused right now, having gotten instantly wet when I stepped into this office. I'm certain my panties are drenched and I hardly care. I'm not stopping for anything.

His face is tense, jaw locked tight and twitching ever so slightly. This is killing him and I know it. He hates not being able to touch me, and the reality of just how much he hates it fuels my actions. That and the fact he's actually allowing this torture to happen, giving me the control which I'm sure isn't easy for him. I begin to move faster, my hips gyrating with purpose against his thigh as my leg brushes against his cock. Reaching down, I palm the front of him and he grunts loudly, his head falling back against his chair and the veins in his neck pulsing. His breathing becomes more strained, blowing sharply across my face as I lean into him. Our lips are close, so close that if I moved in we'd be kissing, but I don't. I drag my body against his instead, rubbing my breasts against his face and down to his chest. My hand cups around his length and he jerks against my touch. I want his hands on me, I want him all over me, but I can wait. Being this close to him, seeing what I can do to make him come apart is making this agony worth it. He flexes his hands and pounds his fists on the arm rest.

"I'm fucking dying," he grunts, dropping his head and brushing his face against my skin. "As soon as that alarm goes off, I'm bending you over my desk and fucking you harder than I ever have. Good luck walking out of here."

Jesus. I stumble a bit at his words. "Do you want to see what you're doing to me?" I ask in my best seductive voice.

He nods his answer, licking his lips.

Dipping my hand down the front of my panties, I slide along my wetness and moan softly against my touch. I swipe my finger across his bottom lip and he opens immediately, pulling my finger into his mouth and sucking softly.

"Kiss me," he demands, his tongue running along his bottom lip. *Fuck it.* I lean forward and brush my lips against his, my soft kiss quickly getting overpowered by his rough one. He assaults my mouth with his, and we're all tongues, lips, and sharp breaths in this moment. I wouldn't even classify this as kissing; this is primal and borderline dangerous. My lips hurt from the contact but I don't care. Nothing could pry me off this man. I bite down on his bottom lip and he groans into my mouth, the metallic taste of blood mixing with our saliva. It's hot, really fucking hot, and I'm praying for the two minutes to hurry the hell up already. The alarm on his phone beeps and my stomach tightens, a soft gasp escaping my lips. *This is it.*

"Touch me," I whisper.

"About fucking time." His hands immediately rip his tie off and spin me in his lap, bending me forward. "Grab my desk and don't let go."

I do as I'm told, quickly pushing to my feet as he stands behind me. My arms are shaking and my legs are struggling to keep myself still and upright. "God, I'm so wet for you," I whimper, hearing the sound of his belt being loosened behind me. I'm more than ready for this and I want it hard. He can make love to me later. Right now, I want dominant Reese and I know I'm about to get it.

He slides my panties down my legs, tapping each ankle for me to lift them. I look over my shoulder and see him slipping them into his pocket, a lustful smirk forming on his lips.

"I wanna make you scream so bad, but I fucking can't. You had to pull this shit at my work instead of waiting 'til I got home to tease me?"

"I couldn't wait."

"Neither can I." He enters me forcefully, the impact knocking the air out of my lungs and causing my body to collapse on his desk. His arm wraps around my waist and pulls me back up. "I said don't let go," he commands, and my hands grip firmly onto the edge of the desk. Slamming into me, he rocks my body forward with each thrust.

"Oh, God," I yell, causing his hand to wrap around my face and muffle my sounds. Each push is more powerful than the next and I'm crying out, unable to control my response to him. My body bends forward as he picks up his pace. His free hand grips my hip tightly, pulling my body back to meet his every push. I close my eyes and feel him, just him. His hand digging into the skin of my hip, hopefully marking me where only he has touched me. His cock and the way it barrels into me. His warm breath, short quick bursts of air on my back.

"If I move my hand, will you be quiet?" he asks and I quickly shake my head. *No way.* "Good girl. I love that you can't control yourself when I'm fucking you." His hips crash against me and I moan into his hand. "My girl likes it rough, doesn't she?" I nod quickly and he drives harder, my body slamming against the desk. My thighs sting from the contact but I don't care. My body is so primed for him and whatever he has to offer, I'll fucking take.

I don't know how he does it, but he manages to keep his sounds to a minimum, the loudest noise coming from the impact of our bodies striking against each other's. The slapping sound fills the office, mixing with my muffled whimpers and Reese's breathing. It really is hot, the sound of our bodies coming together in this heated moment. My core constricts and I feel a tightness forming between my legs.

"Turn around." He pulls out of me and turns me before I can even think to move. Lifting me slightly, he sets me on the edge of the desk and grabs my legs, wrapping them around his waist. He grabs my face and commands my attention. "You remember what I said about these shoes?" he asks, his voice gritty and urgent. I nod, unable to speak due to my ragged breathing, but I definitely remember. He enters me to the hilt and I brace myself on his desk, flattening my hands on the wood. "Do it."

As soon as he begins fucking me, I arch my back to give myself leverage and bear down with my legs, digging my heels into his back. He growls his response, throwing his head back as he barrels into me.

"I'm so close." Reaching up, I grab onto his bicep and dig my nails in as I anchor my heels into him.

His hand grips my neck, pulling my face into his and crashing our mouths together. "Come on my cock. Let me feel it." And at those words and the commanding tone behind them, I lose control.

He thrusts into me harder, gripping my neck with one hand and my hip with the other. I'm biting my tongue to keep myself from screaming, certain he's going to either snap me in half or the desk he's fucking me against. But considering the car currently parked outside, I'm sure he can afford another desk.

"Fuck, yes. I love this pussy," Reese pants, the veins in his neck protruding and his forehead beading with sweat. He keeps his eyes on me, allowing me to watch him unravel as he plunges into me once, twice, and then a third time before he drops his head against mine. I let my legs fall limp around his side, not having the strength to dig them into anything anymore.

"Thank you for my car," I say softly, not missing the way his lip curls up into a half-smile. I reach over and hit the stop button on my phone.

He slowly pulls out of me, holding up a finger for me not to move as he tucks himself away. Opening his desk drawer, he grabs a few tissues and wipes me clean. "I was half-expecting you to refuse it."

I laugh subtly. "Have you *seen* the car? Sam will completely under-stand my reasoning for not driving him everywhere now." I hop off the desk as he tosses the tissues into the waste basket. "You didn't take out a massive loan to afford that, did you?"

He sits down in his high-back leather chair and pulls my panties from his pocket. "Come here." I stand in front of him and he allows me to step back into them, keeping his eyes on me as he slides them up my legs. "Only because you have to walk out of here. Otherwise, these would be mine."

"You know, one of these days I'm going to find your hidden stash of my lingerie. And I will be getting every single pair back."

"Good luck with that." He taps his lap and I scramble onto it, wrap-ping my arms around his neck. "And to answer your question, no, I did not take out a massive loan. We got paid from that account with Bryce."

My stomach knots up temporarily at the sound of that asshole's name. "So, you saw him?" I twist in his lap, glancing down at his hands wrapped around me and checking for any visible bruises or cuts. This is a justified inspection and he allows it, laughing quietly while I do it. When I've thoroughly examined both, I turn my attention back to him. "And you didn't hit him?"

"I didn't see him. Ian met with him. I had some other stuff I was trying to take care of."

"What other stuff?" He gives me the same look he gave me on the couch when he wouldn't elaborate on why this account was so important. Before I took his vague *trust me* reasoning without question. Now I can't hide the slight irritation bubbling inside me. *Why is this such a secret? Is it really that crucial I not find out about anything?*

I shake off these questions, grabbing his face and planting a kiss to his lips. "I should go before Joey and Brooke kill each other."

I stand and round his desk, grabbing my coat and slipping it on. I push the questions filling my head about this account aside, not needing any additional stress. And I do trust Reese. I know he'll tell me when he can, so I'm not going to worry about this.

As I'm securing the belt around my waist, his arms wrap around me and pull me back against his chest. He roughly exhales into my hair before pressing his lips to the shell of my ear. "Three days," he whispers before kissing down my neck as he slips my phone into my pocket.

"Mmm. You keep doing that and I'm never going to leave here."

"Don't give me any ideas." His arms release their hold on me, allowing me to walk toward the door. I grab the handle, glancing once more over my shoulder and seeing him perched on his desk. Hands gripping the edge. Feet crossed in front of him. Cocky, sexy-as-fuck smile growing on his face. It's the same position he was in all those months ago when I came storming into this very office to confront him on being married. I slapped the shit out of him, found out he wasn't married, and then proceeded to blow him behind the very desk I was just fucked against.

So many memories in this office. Mostly sex-filled, but I'm not complaining.

"I'm glad you weren't married," I say, seeing the confusion wash over him momentarily before he realizes the meaning of my words. He doesn't respond, but he doesn't need to because the look he's giving me right now is speaking for him. It's the look I always find him giving me when I catch him watching me. Like he's just now seeing me for the first time. It's a look I don't know if I'll ever get used to, because it still has the same effect on me as the first time I saw it at Justin's wedding. When I stood up from his lap and spun around, getting my first real look at the man who would completely change my life. My bones seem to vibrate while my heart beat fills my ears. I would do anything for this look. For this man. And it takes every ounce of effort I can muster to leave this room. But I manage, giving him a wink and seeing my favorite smile lines appear next to his eyes before I close the door behind me.

I pull myself together enough to give Dave a wave and a smile, getting a very enthusiastic one in return.

"Can't wait for Saturday," he excitedly declares, holding up the wedding invitation he's kept on his desk since I delivered it to him months ago.

"Me either," I reply with a smile that literally makes my cheeks ache. But it's hard to not react that way when someone mentions Saturday.

I step into the empty elevator, hitting the lobby button before I lean back against the wall. Glancing down at my left hand, I study my engagement ring, which I find myself doing a lot lately. I never take it off: not before bed, not while I bake, never. I think it's common for girls to imagine what their ideal engagement ring would look like. To have a specific diamond cut in mind or at least know whether they want platinum or gold. But I never thought about it. I never once had a preference until Reese slipped this ring on my finger in the middle of my bakery kitchen. This elegant, princess-cut diamond is the ring I was always meant to wear. It's the ring I would've picked out myself, but the fact that Reese designed this specifically for me is the main reason I adore it. I can picture him sitting down with the jeweler, having an exact idea in mind and not settling for anything less. I can also imagine how messy his hair looked during that design process.

The elevator stops a few floors down and even though I'm already leaning against the wall and giving plenty of room to whoever is about to enter, I move closer to the corner anyway. As the doors slide open, I'm too busy admiring my ring to register who steps on. But I sense it. I feel the tightness forming in my gut and slowly lift my eyes and lock on to the reasoning behind it.

"Well, isn't this a sweet surprise."

"Fuck," I utter under my breath through gritted teeth, keeping my eyes down and making sure I'm still completely covered. The last thing I need is this grade-A asshole to get a look at what's underneath my trench coat. Out of my peripheral vision, I see him move to the opposite side of the elevator, keeping his full attention on me.

"Is it raining outside?" he asks, and even though I'm not looking at him, I can tell he's wearing that eerie smile that makes my skin crawl. "Because when I arrived here, it was sunny and close to seventy-five degrees out. You must be burning up in that, baby."

Baby. God, this creeper makes me nauseous.

When I don't acknowledge him, he moves closer to me and I instinctively back further into the corner. "Are you hot, Dylan? 'Cause you look hot to me. Need a hand slipping that off?"

At that absurd question, I turn my head and glare at him. "If you step any closer to me, I'll be the only one leaving this elevator with a set of balls." He either doesn't have a pair, or he doesn't value them, because my threat doesn't stop him from moving quickly and bracing himself with a hand on either side of my face. His body is pressed against mine and if this intrusion isn't enough to make me sick, his erection digging into my stomach pushes me over the edge. I clench my teeth and flatten myself further against the wall. "Back the fuck up."

"And if I don't? Removing my balls would require touching them, so by all means." He lifts a finger, trailing it down the side of my face to my neck. "Did you like my flower?"

My breathing was already labored, but now I'm borderline-hyperventilating. *That fucking flower.* I stare up into his eyes, my fists shaking at my sides.

"I was planning on stopping by your shop this week. My father has been craving your tarts and I've been craving something, as well. Think you could fill both our orders?"

"Stay the fuck away from my shop," I hiss as my nails cut into the skin of my palms.

"Or what?" he asks, leaning closer and bracing himself on the wall next to my head. "Nothing stands in the way of what I want, Dylan. Not even your boyfriend."

"What is it? What is your weird-ass obsession with me? I don't want you. I never will. So get the fuck over yourself and find someone else to creep the hell out."

I push against him but he pushes back harder, flattening me against the wall. He tilts his head down, brushing his nose against my forehead. "You want to know what it is about you?"

"I *want* you to get the fuck off me."

"Then do something about it," he snarls in my face.

I could slap this asshole, but I'm suddenly flooded with the urge to do something that'll hurt a hell of a lot worse. Grabbing his shoulders, his eyes enlarge and he drops his finger from my neck as I fist his dress shirt and swiftly bring my knee up, striking him right where I need to with enough force to bring him to his knees.

"Awhhhh, fuckkkkk." He's on his side, rolling in a fetal position with his hands clutching the balls I just crushed.

The elevator comes to a stop at that exact moment, allowing me to step over him and move toward the opening doors. When I hear laughter, I look back at him over my shoulder, seeing his face contorted into a mix of agony and mischief.

"That," he says through a faint voice before blowing out forcefully through pursed lips. "Fuck, yes. That's what it is." He laughs again, but it's snuffed out by more groans as he clutches his groin.

I slam my hand on the elevator door, holding it open. "Stay the fuck away from my shop. And if I were you, I'd get the hell out of Chicago before Reese, my *fiancé*, does a lot worse than what I just did." I glance down at his crotch. "Good luck having kids, douchebag."

I step out of the elevator, hearing the doors ding close behind me. *Hmm. Kneeing assholes in the balls is just as satisfying as slapping them across the face. Maybe a bit more.*

Thanks a lot, Bryce. You've just given me a new favorite go-to move.

Chapter
FIFTEEN

'M PUTTING EVERY SAFETY FEATURE of my new car to the test as I drive back to my bakery. I'm fuming, more mad than I can remember ever being as I weave in and out of traffic and keep the pedal pressed against the floorboard. Thank God this car has those sensors that alert you when you're too close to a vehicle in front of you, because I'm definitely not paying attention to prevent that on my own. My mind is elsewhere, the vision of Bryce cornering me in the elevator and the feel of his finger against my neck overwhelming my thoughts. I've never felt invaded like that before. Not even when Justin put his hands on me. And his hands left bruises. But this? How Bryce touched me? This was different.

I kept my cool for the most part in the moment, but now I'm feeling the aftershock of the encounter. My nerves are completely shot, my chest is so tight I'm finding it difficult to take in a deep breath, and the urge to consume the one thing I've been told to avoid until Saturday is stronger than ever. I know I have to tell Reese about this, and that's making my anxiety level rocket off the charts. It's one thing if Bryce verbally creeps me out; that I can handle. But he put his hands on me. Well, a finger, but still, he *touched* me. And I'm no longer worried that Reese might do something that could get him into trouble, because I know he'll be smart about it and he deserves to know what just happened. I'd sure as hell want to know if some bitch laid a finger on Reese. And I'd be pissed if he kept that information from me, so I'm going to tell him.

After I park my car behind Sam, I storm down the sidewalk and swing the bakery door open, nearly ripping it off the hinges. Joey and Brooke are behind the counter, both of them focusing on me immediately and halting their conversation that, for once, looks pleasant.

"What's wrong? You look pissed," Joey correctly observes. "Did your thank you not get received well?"

"That's not why I'm pissed." Storming into the back, I feel Brooke and Joey on my heels as I grab the glass that's been sitting in the middle of my worktop. Not even bothering to pick the flower out of it, I chuck the glass and its disturbing contents into the trashcan, the sound of it breaking echoing around me.

"Jesus. What the hell happened?" Joey asks.

"Yeah, Dylan. You look ready to murder somebody," Brooke adds.

I ignore both of them and make my way up the stairs, knowing Joey will be following me. I swing the door open and step behind my decorative screen, ripping my coat off and throwing it onto the bed.

"Dylan, what's going on?" Joey asks from behind the screen, genuine concern in his voice. "You're kind of starting to freak me out a little."

I grab some clothes from my dresser and throw them on the bed. "Reese didn't leave that flower on Sam the other night. Bryce did."

"What? Are you fucking serious?" Joey grunts out.

"That asshole from the club?" Brooke's voice fills the room, and I'm momentarily shocked she was concerned enough to follow me up the stairs. But she is Juls' sister, after all, and Juls would definitely follow me.

"Yeah, the asshole from the club. He cornered me in the elevator after I thanked Reese for my car. God, I fucking hate that guy." I button my jeans and grab my shirt just as Joey walks out from behind the screen.

"What do you mean he cornered you? What happened?" Joey asks.

I clench my eyes shut at the memory of it. "He pushed up against me." I open them, turning my head and seeing Joey's alarmed expression. "Right in my face, Joey. I kneed him in the balls, but I should've done worse than that. He put his fucking finger on my neck." I shiver, reaching up and rubbing my skin raw with my hand. "Jesus, I'm so grossed out right now."

"He touched you? Oh, fuck that. I don't care what you say, cupcake. I'm telling Reese about this. And if I ever see that motherfucker again, I'll risk jail time."

"Yeah, me, too," Brooke says, stepping up beside Joey. She flips her dark hair off her shoulder before crossing her arms over her chest. "He seems worthy of a good beat-down. One I'd personally like to deliver."

Reaching for my coat, I grab my phone from the pocket. "You won't have to tell Reese. I already decided he needs to know about this. I was just waiting until I wasn't putting myself and others in danger to tell him. He'd flip out if he knew I was talking on the phone while driving." I sit on the edge of my bed, dialing Reese's office number and placing the phone to my ear. I look up and notice that neither one of my employees have moved from their spot. "Would one of you like to go downstairs in case someone comes in to buy something? We can't all be up here." Joey turns to Brooke who gives him a look like she shouldn't be the one leaving. "Or both of you could go. I don't really need an audience."

Joey snaps his head in my direction, his eyes narrowing on mine. "I take offense to that, but fine." He grabs Brooke's arm. "Come on. I'll show you what to do when someone comes in with a special request. Dylan has a specific way of doing things."

Just as my loft door closes, the phone picks up.

"Reese Carroll's office. Dave speaking. How can I help you?"

"Hi, Dave. It's Dylan. Can I speak to Reese, please?"

"Absolutely. He just went to Mr. Thomas' office, so I'll transfer you to his line. Hold on one second."

Speaking of Mr. Thomas', Juls will definitely be filled in on what I just went through as soon as I hang up from this phone call.

"Ian Thomas."

"Hey, Ian. It's Dylan. Is Reese with you?"

"Yeah, he just walked in. Hold on." I hear shuffling through the phone followed by a muffled "it's your girl."

The tenseness that has set into my shoulders seems to release a bit at the sound of my title. I love being 'his girl', and that's always how Ian labels me. Even during mine and Reese's casual bullshit phase.

"Love. Are you missing me already?"

I smile, my first smile in twenty minutes. "Always. But that's not why I'm calling."

After several seconds, he asks, "Are you going to tell me or am I supposed to be guessing?"

I sigh heavily, mentally preparing myself for the reaction that will surely ruin the amazing, post-orgasmic mood he's floating around with. Mine sure as hell has been ruined. "No. But before I tell you this, I'd like to start off by saying I think I handled this very well and am quite proud of myself."

"Is this wedding shit? Because you know I back you up one hundred percent. Whatever you decide is fine with me."

I let out a small laugh. "No, it isn't wedding shit. I'd actually prefer a discussion with both our mothers' over the one I just had with Bryce."

I don't need to be in Ian's office right now to know Reese's free hand is in his hair. "What do you mean the discussion you just had with Bryce? You saw him?"

I hear Ian's voice in the background, saying something I can't make out before I respond. "He got on the elevator with me when I was leaving your building."

His breathing fills my ear. "Did he? And what did you two *discuss*?"

I can sense the irritation in his voice and suddenly feel like it's being directed toward me. "What's with the attitude? I didn't ask him to get on the elevator with me."

"No, but you picked out that fucking outfit you had on."

I'm on my feet, rage coursing through my body as I begin pacing alongside my bed. "Are you serious right now? I don't remember you complaining about my wardrobe when you had your dick in me. And how the hell was I supposed to know he was in your building? I thought Ian closed the account with him."

"He did. Don't fucking yell at me because you, once again, decided to wear something that could draw you undesirable attention. You could've stripped all your clothes off once you got in my office, or waited until I fucking got home to pull that stunt."

"Yeah, well, that's not my style."

"No shit. What did he say to you?"

My free hand fists at my side as I burn a hole into my carpet with the strides I'm taking. "You know what, Reese? Don't worry about it. I don't need you to fight my battles for me. I fucking handled it like I said I would."

"Tell me what happened."

"No. And if you want to yell at somebody, yell at yourself. *You're* the one who decided to work with that asshole after I told you months ago he creeped me out. Thanks a lot for thinking of me."

"Dylan!"

I hang up my phone before tossing it onto the bed. *What in the actual fuck?* I actually do the right thing here and before I can even tell him what happened, he's blaming me for it? How is this in any way my fault? I'm not the one who agreed to work with that prick. I wouldn't care how *important* this account was or how much money was involved. I would never work with someone who made my fiancé uncomfortable. If anyone has the right to be angry in this situation, it's me. Reese got paid, laid, and has the nerve to take this out on me?

No. Fuck that.

My phone rings on my bed but I ignore it, making my way downstairs. I have no desire to talk to him right now or anytime soon, for that matter. And I'm in desperate need of a cupcake. Nothing else will do right now.

I march through my kitchen with purpose, through the doorway and behind the counter. Brooke and Joey are sitting at my consultation table as I slide the panel on the display case open and reach for one of my chocolate mousse cupcakes with a ganache-filled center.

"What are you doing?" Joey asks, the sound of the chair scraping on the floor following his voice. "Dylan, no sweets."

I straighten up and leer at him. "If you come between me and this cupcake right now, I will end you." Removing the wrapper as quickly as I can, I shove the whole thing into my mouth as Joey rounds the counter, disapproval on his face. "I mhey have annother," I say through a mouthful, closing my eyes and moaning at the chocolaty goodness. *Fuck yes, cupcakes.*

"What the hell is going on?" he asks, snatching the wrapper from my hand and tossing it into the trashcan. "Did you tell Reese?" I reach once again for the display case, but my hand is batted away by Joey before he blocks me with his massive frame. "No more until you talk to me. What happened?"

I open my mouth to give him the rundown of my phone call when the shop phone decides to ring at that exact moment. There's no doubt in my mind it's Reese, and I have no intention of answering. Leaning against the counter, I stare at the phone on the wall as Joey moves toward it.

"It's Reese," I say with a clipped voice after swallowing my mouthful.

Joey ignores me and grabs the phone, putting it up to his ear. He frowns at me before saying, "Dylan's Sweet Tooth." I tap my fingers against my arm, seeing his expression change to indicate I was correct in my assumption. "I'm not sure this is the best time to talk to her. She just inhaled a cupcake and is staring at me like she's going to eat me next."

I roll my eyes as Brooke comes to stand next to me. "What's going on?" she asks softly, her eyes flicking between Joey and myself.

"Boys are idiots. If I were you, I'd go lesbian."

She shrugs slightly. "I've dabbled. It's not really my thing. If there isn't at least one dick involved, I can't get into it."

I slide closer to her, my interest in Brooke's sex life suddenly blanketing all my Reese concerns at the moment. "At least one dick? Have you done multiple?"

"Once. But they were bi and seemed to like dick more than me. I felt like a third wheel."

"Someone actually liked dick more than you? I'm shocked," I reply before laughing under my breath and seeing her eyes light up with mischief. Joey's elevated voice grabs both of our attention.

"Listen here. I don't have to do anything. Dylan clearly doesn't want to talk to you right now and as her best friend, I back her up one hundred percent. Hoes before bros." He leans his shoulder against the wall, bringing his free hand up to his hip. "And another thing, I think it's really shitty that you and Ian agreed to work with that asshole. He's clearly psychotic, given the fact he put his hands on Dylan when he knows you… what?" Joey looks over in my direction, his agitated expression softening. "Uh, she didn't tell you that? Well, yeah, he... hello?" He brings the phone away from his ear briefly before returning it. "Helloooo?" Hanging it up, he spins and tilts his head to the side as he strokes his chin. "Funny thing. Reese apparently didn't know about the elevator incident. Care to explain that to me before he comes barreling through the shop door and hauls you out of here over his shoulder?"

I take the elastic band off my wrist and secure my hair into a pony. "I was going to tell him until he opened his stupid mouth and blamed me for drawing undesirable attention with my outfit. Like wearing snow gear would've prevented that jerk-off from touching me. And for Christ's sake, I had a coat on. It's not like I was strutting around half-naked." I run my hands down my face before stepping up to Joey and poking a finger at his chest. "I'm eating another cupcake. You can either join me or step into the back, but it's happening."

"Well I'm sure as hell going to eat one," Brooke says behind me. "I've been practically eye-fucking them all morning."

Joey's eyes dart over my shoulder, dropping to the display case. He sighs before nodding sharply. "Right. This situation definitely calls for massive sugar consumption." He drops his eyes down to look at me. "But fair warning, I will be pushing you during our run tomorrow to make up for this moment of weakness. And no faking shin splints like today. I was so onto you."

I smile up at him sheepishly. "I have no idea what you're talking about."

Brooke hands us both a cupcake, taking one for herself before sliding the panel closed. She gestures toward the clock on the wall with her free hand. "Wanna take bets as to what time Reese arrives? I'd put money on 2:37 p.m.."

Joey shoves half the cupcake into his mouth before responding. "No way. He'll be here within the next few minutes. I'm saying 2:26 p.m.. What do you think?" he asks, nudging against me.

I take a bite out of my cupcake, glancing up at the clock. "Knowing Reese, he's going to hunt down Bryce before he deals with me. And I'd give him an hour for kill time and dumping the body." I swallow my bite, hearing Joey and Brooke's muted laughs next to me. "I'm going to say 3:32 p.m.."

The shop door dings open, causing us all to spin around quickly. I'm sure we're all anticipating Reese to walk through the doorway, but Mr. and Mrs. Crisp step inside the bakery wearing their brightest smiles and carrying a large, elegantly-wrapped present.

"Happy anniversary," I direct at them, setting my half-eaten cupcake on the counter. I glance over at Brooke who is finishing hers. "Can you grab their cake for me? It's the German chocolate one."

She gives me a thumbs-up, chewing animatedly before she walks into the back. Mr. Crisp places the gift he's carrying next to my cupcake, sliding it closer to me as his wife flanks his side. "And happy wedding week to our favorite baker. This is for you, dear," she says as she straightens out the white and gold ribbon on the top.

"For me? You didn't have to get me anything."

"Oh, it's nothing much. Just something small off your registry," Mrs. Crisp says with a smile. "Don't open it until we leave, though."

Joey brushes his hands off before sliding the gift down the counter so it's in front of him. "What a wrapping job. I can never get my corners straight."

"You can't get anything straight," I counter through a teasing smile. He arches his brow playfully at me.

Brooke comes walking from the back, carrying the anniversary cake I made. She hands it off to me and I hold it over the counter, letting my two favorite customers examine it. Mrs. Crisp gasps softly, putting her hand up to her chest. "Oh, my. Dylan, this is so lovely," she says, lifting her eyes to me. "Thank you so much."

"German chocolate. My favorite." Mr. Crisp grabs the cake and licks his lips. "I might just dive into this on the way home."

"There's extra coconut in the frosting just for you," I direct toward him. His eyes enlarge as his grin spreads across his face. "And thank you for the gift. You really didn't have to do that."

Mrs. Crisp waves me off with her hand, her other tucking into the crook of her husband's elbow. "We're so happy for you, dear, and we hate that we can't make it. Make sure you bring in lots of pictures when you get them developed." She waves goodbye, Mr. Crisp winking at me before they slip out of the shop.

Joey slides the gift back over in front of me. "Go on. You know you want to."

I look at him, then at the gift and decide that yes, I definitely want to. After tearing the paper and handing it off to Brooke who deposits it into the trashcan, I pop open the top of the box. Joey helps me shift the tissue paper around until I feel the smooth edge of something. I grab it with both hands and lift it out, smiling so big my cheeks begin to ache.

I place the hot-pink, brand new, industrial-size mixer on the counter. "Oh, wow. This wasn't on my registry."

"No, but you definitely needed this. I always said you should have more than one mixer," Joey says, running his finger along the top of the handle.

"And it's pink. I love that," Brooke adds. "Every girl needs a pink mixer."

I nod in agreement, lifting it off the counter and carrying it into the back. I slide it onto my shelf next to my beaten-down, ten-year-old mixer I still love as much as the first day I got it. Of course, it pales in comparison to this brand new one, but it will always be special to me.

Brooke comes walking into the back and steps up next to me. "Would it be okay if I watched you bake sometime? I'm really interested in learning how you whip up these incredible creations. That cupcake I just ate was insane."

I grin boastfully at the compliment. "Sure. If you want, I could use some help tomorrow when I start the two wedding cakes. Joey can manage up front without you if you want to give me a hand."

She places her hand on my arm, her face falling in surprise. "You'd let me help make *your* wedding cake? What if I mess it up?"

"Are you planning on messing it up?" I ask.

"No. But I can be a bit clumsy."

I grip onto both her shoulders, gaining her full attention. "I'll let you help out on the *other* wedding cake. How's that sound?" She laughs, giving me half a smile. "Come on, let's go finish those insane cupcakes."

We did just that, Joey grabbing two more and polishing off the rest of the chocolate mousse ones. My eyes kept darting between the clock on the wall and the front door, especially when the bell would alert us of someone walking in. But Reese never came. He never stormed into the shop. He never hauled me over his shoulder in typical Reese fashion. He didn't even call the shop number again. By the time 6:00 p.m. rolled around, I was no longer agitated with my quick-tempered fiancé or fuming over what happened with Bryce. After saying goodbye to Joey and Brooke, I took to the stairs with an emotion I didn't plan on feeling the week of my wedding.

Disappointment.

Chapter
SIXTEEN

AFTER KICKING OFF MY SHOES, I plop down on the bed and grab my cell phone I had discarded hours ago. Seventeen missed calls from Reese, all stopping around the time he called the shop phone. I scroll through his text messages, noting the time on them, as well. His last one to me was at 2:13 p.m. and it wasn't the usual sweet and dirty text messages I'm used to receiving from him. I roll over onto my back, holding my phone out above me as I re-read it.

REESE: *Ignoring my phone calls is really mature.*

Yeah, well… okay, fine. It wasn't my most mature moment. But him jumping down my throat about an outfit he thoroughly enjoyed was a bullshit move, especially after he got his rocks off on it. I get that this situation is irritating and making us both homicidal, but I was not at fault here. And right now, I'd really like hearing that from someone other than my inner self.

I close out Reese's text message and pull up Juls' contact info.

"Hey, sweets. It's so weird you called. I was just thinking about you."

I grab a pillow and stuff it underneath my head. "Oh, yeah? Let me guess. Ian filled you in on my afternoon of fun?"

The sound of chips crunching enters the phone. "Hmm? No. What afternoon of fun? Ian's working late tonight, and I haven't talked to him since before lunch."

"I had a run-in with Bryce after giving Reese a lap dance in his office."

The loud, crinkling sound of the chip bag fills my ear. "Chips aren't cutting it. I need real food. Have you eaten yet?"

"Um, no. But did you hear what I just said?"

"Yes, and you can fill me in on every single detail when you meet me at Fletchers. I'm dying for a burger the size of my head."

My mouth waters instantly. *Carbs? Hell yes. Fuck you, salad. Nobody wants you.* I sit up and swing my legs over the side of the bed, stepping into my ballet flats. "Okay. I'll meet you in twenty."

Standing up, I grab my keys off my kitchen counter, freezing in place when the BMW emblem catches my attention. I should tell Reese where I'm going. Even if I was avoiding him earlier, I'm not anymore. And coming home to an empty loft and not knowing where I am would surely make things worse. I open a text message as I lock my door behind me.

ME: *Going out to dinner with Juls. Be home later.*

❧

AFTER PARKING BEHIND JULS' BLACK Escalade, I walk into Fletchers and spot her at a table in the back. She waves at me with one hand, her other popping a few fries into her mouth.

"Sorry. I hope you don't mind that I already ordered for us. I'm crazy hungry," she says, chewing behind her hand.

"Not at all. You know what I like." I grab a seat, taking a quick sip of my water and watching in amusement as my best friend inhales her plate of fries. "Pregnancy cravings kicking in?"

"Nah. I've just been busy all day with wedding stuff. This is my first actual meal today." She pushes the plate of fries to the middle of the table and wipes her mouth with a napkin. "All right. Spill it." She tosses her napkin onto the table before leaning back in her chair.

"Do you promise not to go into hurricane-mode in the middle of this restaurant?"

"Depends," she replies, motioning with her hand for me to continue.

I take in a deep breath, filling my lungs to capacity. "Reese bought me a car and had it delivered to the shop this morning. But not just any car. A BMW." A knowing smile spreads across her face, prompting me to lean forward with interest. "Did you know anything about that?"

She shrugs dismissively. "I may have given my opinion on car color. He was going mental trying to decide on his own."

I picture his frustrated state and it brings a smile to my lips. "I can imagine. Anyway, I wanted to really wow him with a thank you for such an undeserving gift."

She holds up her hand, halting my speech. "Dylan, you deserve the world and that man will give it to you. Don't sell yourself short."

I feel my cheeks flush at the compliment. Grinning, I issue her a wink and she gives me one in return. "So, I put on my sluttiest lingerie, covered myself with a trench coat, and went to his office." I pause, crossing one leg over the other and seeing a small smile play at the corner of her mouth. "I gave him a lap dance, which he appreciated greatly at the time, and when I was leaving, Bryce got in the elevator with me. I would've been creeped out had he not touched me, but he did. He got right up against me and made crude comments about my outfit. And then he slid his finger down my neck." I mimic his move and Juls shakes her head, her face taut and her fingers tapping on the table.

"What did you do?"

"Kneed him in the balls."

"Good. Continue."

"I knew I had to tell Reese about it, so I called him as soon as I got back to the bakery. And you know what he said? That I shouldn't have been wearing that outfit and that I once again drew attention to myself. I didn't even get to tell him what happened. Once he put the blame on me, I hung up on him. And then when he couldn't get a hold of me on my cell, he called the shop phone and Joey told him Bryce touched me." I glance down at the table cloth, rubbing my fingertip along the seam. "I was so pissed off at him for blaming me for it, but now that I haven't seen or talked to him in over four hours, I'm not pissed. I'm hurt more than anything."

"Because he made it seem like it was your fault for what happened?" I nod in response to her question. "I can see why you feel that way. It wasn't your fault and Reese knows that. But he's extremely protective of you; he always has been. And hearing that you were put into another situation with Bryce when he once again wasn't around to protect you I'm sure infuriates him. And when guys get angry, they say shit they don't mean. Ian does it all the time." She takes a sip of her water, prompting me to do the same. "I can't even begin to tell you how many petty arguments the two of us get into because he says stuff without thinking. I swear to God, I think testosterone has some sort of negative effect on all rational thought." I laugh, grabbing a fry and popping it into my mouth. "I can't believe that fucker touched you. Reese didn't come to the shop after finding out that information from Joey?"

I shake my head. "No. And he stopped trying to get a hold of me. I'm actually considering calling the local jail to see if he's been locked up." I grab the small vase sitting on our table and place it on the empty table next to us. Juls gives me a questionable look and I remember she doesn't know about the flower on my van. "After my fitting the other night, I found a rose on my windshield. I had this gut feeling it wasn't from Reese. That's so not something he would do. He's way more romantic than that."

Juls crosses her arms over her chest and purses her lips. "That asshole put a flower on your van? That's fucking disturbing, Dylan. You better call the police if he comes into your shop."

"I will." I had already decided that. There is no way I am going to let him into my bakery again. That prick has officially crossed the line.

"I was ready to kill that tool at the club when he was running his mouth. But now? I will seriously take pleasure in dismembering him. I'm not just stellar at planning weddings. I'm resourceful, too. I can make a shiv out of practically anything."

I giggle at my heated best friend as the waiter arrives at the table with our meals. And then my laughter fades immediately as I survey the Cobb salad placed in front of me.

Goddamn it.

I grit my teeth, glancing up at Juls who is smiling widely at me, obviously finding my order humorous. "What the hell is this? I thought we were destroying burgers."

"I never said we." She points her manicured finger at me. "You have a dress to fit into, sweets. And as your Matron of Honor and wedding planner, it is my job to make sure everything goes as planned for Saturday." She picks up her giant, heavenly-looking burger and brings it to her lips. "Besides, Joey told me you had three cupcakes today."

I scowl at her as she takes a massive bite. "Seriously? He told you that?"

"Yup," she says through a mouthful.

I grimace, poking my lettuce with my fork. "I don't know how people eat this stuff all the time."

She moans softly, catching an evil look from me. "Sorry," she murmurs.

And I can't help but laugh at the sight of her, thoroughly enjoying her burger and not caring in the least that she's eating it like a caveman. All of her table manners have been left at the door as she takes bites that would rival Reese's. I eventually dig into my salad after my stomach starts growling at me, but I don't enjoy myself nearly as much as Juls. I do however enjoy her company and the conversation that stays far away from eerie elevator encounters. We talk about her upcoming doctor's appointment and how excited she is to possibly hear the baby's heartbeat. We talk about my wedding and the fact that my mother has also been harassing her with phone calls about last-minute alterations, and we wrap up our meal with talk of my honeymoon to the Cayman Islands. Two weeks with Reese in a bathing suit is the second thing I'm most excited about in terms of upcoming events. The fact that it'll be my husband I'll be staring at for those fourteen days is still strongly holding the lead.

As it should.

❧

AFTER SAYING GOODBYE TO JULS, I head back to the loft, expecting to have it out with Reese as soon as I arrive. I mentally prepare myself for our discussion as I set the alarm at the front door before walking through the bakery and up the stairs. But when I step through the door, a dark, empty space greets me instead of his expectant scowl. And then I remember what Juls' said about Ian working late. Reese is probably still stuck at the office, and when he does work late, he usually isn't home until after 9:00 p.m., which gives me another hour before I could be expecting him.

I grab an empty box off the floor and sit it on the bed. Packing should help me pass the time, and even though Reese wanted to do this for me, he shouldn't have to. This is my stuff, and I've accumulated a lot over the past three and a half years. I'm not a hoarder by any means, but I also am not one to throw away anything that holds even the tiniest bit of sentimental value. I've kept every movie stub, concert ticket, and playbill holding a Juls and Joey memory. I've kept every thank you note I've ever received from a customer. But probably my most prized possession is the tin I keep on my dresser that holds all of Reese's love notes to me. I grab it, sitting down next to the box and popping off the lid on the tin. I thrum through the contents with my fingers, scraping along the tops of the cards. Every now and then, I'll blindly reach in and grab one, reading it and reliving every emotion I felt when I first opened the tiny brown card. I have every single note in here, even the first one he sent me that I thought I'd thrown away. But Joey had grabbed it for me while I was delivering my apologetic blow job in Reese's office after slapping him for thinking he was married. I had no idea he kept it until he gave it to me at my bridal shower last month as part of my gift. I cried when I read it that day, which I suppose was funny considering how I reacted to it the first time. But that note started everything. If Reese hadn't sent it to me with the bag of flour, I'm not sure what would've happened between us. Maybe we would've eventually seen each other again at some function involving our two best friends, but maybe not. So even though his first note to me is an apology for fucking up and not one that spells out how much he loves me, it's still my favorite.

Next to the one he gave me with my engagement ring.

After packing up a good amount of clothes and what I won't be using the next three days, I stack the boxes in the corner behind my decorative screen and get ready for bed. It's almost 9:00 p.m., and even though I'd like to stay up and wait for Reese to get home, I know he'll wake me up if he wants to talk about it tonight. And I'm too tired not to crash hard right now. This day has been exhausting, both mentally and emotionally, and as I cuddle up on my side of the bed, I find myself missing not only the wedding stress that was once my only concern, but also the man who blankets me better than any down comforter.

ॐ

A LOUD, PIERCING NOISE JOLTS me awake and upright, and my body immediately goes rigid. I clamp my hands over my ears, muffling the noise as my eyes adjust to the dark room around me. I'm alone, Reese's side of the bed is completely untouched, and it takes me several seconds to realize what's happening. That noise. I haven't heard it before but I know what it is. My shop alarm is going off, and I need to enter the code to stop it. I slide off the bed and run toward the stairs but freeze when my mind draws a conclusion to the reasoning behind the alarm.

Someone's trying to break in.

I drop to my knees beside the bed and grab the baseball bat I've kept there since that psycho bitch threw a brick at my window last summer. Nobody messes with my business, and I am seriously prepared to do damage with this thing.

I run downstairs, keeping a tight grip on the bat as the noise becomes even louder. I go along the far side of the worktop, trying to see through the doorway as my heart rate jumps to a rapid pace. I can't make out anything and I need to stop the alarm before my ears begin to bleed. Mustering up every ounce of courage I have and keeping the bat at a ready position, I run through the doorway leading into the main bakery.

And then I see him.

He's punching in numbers on the keypad, his legs staggering underneath his tall frame, struggling to keep him upright. He stumbles, leaning into the glass window before straightening up again. I drop the bat and step closer, keeping my focus on him.

"Reese?"

He doesn't hear me over the screeching alarm as his fingers continue to enter incorrect codes. I move quickly, putting my hand on his shoulder and stepping next to him. As I press the correct pattern of numbers, the smell of alcohol permeates my senses. The alarm stops abruptly and silence fills the space between us. I turn my head up, seeing unfamiliar eyes staring back at me. Glassy and dilated, they no longer hold the intensity

I'm accustomed to. Even the shade of green seems dulled out, lifeless even. Besides that obvious difference, he's clearly intoxicated, which is not a look I ever imagined seeing on this man. Reese doesn't get drunk. He'll have two, three drinks maybe and then cut himself off. I've never even seen him tipsy before. And as he slouches against the wall, his heavy eyelids closing and his head hanging low, I'm finding myself questioning if I was the only one hurting earlier.

Chapter
SEVENTEEN

"**H**EY. ARE YOU OKAY?" I ask, reaching up with a gentle hand. I stroke the side of his face and see him turn into me, pressing his lips against my palm. His breath warms my skin and I feel the uneven rhythm of it, the quick burst and then the shuddering inhale he takes before he drops his head again.

"Need you," he says through a broken voice.

My heart wrenches in my chest cavity as I stare up at this man who looks defeated and beaten down. And also way too drunk to get behind the wheel. "You didn't drive here, did you?"

"Cab. My car's at The Tavern."

Relief runs through me before I'm startled once again by the sound of the shop phone ringing. I dash over to it to answer, double backing when I think Reese is going to topple over. After he seems steady, I run to the phone.

"Hello?"

"Miss Sparks? This is Lenox Security calling to check to make sure everything is okay. We received an alert that your security system was triggered."

"Yes. Yes, it was, but it was an accident. Everything's okay."

"Okay, ma'am, we just wanted to make sure. Have a great night."

"You, too."

I hang up the phone, rounding the counter and stepping next to Reese. I lift his arm, draping it around my neck and keeping a firm grip on his wrist. My other arm wraps around his waist and pulls him off the wall. "Come on. Let's go upstairs."

Normally when I'm this close to him, I'm relishing in his fresh, citrus scent and setting up camp in the crook of his neck. But right now, he smells like he's hit up every bar in South Side and for the first time since I met him; the urge to nuzzle him is absent. He maneuvers himself with me across the bakery, but I'm doing most of the work as we make it inch by inch. It's a slow effort and when I finally lift my head and size up the stairs we'll have to tackle, my grip on him tightens and a feeling of determination fuels me. I look over at him as I position us at the first step. "You need to help me, okay? It's not that many steps."

His lips twitch into a smile before he drops his head to the side, bumping it against mine. "You're so pretty."

I chuckle, lurching forward and trying to bring him with me. "Thanks. Come on. Lift your feet."

"I stare at you sometimes when you don't see me. I like doing that."

"Oh, yeah?" I sound surprised, but I'm not. I know Reese stares at me. I always feel his eyes on me when he does it. And I like that game we play, where I pretend I don't notice and let him watch me. He does the same when I partake in my own obsessive gazing. I know he sees me. His lip will twitch or he'll coincidentally adjust himself as I'm studying him, drawing my attention off his face.

I'm on to his tactics.

He lifts his left, then his right foot, putting us both on the first step. "I stared at you on my phone tonight. I didn't really like it."

We make it a few more steps as he leans further into me, causing me to let go of his wrist and grip the handrail instead. "Yeah? Let's get you upstairs and then you can tell me why you didn't like it."

"I didn't like it, Dylan."

"I know. Come on. Just a little more. We're almost there." We get two steps away from the door when Reese suddenly drops to his knees, pulling me down with him. "Reese! Hold... what are you doing?"

He turns awkwardly until he's sitting on the step. His head drops between slouched shoulders, and I see the slight shake of his hands as they hang over his knees. I slide next to him, placing a hand on his thigh. He lifts his head and turns to me, the worry in his eyes evident. "I can't just stare at pictures of you. It's not enough."

"Well, I'm right here. You don't have to stare at pictures. Let's go upstairs and you can look at me all you want." I go to stand when his hand grabs my wrist, halting me.

"I watch you all the time." I lower myself back down as he drops his gaze, staring off at nothing. "If I'm not touching you, I want to be."

"I know the feeling," I interject, gaining his attention immediately.

His face hardens. "No. You don't." I open my mouth to argue but stop myself when I see the conviction in his eyes. "It's constant, Dylan. You invade every thought I have even when they have nothing to do with you. I'm not just in love with you. I'm kind of obsessed. And the thought of somebody else watching you the way I do, or needing to touch you like I do…" He pauses, squeezing his eyes shut. "I'm terrified."

I scoot closer, crawling into this lap. His eyes open and refocus on mine as I cradle his face in my hands. "He barely touched me. I'd never let him or anyone else put their hands on me the way you do." He tries to shake his head but I stop him. "You don't need to be scared. I got him good. And I'll do worse if he tries it again."

His hands grab my wrists and pull down, removing my grip. "I'm not scared he'll touch you. I'm scared of what I'll do when I find him."

I'm familiar with that feeling. It consumed me until Reese took it away. Now it's my turn to comfort him.

I look down at his hand resting in my lap. "I used to be scared of what you would do to him. It's why I didn't tell you about seeing him at the club. But then you told me something that took away that worry. Do you remember?" He registers my questions with a slight shake of his head. I shift in his lap, placing my hands on his shoulders and apply gentle pressure. "You said you were a smart guy, and you would never do anything that could get you into trouble. And I knew that was true. I also knew you would never do anything to hurt me. And getting yourself taken away from me because of what you want to do to Bryce would hurt me. You're not the only one who couldn't survive on just pictures to stare at." He rakes a quick hand through his hair, leaving it a right mess. "Is this why you went out drinking?"

He frowns. "I hated what you said to me. About me working with Bryce after knowing how he made you feel. It killed me to hear you say that. Because I know how it looks. I fucking know. And I just wanted to stop thinking about everything." He squints, flattening his hand against his temple. "It didn't help."

"I didn't mean it. I was just angry because I thought you were blaming me for what happened."

He grabs my face with both hands and forces me closer, putting us inches apart. "I'm sorry I yelled at you. I didn't mean to say that. I'm just so fucking frustrated that this shit is taking so long. But I'm close. I'm so fucking close, Dylan. It's almost over, okay?"

I don't question what he's saying to me. I know he won't tell me anyway, and I don't want to focus on this anymore. I slide off his lap, standing and reaching for him. "Come on. Let's go lie down."

We make it up the stairs, me still supporting a good amount of his weight. I shuffle him toward the bed, dropping his arm from around my neck and giving him a light shove. "Go ahead and get on the bed. I'll be right there."

He grabs my waist with both hands, pulling me against his chest. "Come with me."

I laugh against his dress shirt before turning my gaze up to him. Tender eyes meet mine. "I am. I just need to get you some water."

He grumbles incoherently before letting me go. Grabbing a glass from the cabinet, I fill it with some tap water and toss a few ice cubes in. As I round the counter, I spot Reese's long legs hanging off the edge, the rest of him face-planted in the middle of bed. I set the glass on my nightstand and pull his shoes off, dropping them on the floor.

"Roll over, handsome," I say, kneeling next to him and nudging his side. He moans but doesn't move. Not in the slightest. He's dead weight, and I can't help but recognize the fact that even a passed-out, face-down Reese is better-looking than any other guy put in this scenario. I shove my hands underneath his body and push as hard as I can, rolling him onto his back. Eyes closed. Hair a right, sexy mess. I take a moment to appreciate the sweet look on his face, which will most likely be nowhere in sight tomorrow if the hangover I'm predicting decides to show up.

His heavy, even breathing fills the air as I tug off his khakis and socks. I loosen his tie, unbuttoning his dress shirt and placing them with his pants. I grab the pillows and tuck one under his head, knowing full well there is no way I'll be able to shift his body up the bed to lie how we usually do. So we're going with this arrangement tonight.

Placing my pillow next to his, I get settled on my side and tuck my hands under my chin. I stare at his profile until my eyelids become too heavy to hold open anymore.

ر

NORMALLY WHEN I WAKE UP after having passed out next to Reese, I'm used to seeing an empty side of the bed next to me. He's always up before me during the week, getting in his own workout at the gym before he heads into the office. And even though he came home drunk last night, I still expected to wake up alone. He's so dedicated, it wouldn't surprise me in the least if he pushed through it with the worst hangover in the history of hangovers. But before I even open my eyes when my alarm goes off, I know he's next to me.

I'll always feel his presence before I see him.

I sit up after turning off my alarm, spotting him lying on his side. That's also different. Reese is usually sprawled on top of me when I wake up, his head pressed against my chest and his long legs tangled with mine. I decide to let him sleep while I run with Joey. If Reese is sleeping in, he must need it.

After putting on my workout clothes and stepping into my Nike's, I press my lips to his forehead, hearing him moan softly into his pillow. I make my way downstairs and see Joey's tall frame stretching on the other side of the glass.

"You are not going to believe who I ran into last night," he says as he pulls his arm across his chest.

I lock the door behind me and tuck my key into the pocket on the inside of my shorts. "Who?"

"Your loser ex-boyfriend."

I pull my knee up to my chest, feeling my muscle tighten. "Get the hell out of here. Where?" I haven't seen Justin since he made the mistake of coming to my bakery to apologize for putting his hands on me last summer. I was in no mood for him or his apology, and Reese just so happened to be there. I've never seen my stupid ex look so terrified before.

It was a good look on him.

"The market. He seemed to be shopping for one, so you know I had to pry. And upon further inspection, I noticed he wasn't wearing a wedding ring."

I shrug impassively, switching legs. I'm not surprised if his cheating marriage failed. Nor do I give a shit. "Did you say anything to him?"

He pops his gum before smiling cunningly. "Nah. The little chicken-shit practically sprinted down the frozen food aisle when he spotted me. I'm sure he saw your engagement announcement in the paper, though. That advertisement took up the entire page."

I laugh as I roll my ankle on the pavement, loosening it up. Reese made sure to send in the biggest photo he had of the two of us to the local newspaper several months ago. When I insisted on something a bit smaller out of sheer modesty, he distracted me the way he usually does and I forgot all about it until it was published. Well, until he had it framed and delivered to me.

I stretch my neck from side to side as Joey moves down the sidewalk, motioning for me that he's ready to start running. I jog up to his side and we take off at our usual pace. The fact that Joey gave me a warning yesterday about pushing me during this run stays locked away inside my head. If he doesn't remember it, I'm not reminding him.

"So, what happened with Reese last night after he got home? Was he pissed about Bryce?"

"Oh, you're not going to believe this. He showed up drunk and woke me in the middle of the night with the shop alarm going off. He couldn't even enter the code, he was so plastered."

Joey flicks his head toward me, his mouth dropping open and the wad of gum nearly falling from his mouth. "Shit." He pushes it back in before responding. "Reese was drunk? Are you serious?" I nod and he continues. "What kind of a drunk was he? Sloppy? Horny? I looove when Billy gets drunk. He's extra frisky."

I nudge him hard in his side and he flinches. "No, he wasn't horny. He was actually kind of sad."

"Ughhhh. I hate depressing drunks. My mother's like that."

We round the corner and start up the big hill, causing us both to grumble our exhaustion until we make it to the top. I steady my breathing after taking in three deep breaths. "What do you think Reese could be doing with Bryce that would make working with him so important? He keeps telling me to trust him and that it's almost over, but I don't understand why he can't just tell me."

Joey thinks silently for several seconds, the sound of our feet striking the pavement becoming more prominent. "I don't know. I feel like we're in a fucking episode of The Sopranos, only with accountants instead of Mob bosses." He ducks his chin into his T-shirt, wiping the sweat off his nose. "Maybe he doesn't want you to be involved if things don't work out the way he's hoping. Like maybe he thinks Bryce will retaliate by hurting you if he finds out Reese is up to something."

"But what could he be doing? Like you said, he's an accountant."

"I don't fucking know. Tax shit? Whatever it is, it must be worth it to Reese. I don't think I could work with some guy who hit on Billy. I'd go crazy. I can't imagine how hard that must be for him."

"I think that's why he got drunk." I picture those desperate eyes he had last night while sitting on the steps, stripped down and raw. I never want to see him like that again. And I suppose Joey's right. Reese could be keeping me in the dark to keep me protected. Bryce does seem like the type to lash out, and if he wanted to get back at Reese, he could do it by getting to me. But I'll never let that happen. I'll never let that douchebag anywhere near me. And God help him if he decides to take it out on Reese. If he lays one finger on my fiancé, I'll be the one spending my honeymoon in jail.

A sharp slap on my ass breaks me out of my mind set. "Ahh! What the hell?" I shriek, rubbing my left cheek.

"Cupcakes, cupcake. I told you I'd be pushing you today. Think I forgot?" He drops back and gets directly behind me. Another slap and

I'm arching away from him, hissing in pain. "Move it. Or you'll get to explain to Reese why you let me spank you. I'm sure that'll go over well."

Laughing, I pick up speed and put some distance between us, but it's fleeting. Joey catches up within a few seconds and we continue our run with him on my heels. I'm rewarded with a few more slaps when I absentmindedly slow down, but I'm not used to this pace. This is the speed which renders you unable to speak to your running buddy. My legs are burning, as are my lungs, and I'm sweating more than I ever have in my entire life. And it isn't even sixty degrees out yet.

But I don't complain.

I don't quit on Joey and give up even though my body is screaming at me to do just that.

I have a dress to fit into, so I muster up every ounce of willpower in my body and push through my run. Because let's be honest, the chance of me sneaking another cupcake before I walk down that aisle is looking pretty good right now.

Chapter
EIGHTEEN

'M DRIPPING SWEAT AFTER WHAT feels like the hardest run of my life. After saying goodbye to Joey, I head upstairs and expect to see Reese still passed out in bed, but it's empty. I see the light creeping from under the bathroom door and kick off my shoes before I make my way into the kitchen. As I'm pulling a bottled water out of the fridge, I hear the reason behind Reese being out of bed. The unmistakable sound of him throwing up has me rushing to the door, twisting the locked doorknob.

"Reese?"

The toilet flushes and then I hear his gravelly voice, barely above the noise. "Yeah?"

I jar the knob again, tossing my bottled water onto the floor. "Open the door."

"No. I don't want you in here."

"Well, that's too bad," I scoff, grabbing one of my kitchen chairs. I climb up on it, skimming my hand along the top of the door jam and feeling for the key I keep up there. Once I grab it, I jump down and move the chair out of the way. "I'm coming in. I can handle vomit."

"Dylan, please don't come in here," his raspy voice begs me.

I wiggle the key around until I feel it unlatch the door. I turn the handle freely this time and swing it open, spotting Reese on his knees.

He's slouched over the toilet, shirtless and only in a pair of boxers. His head is resting on his forearm and he doesn't bother to lift it when I enter the room. I place the key on the bathroom counter and crouch down behind him, placing my hand on his back.

"Are you okay?" I ask as I begin rubbing my hand along his clammy skin.

He coughs a few times, dropping his head and spitting into the toilet. "I asked you not to come in here. Why would I want you to see me like this?"

"In two days, I'll be vowing to be with you for better or for worse. Or did you forget about that?" He tilts his head to the side so our eyes meet. "You took care of me when I was like this. Now it's my turn."

He's either too weak to give me a rebuttal, or the fact that I've reminded him of how many days we have left is soothing him. I run my fingers through his hair, which is sticking out every which way, feeling the dampness of his sweat on my hand. He looks thoroughly exhausted, with bags under his eyes and his complexion looking paler than I've ever seen it, but somehow, he pulls it off. Not that I'm the least bit surprised.

I place my lips to his shoulder. "You're beautiful even when you're hung-over."

He drops his chin, smiling. "You're beautiful even when you ugly-cry."

His words have me wanting to feel his mouth against mine, even if he has been puking his guts up. But I bite back the urge and settle for a wink instead, which prompts his smile to grow the tiniest bit. I stand and grab a washcloth from the cabinet, wetting it at the sink. "I'm going to get you some water," I say as I lay the cool rag on the back of his neck. He acknowledges me with a subtle nod before closing his eyes.

I grab the bottled water I had discarded and return to the bathroom just as a wave of nausea hits Reese. He arches over the toilet, gripping the seat with his hands. His back goes rigid, every muscle flexing as he proceeds to vomit and dry heave. I kneel behind him and hold the rag against his neck, rubbing his upper arm with my other hand. This round lasts several minutes, and when he slouches down, seemingly finished, I pick up the water bottle and unscrew the cap.

"Here."

He looks over his shoulder at me and takes the bottle. After swishing the water around in his mouth, he spits it into the toilet and repeats the action several times. He tries to stand, but I stop him with a firm hand on his shoulder.

"Are you done?"

He nods, pushing to his feet. "I think so. That shit sucked. I haven't thrown up since I was little." I follow him over to the sink, watching as he splashes some cold water onto his face. He grabs his tooth brush and slicks some toothpaste on it, connecting with my eyes in the mirror. I see his rake down my body. "How was your run?"

"Difficult. I had cupcakes yesterday and paid for it greatly." I begin stripping out of my sweaty clothes while Reese continues brushing his teeth. "Are you going into work today?"

"No. I took a sick day. I need to go get my car and then I thought maybe I'd watch you bake." He spits into the sink and rinses off his tooth brush. "If that's okay with you."

I smile, tossing my clothes into my hamper. "That's definitely okay with me. You haven't watched me bake in a while." I reach into the shower and turn it on, testing the temperature. "But you'll have to disappear when I start working on our wedding cake. That is off-limits."

He steps up behind me, wrapping his arms around my body and pulling me against him. His hands splay across my lower abdomen, protectively caressing it. Like he knows without a doubt there's something in there worth protecting. When I look down to watch, I see the sweat pooling between my breasts. Suddenly grossed out, I try to slip away but his grip tightens. "What are you doing?"

"I'm all sweaty." I continue to squirm in his arms but freeze when his lips touch my neck.

"I like you sweaty."

"You like me sweaty when *you're* the reason for it."

"Hmm. Let's explore that."

I turn in his arms, staring up at him with disbelief. "Don't you feel like death? How can you even think about sex right now?"

He shoots me a baffled look. "You're naked and I'm touching you.

But honestly, you could be on the other side of the room in a fucking parka and I'd be thinking about it. I'm always thinking about it. Hangover or not."

I flatten my hands against his chest and push. "Rain check, handsome."

"With frosting?"

His request has my insides burning as much as my legs were on that run. We haven't played around with frosting in a few weeks. Usually, the urge to lick it off me hits him in the middle of us fooling around, sending him sprinting into the kitchen for the ready-made tub I keep on hand for such occasions. He's too impatient to wait for me to whip up a batch, which he proved when he bent me over my worktop and fucked me while the neglected, half-put-together icing went untouched. That happened a few days after we reconciled. And now, you'll always find a tub of it in both our fridges.

I shoot him a cheeky grin and nod. At my promise, he drops his arms and returns to the sink, allowing me to finally step into the shower.

The loft is empty when I step out of the bathroom with a towel wrapped around me. I slip into a sundress, one that cinches at my waist, and step into my favorite pair of strappy sandals. After applying some tinted moisturizer and mascara, I blow-dry my hair partially and clip half of it back.

Reese is sitting on a stool pulled up to my worktop, dressed in a pair of running shorts and a T-shirt. He lifts his head at the sound of me coming down the stairs, the apple turnover he's about to bite into stopping inches from his mouth. I grab my apron off the hook by my shelving unit and slip it over my neck. I know he's still looking at me. Even though I'm pulling out the racks of pastries, muffins, and cupcakes with my back to him, I feel it burning into the back of me, no doubt appreciating my outfit. I glance at him over my shoulder, prompting him to lift his gaze.

"I love you in dresses," he says before finally taking a bite of his turnover.

"I know," I reply. "Wait 'til you see the one I'm marrying you in."

His eyes lose focus momentarily as he drops his hand to his lap.

Clearing his throat, he adjusts himself discreetly and I feel my face heat up as I place the racks on the worktop. I love that the very idea of me in my wedding dress gets that kind of reaction from him, even though he has no idea what the dress looks like.

"Do you need any help?" he asks after regaining his composure.

"Sure."

He shoves the rest of the turnover into his mouth, standing up and wiping his hands on his shorts. We each carry a rack up front and fill the display case. As Reese meticulously arranges the cupcakes in a way only he would do, the shop door dings open and Joey walks in, followed by Brooke.

"Well, isn't this a nice surprise," Joey says as he steps up to the counter. I see the side of Reese's mouth twitch into a smile as he straightens up and greets both of my employees with a tilt of his head.

Brooke places my cup of coffee on the counter. "Sorry, Reese. I would've gotten you one if I knew you'd be here this morning."

He shrugs before grabbing my cup. "That's okay." I watch as he takes a sip of my usual order, which is entirely too sugary for his taste. Reese is a black coffee kind of guy, and the look on his face is priceless as he swallows his mouthful. He holds the cup out to me with a frown. "Jesus Christ. That tastes like ice cream."

"Mmmm. Just the way I like it." I place the cup to my lips and take a sip. "So, Brooke. How was your date last night?"

Her smile fades instantly, hardening as the memory of it washes over her. "Painful," she grits out. "I swear to God, I'm done with dating sites. The guy last night, Dustin, was a major let-down in the package department. One look and I was like," she brushes her hands off in front of her, holding them out with her palms facing us as she steps back. "I'm out." The three of us burst out laughing as she moves toward the kitchen, smiling over her shoulder before she slips into the back.

I take another sip of my drink, moaning against the brim. The caffeine perks me up instantly, and the caramel might just be enough to curb my sweet tooth for the remainder of the day.

Maybe.

Doubt it.

Joey drums his fingers on the counter, his eyes flicking between me and Reese while his lips stay curled up into a sly smile. "And how is my favorite soon-to-be-married couple this morning? Anyone getting cold feet?"

I lift my eyes to Reese, catching the look he gives as his response.

"Right. What a ridiculous question," Joey says through a laugh.

I reach behind my back and untie my apron. "Reese and I need to go get his car this morning. Can you handle things? We shouldn't be long."

Joey nods, running a hand through his hair. "Yeah, no problem. Just don't forget about the other wedding cake you need to start on. Besides your own." He adds that last part with a playful smile.

"I haven't." Spinning around, I take another sip of my coffee and place a hand on Reese's arm. "Come on. You ready?"

"Yeah, let me run upstairs and get my keys."

I slip my apron off and toss it under the counter as he disappears into the back. Brooke walks back up front, wearing her biggest smile.

"This is adorable. I love that he's here."

"Me, too," I reply. I *really* love that he's here. In fact, I'm tempted to ask him to take another sick day tomorrow. I smile at her, remembering what I promised yesterday. "When I get back, it's you, me, and a wedding cake."

She claps her hands excitingly in front of her. "Oooo, yes! This is going to be awesome! What kind of cake are we making?"

Joey holds his hand up, halting my response. "One that doesn't sound appetizing at all. Banana cake with caramel cheesecake mousse." He grimaces, sticking a finger in his throat to mimic throwing up.

I shove his shoulder. "It's going to be a beautiful cake. The bride wants sugared orchids cascading down one side. I love that. And those flavors work really well together." Reese walks back through the doorway, twirling his keys on his finger. I walk around the display case to join him. "We'll be back soon. Play nice, you two."

Joey wraps his arm around Brooke's shoulder. "Who? Us? There's nothing but love here."

I stop at the door, eyeing him suspiciously over my shoulder. Brooke is staring up at him with her own, as he wears the biggest teasing grin

I've ever seen. "Did you get laid last night?" I ask. His playful eyebrow wiggle answers for him. Brooke pushes away from him, scoffing in the process as I roll my eyes. "Later, bitches."

⌖

"SO, WHAT EXACTLY DID YOU drink last night? Do you remember?" I ask as I weave in and out of traffic.

"I remember everything."

I glance over at him, seeing his set profile. "You do?"

He runs his hands down his face, dropping them to his lap before responding. "Yeah. I know I drank whiskey. A lot of it."

"Do you remember getting home?" I steal another glance and see him drop his head against the seat.

"I remember everything, Dylan. The way you looked at me after you stopped the alarm. The conversation on the stairs. Everything. I promise you'll never see me like that again."

I pull over in front of The Tavern and put the car in park before I grab his hand. He immediately threads his fingers through mine, keeping his eyes focused on them. "I didn't mind taking care of you. Not last night and not this morning either. It's my job."

His eyes meet mine, flashing with assurance. "It won't happen again. The only thing that makes me lose control is you. Nothing else. Okay?"

I give his hand a gentle squeeze while his other grabs the door handle. "Okay. I'll meet you back at the shop?"

He leans over, pressing his lips against mine. What starts off as the lightest touch quickly dissolves into a searing connection. I fist his shirt with both hands, holding him to me as he devours my mouth. His lips tease my jaw, my neck, the delicate skin below my ear. He has me worked into a wild frenzy in a matter of seconds. Breaking away, he pants loudly against my mouth before licking his bottom lip.

"You taste like your coffee."

"Sorry."

He smiles. "Don't be. I love how everything tastes on your tongue." His lips meet mine once more, briefly, before he opens the car door. "I'll follow you."

"Good luck keeping up," I tease, earning myself a warning look before he steps out. He closes the door, and I watch him walk to the driver's side of his car through my rear-view mirror. I lick my lips, tasting the combination of sugar and coffee.

Apple turnover, caramel macchiato, and Reese Carroll.

I'm doubting anything has tasted better.

⤳

"WHY DO YOU USE EGGS at room temperature? I never got that."

I register Brooke's question over the sound of my brand new mixer, which is an absolute dream. Not only does it have all these settings my old mixer failed to come with, but it's also whipping my ingredients in record timing. After depositing the bags of flour and sugar onto the worktop, I answer. "Because they mix better into the batter. And it makes the finished product fluffier. I can always tell when someone doesn't use room temperature eggs."

"It's a tragedy when cold eggs are used," Joey adds, sticking his head through the doorway. "Brooke, grab me the container of blueberry muffins. We're almost out up here."

I measure out my dry ingredients as Brooke hands off the Tupperware container. She returns to my side, brushing the flour along the wood with her finger. "Do you always make wedding cakes a few days in advance?"

"I like to. Especially if I have more than one to make. We'll knock out the cake layers today, and I'll freeze them overnight. That will help lock in the moisture. And tomorrow afternoon, we'll focus solely on assembling the cakes and all the intricate detail work." I look over at her with a playful expression. "The fun stuff."

"This is so cool. I can't wait to see the finished products."

I see that familiar excitement beaming off Brooke that I always have when I make wedding cakes. Maybe this will be her niche. Maybe she was always meant to be a baker. I step to the other side of the worktop, motioning toward the measuring cups I've readied for her. "Can you add those in after the batter turns a light, golden color? That's when you know the caramel is fully mixed."

"You're not going somewhere, are you?" she asks with wide, startled eyes.

I laugh, grabbing the bowl of bananas in front of Reese. He lifts his eyes off his phone screen to give me a quick wink before returning to his task. Whatever he's looking at, it's kept his attention for the past hour.

Looking over at Brooke, I shake my head and begin peeling the twenty-five bananas I made Joey run out and get this morning. "No, I'm not going anywhere. We're doing this together."

She opens her mouth to respond when the sound of Reese's cell phone ringing halts her.

He stands abruptly, nearly knocking his stool over but grabbing it before it crashes to the ground. He frantically brings the phone up to his ear. "Reese Carroll." His eyes drift from the stool to my face, and I see his chest rise with a deep inhale. He mouths "I'll be right back" and takes quick strides across the kitchen, taking the stairs at a rapid pace.

"Jeez. Must've been important," Brooke jokes, but at her word usage my mind begins to wonder if this urgent matter has anything to do with Bryce. I feel my pulse quicken at the thought but quickly focus on my task. I have two cakes to make, and one can't even be started until Reese disappears. He can't see the ingredients I'm using for our wedding cake. It will definitely give away my surprise to him.

I'm slicing the bananas and depositing them into a big mixing bowl when Reese comes running back down the stairs. His heavy footsteps gain my attention, spinning me around. He's dressed in his work clothes now, wearing one of my favorite gray-plaid ties of his. Hands grab my face and he plants the sweetest, gentlest Reese kiss to my lips, melting me like the caramel sauce I used in the batter.

He pulls away, and I see the sheer thrill pouring out of him, like he's just won the damn lottery or something. He smiles and I melt further at the sight of my favorite lines next to his eyes. "I need to run to the office."

"You seem very happy about that."

He laughs, kissing the corner of my mouth. "I am," he whispers against me. "Two days, love. Two days and you are *mine.*"

His words send a chill through me. I'm his already but God, the way he says *mine* like I'm not even close to being his yet makes my mouth go dry. I watch him walk away with the biggest smile I've ever seen on his face. And I know it has nothing to do with going to the office.

Chapter
NINETEEN

L
UCKILY WITH REESE'S SWIFT DEPARTURE, Brooke and I were able to throw together not only the cake layers for the other wedding but for mine, as well. I had a great time cooking with Brooke, and she seemed to pick up on things like a natural.

I've never seen any bit of my best friend in her sister, and I've known them both for over ten years. Brooke always seemed so brash and extroverted. She never let you get a word in usually, especially if it contradicted what she was trying to get across. And even though she seemed popular in school, she never had any friends who stuck around. Joey, Juls, and I have been together for as long as I can remember. Yes, there were others who floated in and out of our lives, but the three of us always stayed true to each other. Brooke didn't seem to have that, not even now. Her closest friend was Juls from what I observed. She and I were always friendly, but this is the most I've ever talked to her. And as we spent the afternoon with just the two of us in the kitchen, laughing and talking like we've done it for years, I find myself forgetting who I'm with.

I see glimpses of her sister shining through. The way she focuses on her task but still keeps the conversation going, not allowing for a dull moment. The way she reaches over and brushes the flour off my cheek I had absentmindedly smudged on. But most of all, I see it in the way she tears up when she asks me to recount how Reese proposed to me. Juls always has the waterworks on reserve, especially for romantic moments. And Reese's proposal can never be topped, in my opinion. So even though I spend the afternoon with Brooke Wicks, it feels like Julianna Thomas is standing next to me.

I'm wiping off my worktop after putting away all my baking supplies. Joey and Brooke left a little while ago, and the shop is quiet.

Too quiet for me right now.

I'm antsy, and the anticipation of Reese getting back and hopefully returning with that same smile plastered on his face is making me fidget. I'm trying to stay busy, but I'm certain I've wiped down my worktop at least five times now. If it isn't disinfected at this point, it never will be.

At the sound of the shop door opening, I lift my head and glance through the doorway. Reese comes walking into the kitchen, his tie loosened and his sleeves rolled up to mid-forearm.

I drop the rag on the worktop, spinning around and greeting him with a smile. He's storming toward me with purpose, determination in each step. I grip the edge of the wood, recognizing the feverish look in his eyes. My lips part, but not to speak because I can't. Not when I know he's about to kiss me, and I know that's what he's about to do. My mouth becomes parched as he presses his body against mine, his hands flattening on the wood behind me. Boxing me in. Keeping me right where he wants me.

His mouth molds to mine with desperation, rendering me speechless. I tremble against him as his tongue invades my mouth, easily gaining entry. I lift my hands to hold him to me but only get halfway up my body before he grabs my wrists and slams my hands back down on the worktop.

"No, love. It's your turn not to touch me."

"What? No, let me touch."

He shakes his head, releasing my wrists. I keep my hands where he's put them and watch as he reaches up and undoes his tie.

I know what's coming. I know I'm about to get my last look before he does whatever the hell he wants with me.

God, how fucking lucky am I?

"Wait," I plead as he holds his tie between both hands, ready to take away my sight. He tilts his head, waiting for me to speak. I hit him with a smile first, loosening the tightness that's set in his face. "Tell me what's going on? What was the phone call about earlier?"

He keeps the tie in one hand and brings the other up to my face. I lean into it, blinking heavily as he moves closer. "Do you remember when you asked me if I worked with Bryce? Because you didn't want to have to see him if you came to visit me?" I nod, thinking back to that day on Reese's couch. "The thought of some guy making you uncomfortable drove me insane. Even then, I was so possessive over you I would've killed him if he so much as looked at you again. I shot him down every time he wanted to hire me after that. I didn't want to be near him. But then I found something." He takes his hand off my face and rakes it through his hair. "I was looking through the file I had on him and something caught my attention. Bryce is a smart guy. He's successful with his investments, but some of his figures weren't adding up. He told us the last time Ian and I worked with him that people donate to his company. Anonymously. Which can happen but he had a lot of donations and the figures weren't small. I showed it to Ian and told him if Bryce asked to hire us again, I wanted that account."

"You thought he was doing something illegal?" I ask.

"I *knew* he was doing something illegal. But I needed access to all of his monies to prove it. So I've just been biding my time, hoping he would pursue our company to work with him again. I didn't know if it was going to happen. I turned him down a lot after I met you, but he finally came to us." He reaches out and tucks my hair behind my ear. "I took a major risk in working with him. I knew he'd try to get to you once he got around me again. Bryce likes to push people's buttons, and he's good at it. Every fucking time I met with him, he brought you up, but I couldn't react. I couldn't lose that account when I didn't have what I needed yet. Ian got this guy, some private investigator, to work with us. I was supplying him with what I thought could bring Bryce down, but he was taking forever with it. He kept needing more documents or telling me what I gave him couldn't be deemed illegal. I was getting impatient. I couldn't have something happen to you." Both hands grab my shoulders. "It killed me to work with him, Dylan. You have to know that."

"I know. It's okay."

"It's not okay." His hands slide down so that he's gripping my elbows. "I saw what he did to you in that elevator. After Joey told me he touched you, I called security and asked to see the surveillance footage. I saw how you reacted to him. And I fucking saw him touch you." His eyes close tight momentarily. I reach up and touch his cheek, seeing them flash open. "I lost it. I searched that entire building for him. I didn't know if he was still there but I knew if I found him, I'd kill him. Ian tried to calm me down but I didn't want to hear it. He *touched* you. He touched what was mine. And it was my fault. I brought him back around. I put my need to get to him before you. And I hated myself for it."

"It wasn't your fault. You didn't bring him back around. Joey told me the other day that Bryce had stopped in the shop a few times before you took on that account with him. He was always there. You were trying to protect me. Don't ever hate yourself for that."

He sighs heavily and rubs his eyes. "I'm honestly glad I didn't know he's been in here. Thank you for not telling me about that."

"You're welcome," I say, biting back my smile. "I hate keeping stuff from you, too."

"Well, it doesn't matter anymore. That phone call I got earlier was from the PI. He discovered that Bryce has been embezzling funds from clients' accounts. That's what all those anonymous donations were. I had to go into the office to give him everything I had on Bryce. He's done. I fucking got him."

I feel a lightness take over my body, like the biggest weight has been lifted off my shoulders. "He's getting arrested?"

He nods. "He's looking at twenty-five years." He presses himself against me again, wrapping his arms around my waist. "I'm sorry I couldn't tell you. The PI told us we couldn't say anything to anybody. It fucking killed me to keep that from you, but I needed this to work. I needed to do something that would keep him away from you permanently, and killing him wasn't an option."

"Thank you for what you did."

He brings our foreheads together. "I will always protect you, Dylan. We might not be married yet, but I said my vows to you a long time ago."

I reach around and slide the tie out of his hand, holding it between us. "And I will always trust you. With everything. Including what you're about to do to me."

He takes the tie from me as all the softness fades from his features. I see the transformation happen immediately, like a switch has been flipped inside him. The predatory shift in his eyes. The way his nostrils flare and his jaw twitches just below his temple. This is dominant Reese. This is the man who takes what he wants and right now, I'm his target.

"Close your eyes."

I obey instantly. There is zero thought involved. Nor is there any part of me that wants to fight him. I want this; I want everything from his man. He's never taken away my senses before, leaving me vulnerable, but I trust him completely. He could do anything to me right now and I wouldn't object.

The silk material of the tie slides over my eyes. I turn my head and press my lips to his arm as he secures it behind me with a knot. I feel his hands on my waist as he lifts me off the ground and plants me on the edge of the worktop.

"Lie back. I want you to keep your hands flat on the table, and I don't want you to remove them. Do you understand?"

"Yes," I answer, lying back on the wood. I flatten my palms out next to me and wait for my next instruction. I feel his body settle between my legs as his hands slide up my thighs, teasing the bottom of my dress.

"Do you know the exact moment I knew I loved you?"

I gasp softly, not expecting him to go there right now. Not at all anticipating him using my question to him on me. My body and mind are prepared for sex, completely primed and ready, even if it is in a way I've never experienced before. But this? His words I cherish more than anything he could possibly give me? I'm not at all prepared for this admission.

I don't answer; I'm not sure I can right now. Every muscle in my body is taut and I keep finding myself holding my breath, not wanting my suddenly erratic breathing to muffle what he's about to tell me. This might very well top the vows we're going to be saying to each other in two days. And we picked out some pretty emotional ones. I cry every time I read through them.

"You're nervous," he states. "Is this something you don't want to know?"

I smile, releasing my bottom lip from between my teeth. "No, I do. Of course I do. I just wasn't expecting you to get all sweet on me right now."

"It'll be brief," he replies. "You told me when you knew, so it's only fair you know how long it's been for me." His hands move up my body on top of my dress, skimming over my breasts. The weight of his touch feels different now that I can't watch him. All my energy is focused on his hands and where they might go. One palm flattens on my chest, resting there.

"What are you doing?" I ask when he doesn't move his hand.

"I want to feel you react to what I'm about to tell you."

I shudder underneath him. "Okay."

He gives me a few seconds to calm down a bit. I need it. If he wants to feel my reaction, then my heart rate needs to slow the hell down. I take in several calming breaths, feeling everything settle.

And then, he speaks.

"I knew I loved you when you sent me that text, asking if I would stop whatever I was doing to come to you and I didn't have to think about it. At all. Dylan, before I even finished reading your question, I was grabbing my keys and heading to the door."

I feel my tears being absorbed into the material of the tie. Not being able to see him while he tells me this is doing things to me. I'm purely focused on his voice and the raw honesty in it, not his eyes that usually hold onto me. I feel like my entire body is quivering beneath him while I try to anticipate his words. And I know he's feeling my reaction to him. My heart is slamming so hard against my sternum my bones feel like they're vibrating.

"Love," he continues in a much softer voice, "I could've been on the other side of the country and I would've found a way to get to you if you asked me. Nothing was more important to me than you. And nothing ever will be. You said you knew you loved me on my birthday, right?"

"Mmm hmm." I reach up and wipe the tear that's escaping from underneath the blindfold. "Why?"

"Because I think you loved me that night, too."

There's no stopping the tears now. It's a useless act. I nod repeatedly as I reach up and cover my face with my hands. I'm crying because he's right. I did love him then. I knew it when I had to see him that night after being so damn adamant about not seeing that much of each other. But I was determined to fight those feelings, and I buried them deep. But he knew. He always knew.

"When I opened my door and saw you standing there, I knew it wasn't just me. Even though you would've never admitted it, you loved me then, too."

My entire body shakes with my cries, and I feel his palm slide up my chest and around my neck. He grips me there, pulling me to a sitting position. I drop my hands to bury my face in his neck but stop when I feel the tie being pulled down. My eyes slowly flutter open, adjusting to the light as his thumbs wipe away my tears.

"I did love you then," I whisper, fisting his dress shirt as he cradles my face in his hands. I sniffle loudly, slowly calming myself and staring into his bright green eyes. "I was so scared to love you, but I did. You're kind of impossible not to fall in love with, damn it."

He laughs, running his finger along the tie, which is now around my neck. "I love how you reacted to that. Your heartbeat sped up like crazy."

"Well, that's nothing new. If you're in the same room as me, it goes haywire." I strain my neck to steal a kiss. "Thank you for telling me that."

"You're welcome. Now," his hands trail down my side, stopping at my waist. "We need to go upstairs and get a new tie. You soaked this one."

I cock my head to the side, arching my brow and going to the dirtiest place in my head because he's easily set me up for it.

He notices my reaction and smiles. "Go ahead. Say it."

"Say what?"

"You know what."

"Nope. Sorry. I have no idea what you're talking about."

"Really? I find it hard to believe that right now, you're not dying to say something involving the word 'soaked'."

I giggle, dropping my gaze to the buttons on his dress shirt. I tease them with my fingers. "It sounds to me like *you're* the one with the perverted mind right now. Not me."

"Is that right?"

"Yup."

"Okay." He quickly slips a hand between my legs and presses against the front panel of my panties.

"Oh, God." My head rolls to the side as I grip onto his arms. *Holy shit.* I shudder when he moves along the lace material, teasing me with the tiniest bit of contact.

"Don't say it then," his deep voice taunts me. "Don't tell me you're not completely soaked for me right now. That I couldn't make you come all over my hand if I wanted to."

"If I don't say it, are you… Reese… shit… are you going to stop?"

"Yes."

I shift my eyes up to meet his. "Okay. Say your line again."

"We need a new tie. You soaked this one."

"That's not the only thing that's soaked!" I reply animatedly. "I'm soaked. Really soaked. My panties are pretty much useless at the moment. You should probably just remove them. They're not doing me any good right now, and they are definitely in your way. Did I mention the word 'soaked'?"

He smirks before his face breaks into a smile. "Pervert. I knew you couldn't resist going there." He slides his hand out and grabs the back of my thighs.

"Can we get back to getting a new tie? You've teased the hell out of me and if you don't finish what you've started, I'll take matters into my own hands. Or more specifically, fingers."

His brow furrows. "Nobody finishes what I start when it comes to that pussy. Not even you. You come when I make you. And it will be happening on my cock and in my mouth, not on your fingers."

"Fine by me," I reply, scooting to the edge of the wood. "As long as it happens in the next five minutes. Otherwise…" I pause, shooting him a teasing look.

He grabs me off the worktop and flings me over his shoulder. I squeal, wrapping my arms around his waist as we move toward the stairs. "Otherwise nothing. You hurry me along in any way or threaten to handle your own orgasms and you won't be coming at all. I'll tie you to the bed and make you watch me handle my own situation all over your tits this time."

"All I heard was bed. Your ass is distracting me." I give it one good smack as he starts up the stairs.

"Speaking of asses, I plan on fucking yours tonight."

My eyes widen as my body becomes instantly rigid. *Fuuccckkk. Anal? Am I ready for that?*

He senses my apprehensiveness and rubs his hand on my bare thigh, soothing me. "Relax, love. Trust me with your body. I'll always make it good for you."

"Oh, God," I nervously mumble, dropping my head against his back.

"You'll be screaming that a lot in a minute."

I laugh against his shirt, instantly relaxing and leaving my nervousness on the stairs.

Chapter
TWENTY

'M NAKED, LYING IN THE middle of the bed with my hands above my head. I was given three instructions after Reese set me on my feet and removed my dress and panties. Three instructions I eagerly obeyed.

"Get on the bed, grab onto the bed posts, and don't let go."

My hands are wrapped around two wooden spindles as I watch him standing at the foot of the bed. He hasn't taken away my sight yet and right now, I'm extremely grateful for that as I watch him slowly remove his dress shirt button by button. He's taking his time and he knows what it's doing to me. He also knows that if he hadn't told me to keep my hands where they are, I would be ripping that shirt off him in record timing.

I take in the sight of him shirtless. The leanness of his body which is sculpted with that perfect amount of muscle. Broad shoulders and slightly-tanned skin. The hard lines of his abs which my hands are yearning to roam over.

My grip tightens around the wood.

His fingers loosen his belt as his eyes roam my body, slowly taking in every inch of me. Lower, lower, until he suddenly flicks them up to meet mine.

"Bend your knees and spread your legs." I do as I'm told. "Wider."

I drop my knees to the side as far as they can go, leaving myself completely open. My pussy is throbbing for him, aching to the point of being agonizing as he studies me. His eyes are locked between my legs, and the view seems to speed up his movements. Bending at the waist, he drops his pants and boxers and steps out of them. As he takes a few steps toward my dresser, I close my legs a few inches.

"I didn't tell you to do that," he says, looking at me over his shoulder as he opens my top drawer. "Open them."

I submit to his command and lower my knees so they are inches from the mattress. I see him slip out one of his ties before he walks to the side of the bed, authority in each step. There is zero trace of the man who told me minutes ago when he knew he loved me. That tenderness is gone. He's exuding control right now, and I've never seen anything hotter.

Looming over me with the tie in one hand, he slides his other hand up my arm and wraps it around one of mine, gripping me and the post. "Keep them here. If you move them before I tell you to, I'll tie them in place. Do you understand?"

"Yes."

"Good." He presses his lips against mine, searing me with a brutal kiss. "These will be the last words I say to you before I take you in the way I've been dying to take you. You won't be able to see or hear me until I want you to. Understand?"

"Yes." My voice comes out steady, devoid of any apprehension.

He leans back and drapes the tie across my eyes, blinding me. "Right now, I want you to concentrate on feeling everything I give you. Nothing else."

I lift my head, allowing him to secure it behind me. And then the bed dips as his weight is removed, leaving me alone with only the sound of my breathing filling my ears. But it's not uneven, nervous breathing. The pace of my lungs taking in air is quickened due to the eagerness I'm feeling. I want to experience this with him, everything he's about to give me in a way I've never had. I'm not tense. I'm ready.

So fucking ready.

The sound of movement in the kitchen has me turning my head in that direction.

A cabinet closes.

The soft clink of ice hitting the bottom of an empty glass.

I expect to hear the tap water running next, but I don't.

I gasp as my ankles are grabbed. My legs are straightened on the bed and then his hands are gone. I strain to listen, looking down the length of my body even though I can't see anything. I imagine him standing at the foot of the bed, glass in hand as he stares at me. He's hard. Painfully hard. Stroking himself to ease some of the ache. My grip tightens further as I clench the muscles in my core.

Is it possible to orgasm from anticipation alone? Because I might just be the first.

"Oh, shit." I jerk when I feel the stark chill of ice on my skin, trailing up the inside of my leg. My legs are spread wider and then his body fills the space between them. I think I know where the ice cube is going. I'm positive actually, but just when I think he's going to dip it between my legs, he avoids the area entirely.

I feel his free hand wrap around my hip, holding me in place. The ice cube glides over my stomach and up to the crease between my breasts. The heat of his mouth follows the path, warming my skin. I tilt my head up as he moves along my collar bone before circling my nipple.

"Reese."

I bite my lip to contain myself. I want to squirm. To thrash about because this is almost intolerable.

But I don't.

I whimper as the ice cube moves over my nipple. The bite of it is severe, but it feels too good for me to protest, especially when his mouth latches on and takes away the chill. He doesn't moan into my skin like he usually does. He doesn't give me any sign that he is enjoying this. But I knew he wouldn't. He warned me I wouldn't hear him, and apparently, sounds are included.

He moves slightly and I know he's marking me. I'm familiar with the pull of that spot. Alternating breasts, the pattern is repeated. Cold then warmth, and then the chill is gone, as is the heat of his body over mine. I feel the hair on his legs brush against mine as he shifts, and then his hands are wrapped around my thighs, spreading me open. I figure the ice has been discarded, no longer needed. I wait for the heat of his mouth to press against me. His warm breath. The scorch of his tongue.

"Fuck!" I arch off the bed, almost letting go of the posts when he runs up my length. His tongue is frigid, mimicking the sensation of the ice cube and melting into me just like one. The feeling is overwhelming as he dips inside me, tasting ever inch. His mouth never warms, and I know it's because the ice is in his mouth, which is confirmed when I feel the sharp edge of the cube press against my clit.

"Holy shit, Reese."

He dips lower, pressing the ice cube inside me with his tongue. In and out. He's fucking me with it, driving me toward my climax with this new sensation. I'm barely keeping my composure as my insides become liquid. My thighs are shaking against his head as I try to control my trembling. I'm close, moaning his name and gripping so tightly onto the wooden posts I'm certain they're about to snap off. Then the chill is gone, followed by the sound of him crunching on the ice. Seconds go by and I think maybe he isn't going to allow me to come. I take in several deep breaths, feeling my orgasm slip away from me until he buries his face between my legs.

His mouth still has the slightest chill, but his warmth is taking over. He fucks me with his tongue until I'm begging and incoherently pleading with him to make me come. He runs up and down my length, spreading me open with his fingers. His tongue swirls around my clit, flattening against it then flicking it in that rhythm I like. I'm once again right at the brink of orgasm and he knows it. He must, because that's the moment he chooses to prop my ass up with his hands and lick along my rim.

"Oh, shit! Wait, wait, don't...oh, God, just... Reese, I don't...un-ghhhh."

He's never done this to me. The only time he's ever gone anywhere near my ass is with his finger. I clench out of reflex; it's automatic. He shouldn't be there with this tongue, and it definitely shouldn't feel this amazing.

Right?

Wrong. So fucking wrong.

He's licking me like he works my pussy, and it feels unlike anything I've ever felt. My heart is thundering in my chest as I replay his words to me over in my head.

"*Right now, I want you to concentrate on feeling everything I give you. Nothing else.*"

So I do. I concentrate on this new sensation, blocking out my instincts and not letting any anxiety overpower me. I feel his hands shift, one elevating me while the other moves around my waist. At the brush of his fingers against my clit, I lose it. I throw my head back, screaming his name until my voice breaks. And then I feel him press against me with his tongue, slipping inside, and my orgasm stretches out, rocking me with a blinding intensity. Paralyzing me. I feel shattered. Stripped of all coherence.

And it's incredible.

I don't even realize he's lowered my body back down until my blindfold is removed. I open my eyes, meeting his. There's apprehension in them. Not much, but I see it. The uncertainty of what he's just done to me. But when I smile at him, one that I'm sure looks completely dopey because that's how I feel, his insecurity vanishes.

"You can let go of the bed," he says as he kneels between my legs.

I do and shake my hands out, bringing them down to my sides. He reaches across the comforter and picks up a bottle I hadn't known he put on there. One I've never seen before. I really don't want to be nervous right now, because I do trust him, completely, but I know what that bottle is. I know what he needs it for. And I do a shit job at concealing my worry because he sees it, prompting him to drop the bottle and lean over me. His hand conforms to my cheek.

"I would never hurt you, Dylan. You liked what I just did, right?"

I nod and lean into his palm. "Yes. I didn't think I would, but I definitely did."

He gives me half a smile. "Trust me. I'd never lie to you. This will feel a little uncomfortable at first, just in the beginning, but it won't hurt. And then it's going to feel really fucking good. Okay?"

"You've done this before?" I ask, hearing the slight hurt in my voice. *Jesus, Dylan. Don't go there right now. Who cares what he's done before you.*

"I haven't done it with you. You are the only woman who matters. And the only one I want to experience this with." He picks up the bottle and flips the cap open. "I'll tell you what to do. Just listen to my voice and keep your eyes on me. If you have to close them you can, but when I'm all the way in you I need you to look at me."

"Okay," I reply, watching as he spreads the lube on his cock. "Did you like what you just did to me? I mean, you were... you know."

He squirts a bit of the liquid onto his finger before tossing the bottle to the other side of the bed. "I like everything I do to you." I flinch as he spreads the cold liquid along my entrance, applying the tiniest bit of pressure. He watches me as he slips one finger inside, flattening his other hand on my pelvis. His thumb begins rubbing my clit as he moves his finger in and out of me.

"Mmm." I close my eyes and take in the sensation, trying to stay relaxed.

"Two fingers, love."

He pulls out of me and then I feel the slight sting as he stretches me. But he enters without restriction and begins moving his fingers around in slow circles. "Feel good?" he asks.

I open my eyes. "Yes," I answer honestly. "So good. Can you do another?"

His thumb rubs against my clit as he slides his fingers out. I scrunch my face when he re-enters me, clamping my eyes shut. He stills inside me, letting me adjust to the foreign size. And it doesn't take long until I'm begging him to move. He stretches me further as my eyes shoot open, immediately seeking out his cock.

I want it.

There.

"Reese, please."

His eyes flash with a new desire. Maybe he wasn't expecting me to beg for this. Maybe he just assumed I'd go with it and then hopefully enjoy myself. But here I am, begging because I need to have him in this way.

He slides his fingers out and grips the base of his cock. "Hold your knees back for me." I do as requested as he positions himself. His eyes trail up my body, landing on mine. "You want this. You just begged for it. Focus on that." He presses against my opening, meeting the tight ring of muscle, and I suddenly feel like my insides are burning up. "This is the uncomfortable part."

"No shit," I respond, letting go of my legs and clawing the comforter at my sides. I can't relax.

I'm no longer finding the urge to beg.

This fucking sucks.

"Dylan, you need to push against me."

"What?"

He grips my hips, steadying himself. "Push against me. Like you don't want me in."

Well, that's not hard to imagine.

I swallow loudly, trying to loosen up. "Okay, okay. Just... fucking hell, just wait a second."

He muffles a laugh above me but I don't respond to it the way I normally would, by telling him to fuck off unless he wants to switch positions. Instead, I do as he asks and push, feeling him slip further in. Inch by inch. I watch as his face contorts into one of immense pleasure, and that drives me. To want it more. To pull my knees back so my thighs are against my chest, opening up to him.

"Fuck, yes." He growls, deep and guttural as he slides in to the hilt. "Christ, you're so fucking perfect."

I wasn't sure what I was expecting to feel, but it wasn't this. A wave of heat washes over me at the sensation of him all the way in me. "Oh, my... Godddd."

And then he starts to move in and out as he works my clit with his thumb. I keep my eyes on him even though the intensity of the pleasure I'm feeling is urging me to close them. It's too much. I need to take away some of this stimulation before I break so I close them, but it's brief.

"Dylan, look at me." I do, and he takes over holding my legs back as he thrusts into me. "Feel it. Feel how I make *every* part of you feel good. You want this. You want me here."

"Yes," I answer, but it comes out as a plea. To keep fucking me. To never stop. To love every part of me, because that's what he's doing.

His breath comes out uneven, ragged. He's gasping above me, struggling to not lose control yet. And seeing him like that gets me right there with him.

"Reese."

"Fuck, I can't... Dylan, I can't stop."

"Don't stop. I'm so close."

His movements become urgent, slamming into me with a crucial force. Pushing me up over the edge. And he's right there with me.

"Coming," I barely choke out as my orgasm moves through me like a tidal wave. I need to see him. I need to watch him lose it even though my eyes are straining to remain open while I ride this out.

"Holy fuck. Oh, my God, Dylan. Fuuckkk!"

He keeps his eyes on me, giving me the satisfaction of seeing him unravel. And it's unlike anything he's ever done. He's wild. Screaming out my name between moans. Throwing his head back and flexing every muscle in his upper body. He gives me everything in a way I've never seen. It's chaotic almost, the way he lets go, but it's beautiful.

When his orgasm subsides, he drops my legs and pulls out of me. Arms wrap around me as he sits back and pulls me against his chest, burying his head between my breasts. I feel him tremble against me and thread my fingers through his hair.

"Thank you, love. Thank you for giving me that."

Dropping my head, I press kisses into his hair. "See, that wasn't so bad. I told you you'd like it," I tease.

He lifts his eyes to me, stunning me with that sweet face. "I love you."

"Love you, too." I brush my nose against his. "Now what? Should we box up more of my stuff? I feel like we still have a lot to do."

He cocks an eyebrow, looking around the room. "Anal sex and getting you ready to move in with me permanently? Fuck yes. That's my kind of Thursday night."

I throw my head back, falling into a laughing fit as his arms tighten around me, pinning our bodies together.

Close, but never close enough.

Chapter

TWENTY-ONE

'M GETTING MARRIED TOMORROW.

   I'm finally becoming Dylan Carroll.

   Holy shit.

Okay. Focus, Dylan.

I'm chopping up the bars of semisweet chocolate I'll need for my wedding cake frosting while Brooke watches the mixer with keen interest. She completely lost her shit this morning when I told her she would be in charge of making the caramel buttercream frosting for the other wedding cake. I've been right beside her, supervising everything, but this really is her baby and she's studying it with a mix of pride and restlessness.

"Can you grab the peppermint extract off the shelf for me?" I ask, breaking into her trance. She gives her frosting one last glance before she grabs the bottle I've requested and places it next to my cutting board. "Thanks. How's it looking?"

She begins to twirl a strand of her hair, a nervous habit I've picked up on today. "Umm, I don't know. Like frosting? It might taste like ass, though."

"Oooo, I love ass," Joey rejoices as he carries in a gift bag. I blush instantly and he notices. "Hmm. Care to elaborate?"

"Nope," I state firmly, shaking off my reaction to the word ass.

Really, Dylan?

He places the bag in front of Brooke and she surveys it peculiarly. "Here. This is my thank you for the shirt you got me. Which I look amazing in, by the way."

I roll my eyes at his astounding modesty.

"Oh. You didn't have to get me anything." She stops the mixer, sliding the bag closer to her and peeking inside. I've placed my knife down, not wanting to miss the reaction to what I already know is in the bag. Her mouth drops open as she pulls out the apron Joey special-ordered for her. "You got me my own apron?" She holds it out, and I see the moment she notices her name on it. Her eyes well up with tears at the sentiment, just like any Wicks girl. "Thank you so much!" She flings her arms around Joey's neck, clutching onto her apron.

Joey looks over at me and smiles as he returns the hug. "I was the last person who thought you should be working here, Brooke. But you've actually done really well. And you're a natural back here with my cupcake."

She spins around and slips her apron on, tying it around her neck. "Look, Dylan! It matches yours!"

"Apron sistas," I sing, seeing Joey grimace behind Brooke.

"Goddamn it. I knew I should've ordered me one," he mumbles as he turns around and disappears up front.

I stifle my laugh, dumping my chopped-up chocolate pieces into a mixing bowl. I brush my hands clean on my apron and walk over to examine Brooke's frosting. Dipping a teaspoon into the bowl, I pop a small amount in my mouth.

"Well?" she asks fretfully. "Oh, God. Please, tell me we have time to make another batch of this?" She slaps a hand over her eyes. "I will never forgive myself if I've ruined some girl's wedding cake."

I grab her arm and pull her hand down. "It's delicious, Brooke. Really. Try some." I hold out a spoon and she takes it after studying it for several seconds, the obvious shock pouring out of her.

She dips it into the bowl and tests her creation. Her eyes flutter closed. "Mmm. Holy shitballs." They pop back open, full of wonder. "I made that?"

I hold out my hand and she high-fives me. "Told you you could do it. Don't doubt yourself back here." I walk to the fridge, grabbing the heavy cream and catch her taking a picture of her frosting with her phone.

I love that: her excitement, her pride over what she's created.

I'm so glad I hired Brooke Wicks.

After setting a large saucepan on the stovetop, I pour in the heavy cream and turn on the heat. Once I get it to a boil, I can add the peppermint extract and strain the mixture into the chocolate. Then it has to cool before I can frost my cake.

My wedding cake.

Both cakes are already assembled and ready to be iced. I've timed everything perfectly, allowing us to frost the other bride's cake while my icing cools. The sugared orchids are already assembled for her cake. I tackled those bright and early this morning, knowing they would take me several hours. They turned out amazing, incredibly life-like, and I sent a picture to Reese so he could see what had me skipping my run today. His response was just as sweet as the flowers.

REESE: *You amaze me, love. You always have.*

And then he sent me one more a few seconds later.

REESE: *One more day.*

I turn the heat off for the cream and carry the saucepan over to the worktop. I slowly pour the mixture into my mixing bowl, whisking the contents as they melt together. As soon as the cream touches the chocolate, that familiar smell permeates my senses, filling me with the memory of this frosting. The only one I have besides the time I made it for Mrs. Frey's anniversary cake. Reese hasn't had this frosting since he ate it off my body on this very worktop, and when I was deciding on what to do for my own wedding cake, I knew I had to incorporate this flavor somehow. However, it's not going to be hot pink this time. At least, not on the outside of the cake. I've tweaked the recipe to leave out the shaved peppermint sticks, opting for the flavor from the extract instead. And with a little help from some food coloring, I'll have a beautiful white-mint chocolate wedding cake, as opposed to a pink one.

The shop door dings open as I set my empty saucepan back on the stovetop. Juls comes walking into the kitchen, carrying a small envelope with Ian right behind her. She's dressed chicly as usual, while Ian is wearing the same attire I'm used to seeing Reese in.

"Is someone getting married tomorrow?" Juls asks, walking toward me. She stops when she sees Brooke's apron. "Aww, I love that."

"Joey got it for me," Brooke states, smiling over at my thoughtful assistant as he walks into the back.

Juls darts over to him and wraps her arms around his waist. "You're the sweetest, JoJo."

"Christ, it's just an apron. I didn't propose or anything," he counters.

"Babe, hurry up and show Dylan what we came here for. I need to get back to the office." Ian walks over to the assembled cakes and studies them, leaning in closely. "These will get frosted, right?"

"Yes," all four of us answer in unison, the obvious implication evident in our voices.

He straightens and stares at us like he hasn't just asked a ridiculous question.

Who the hell wouldn't ice a wedding cake?

"Okay, are you ready?" Juls asks, opening her envelope and waving over Joey and Brooke. We all three huddle around her as she pulls out the tiny black and white photo and holds it out for us to see. "Look at my little nugget."

"Oh, my God!" I snatch the photo out of her hand and run my finger over the image. Tracing over the tiny splotch, because that's exactly what it looks like, I can't contain the magnitude of emotions beginning to course through me.

My best friend is having a baby.

When I glance back at her, it's through teary eyes. "Juls! I love your little nugget!"

"Give me that." Joey grabs the picture and studies it with Brooke. He gasps, looking from the picture to her stomach. "Can you feel anything yet?"

She shakes her head, wiping underneath her eyes. "No, not yet. But we heard the heartbeat today. That was amazing." Ian comes up behind her and wraps his arms around her waist. "Wasn't it amazing, babe?"

He kisses her neck. "It was. I wish I could've recorded it." He removes one hand from around Juls and takes the picture away from Joey. "Let me see my baby again."

I watch as the proud father-to-be looks at the sonogram with his wife. He whispers something into her ear and she nods, tearing up again. It's a private moment and I let them have it, turning around and busying myself.

At the sound of the shop door, Joey disappears up front, returning moments later and carrying the familiar white box. He sets it down on the worktop in front of me. "Not sure how he's going to top a set of car keys," he says jokingly, tugging at the white ribbon.

I open the box and pull out the card, not bothering to contain my excitement. I can't. I'm marrying this amazing man tomorrow, my best friend just showed me a picture of her little nugget, and I have the two best employees a girl could ask for.

I know tomorrow is going to be the best day of my life, but I'm finding it hard to imagine topping this moment.

I open the card as Joey sifts through the tissue paper, stopping to read over my shoulder.

Dylan,
You asked me to keep my eyes on you before when you danced to this song, and I've never taken them off. Dance for me now.
X, Reese

Joey pulls out Reese's iPod and darts up front with it as I tuck the note into my apron pocket. He returns moments later with the docking station, plugging it in and setting everything on the worktop. "I love how he knows we dance on Fridays. Could he seriously be any more perfect?"

"No," I answer, earning myself an annoyed look from him.

He cues the song up and seconds later, Beyoncé's "Naughty Girl" fills the kitchen. Juls, Brooke, Joey, and I all begin dancing around the space and when I glance over at Ian, he's holding his phone out with it focused on me.

"What are you doing?" I yell over the music, moving in between Juls and Brooke.

"What I've been instructed to do." He smiles and motions for me to keep going.

Oh. Well then.

My man wants me to dance for him? Okay. I can do that.

I playfully spin around, bringing my eyes back to Ian's phone every few seconds, pretending I'm looking right at Reese. Imagining him sitting behind his desk and watching me with that focused stare of his. I don't dance sexy at all, because I'm still kind of dancing for Ian and that would be entirely too weird, so I keep it fun, letting Joey spin me around and dip me. Grabbing onto Brooke and waltzing her around the kitchen. It's the best Friday dance party I've ever had with the most amazing people I've ever known.

After Ian and Juls leave, Brooke and I get started on icing the wedding cake for the other bride. That part itself is relatively easy, considering the bride didn't request any intricate piping work or anything besides the sugared orchids. And those won't be added until tomorrow morning. My cake, however, contains a ton of complex detailing that will take me the rest of the day to create. I wanted my cake to be very romantic, yet still traditional in a sense. Nothing modern or edgy. I was inspired by my dress when I came up with this design, wanting to mimic the lacework I instantly fell in love with. And sticking with the theme, which made my mother overly-ecstatic, I decided on a pale-gray lace pattern which will adorn my five-tiered cake, tying it into the bridesmaid dresses.

It takes me five-and-a-half hours to finish my cake, leaving me with just enough time to take a quick shower and get ready for my rehearsal. Reese is driving straight to the Whitmore from his office so I'll be meeting him there, which is perfect because I wanted to surprise him tonight with my outfit. I actually had something else picked out to wear tonight: a deep plum-colored halter I picked up a few weeks ago. But when he surprised me earlier today with my dance party song, the memory of that day inspired me.

Apart from the engagement ring on my finger, I look exactly like I did the day I met Reese. My black strapless dress still looks brand new, considering I haven't worn it since that day. My hair is falling in soft curls over my shoulders, and my makeup is fresh and elegant. After grabbing my clutch, I walk toward the door but stop, taking a look around my living space.

It doesn't look like my loft anymore.

The only thing left in it that hasn't changed yet is my bed, which I'll be sharing with Juls and Joey tonight at our last sleepover. Everything else is packed away in boxes, except for what I'll need to get ready tomorrow. All my pictures are gone, my kitchen counters are bare, even my decorative screen is folded up and leaning against the wall. Reese is having all my stuff delivered to his condo tomorrow while we get married, that way we don't have to worry about it. Then my landlord will be making some changes to the loft so the future tenant doesn't have to go through the bakery to get to it, which I'm extremely grateful for. For security reasons alone, I wouldn't want someone walking through my shop all the time who doesn't work for me. I suppose until it gets rented out, I could still come up here if I wanted to, but I'm not sure I will. My new life starts tomorrow, the one I've been counting down toward, and I'm excited to move in with Reese and put my single life behind me. So tonight, with my two very best friends, I'll soak in my last night in my loft and every memory it holds.

I can always take those memories with me.

Chapter
TWENTY-TWO

WHEN REESE AND I FIRST sat down to talk about where we wanted to get married, I never thought the Whitmore could be an option. I knew how expensive it was, at least from what Juls told me after planning Justin's wedding here. And I'd never hit my parents up for that kind of money. To be honest, I could get married to Reese in his condo and it would be perfect. I don't need a fancy venue to make tomorrow the best day of my life. So I threw out other options, such as the church Juls and Ian got married in and a small reception hall down the street from it. And while I did this, Reese just sat back with a smile on his face, letting me list off any and every idea I could come up with. When I asked what he had in mind, he told me he wanted to marry me where he first saw me, and that money wasn't an issue; he wanted to pay for it. I almost argued, but seeing how much marrying me there would mean to him, silenced me. I couldn't argue with that look; I never can. It's this perfect blend of honesty and love. And it's a look that I would do anything for, including letting him pay for everything.

I park my car next to Joey's Civic and lock it up. Joey and Juls are waiting for me by the doors, and as I get closer to them, I see their reaction to my outfit.

It's emotional.

Really emotional.

"He's going to lose it," Joey says after dabbing his eyes with a tissue.

"Seriously, sweets. I'm not sure Reese is going to agree to stay with the guys tonight at my place after seeing you in this." Juls brushes my hair off my shoulder, letting out a few sniffles.

"Well, staying with us isn't an option. My bed isn't big enough for four."

Joey holds the door open for us and Juls and I step inside. I glance over my shoulder at him. "Did you pick up the dresses and your suit? And the ring? You have his ring, right?"

He frowns. "Please. Like I'd drop the ball on something like that." He looks past me and practically starts to glow. And I don't need to follow his gaze to know who he's looking at. Joey only reserves that look for one man. Even though he likes to complain that Billy doesn't shower him with Reese-style gestures, there's no mistaking the effect he has on my dear assistant.

I watch as Billy walks up to us, giving Juls and me a smile before grabbing Joey's face. They share a kiss, one which causes my skin to flush. One which causes Juls to sigh. And one which seems different from the other kisses I've seen them share.

"I'm pretty sure people have had sex in this building. In fact, I know they have. In case you two need a minute," Juls cracks, causing us both to laugh.

Yup. I've definitely had sex in this building.

Billy and Joey turn to us, breaking their kiss. "A minute? I'm not a fucking virgin," Joey snaps.

Billy laughs, releasing Joey and walking to me. He leans in, dropping his voice. "Can I talk to you for a minute?"

"Sure," I answer, looking over at Joey and Juls. "I'll meet you in there. Tell Reese to give me a minute."

Joey looks strangely between Billy and me. "Umm, okay."

"It's something Reese wanted me to tell Dylan," Billy says.

Joey nods, wrapping his arm around Juls and ushering her toward the back room where the ceremony will be held.

I look up at Billy. "It doesn't have anything to do with Reese, does it?"

He smiles. "No. I wanted to ask your permission to do something at the reception tomorrow. For Joey. It's your day and I completely understand if you don't want me to do it." He reaches up and straightens his tie, looking over at the door Juls and Joey walked through moments ago. "This is the grandest gesture I can think of," he says in a low, guarded voice.

I almost fall apart in tears but I manage to hold it in, saving my makeup in the process. When he looks back at me, I answer. "You never have to ask my permission to do anything that will make that man smile. Do you need my help?"

His shoulders seem to relax as he shakes his head. "No, I got it. Thanks, Dylan." He grabs my hand and loops it through his arm. "Come on. I'm sure that man of yours is waiting." I glance up at him and see his eyes trail down my dress. "Have I seen you in this before?"

"Mmm hmm."

"At the wedding. Right? Your ex-boyfriend's?"

"Mmm hmm."

He opens the door and lets me walk ahead of him. "Oh, shit. Reese is going to lose it." I chuckle at the very words Joey used minutes ago as we step inside The Great Hall.

Rows upon rows of chairs line both sides of the aisle, the end ones adorned with mini versions of the white gardenia bouquet I will be holding tomorrow. The lights are dimmed and all around the room, candles are lit, and giving off a warm glow. I let my eyes wander, taking in all my best friend's hard work. It's perfect. Every little detail. And then I give in to the temptation waiting for me in the group gathered up front.

Everyone is watching me, stopping all conversation when I stepped into the room with Billy. I'm just now registering that he has left my side when I see him standing by Joey. My parents and Reese's mom and dad are together, along with Reese's sister and her husband, who I met a few months ago at a family dinner. Juls is with Ian and they're all over each other, as usual. But I don't linger on them, or anyone else besides the man who is standing out amongst them. Dressed in a dark-gray suit, Reese seems to be the one unable to move as he takes in my outfit.

The very outfit I fell into his lap in.

I save him the trouble of coming to me and begin walking up the aisle, tucking my clutch under my arm. I'm ready to get through this as quickly as possible. I want this night to be over. I want it to be tomorrow already. But as I try and get past the cluster of people to get to who I really want to talk to, my mother grabs me.

"Sweetheart! You look stunning," she says, kissing me on my cheek. *Shit. So close.*

I'm passed around like a damn baby, getting showered in affection while my eyes strain to stay on Reese. I have to pull them away from him to talk to his sister and brother in-law, exchanging pleasantries and trying not to seem rushed about it. I don't want to be rude, but Jesus Christ, I'll see everyone tomorrow. Maggie and Phillip, Reese's dad, steal me next, gushing over me in the sweetest way possible. And then by some miracle, the preacher decides to cut in just when I think I'm going to be stuck in this conversation forever.

"Miss Sparks, are you ready to begin?"

"Yes!" I yell excitingly, hearing everyone react to my enthusiasm. I get within a foot of Reese and take his hand, positioning myself directly in front of him while the preacher moves around us. "Hi," I whisper.

He smiles. "Hi, yourself. Nice dress."

I feign humility. "This old thing? I wasn't sure if you'd like it or not."

"Shall we begin?" the preacher asks.

Reese looks at him. "One second." He pulls me in and presses his lips to my ear. "You're driving me crazy. I'd prefer not to get hard in front of my parents."

"Well, then you shouldn't have invited me."

He releases me with a smirk before nodding at the preacher. "All right. Let's go."

We run through the ceremony and even though I don't want to, I bawl my eyes out when I recite my vows to Reese. When I promise to cherish him forever, to love every part of him with every ounce of myself, I cry harder. Juls and Joey's sobs behind me blend into mine, while I hear the faint sound of everyone else's emotions getting to them as they watch from their seats. And then I really become a wreck when he repeats them. But unlike me, Reese doesn't cry. His voice isn't a quivering mess. He doesn't have to pause to try and pull himself together. But even though he doesn't react the way I do when he recites them, his words seem to hold more sentiment than mine. As if this is the only time I'll hear them from him. As if he isn't going to be reciting them again to me tomorrow.

He vows to always be mine, to honor me and stand by my side through everything life throws at us. To make me laugh and to hold me when I cry, prompting him to pull me against him since I am, indeed, crying. He finishes his vows into my hair while I cling to him like he's my life line. His scent soothes me as I nuzzle him long after he finishes talking, relishing in the way my body fits perfectly against his. And everyone gives us that moment. No one asks if we'd like to continue with the mock ceremony. No one clears their throat to speed things along. We don't break contact until we're both ready, which feels like hours instead of minutes.

After finally separating, we finish the ceremony and share a brief kiss, one I know will be much longer tomorrow. Everyone pairs up and walks back down the aisle, Reese and I leading the way. We say goodbye to my parents and Reese's family before he and I walk through the parking lot, our friends a few feet behind us.

"So, did I surprise you with my dress?" I ask as we stop in front of my driver's side door. I lean my back against it and tug at his suit jacket, bringing him closer to me.

"You always surprise me, love. Especially when you're in *that* dress."

"Oh? I surprised you in this before?"

He puts a hand on either side of me, bringing our foreheads together. "Well, I wasn't suspecting to get knocked on my ass by a wedding hookup. So, yes, you surprised me."

"See you two at The Tavern!" Juls yells, gaining our attention. We wave to her and the rest of the group as they all walk to their vehicles.

"I was just as affected, you know," I say, bringing his attention back to my face. "I couldn't stop thinking about you, which annoyed me because I thought you were married. But don't think you were the only one who got knocked on their ass," I repeat his words to me with a playful tone. "Thank you for my delivery today. Did you see the video?"

He presses his lips against mine. "I did. I watched it at least ten times before I left the office. You looked so happy."

"I am so happy."

"So am I," he replies against my mouth.

I bite at his bottom lip. "We should probably get married then. Since we're both *so happy.*"

"Makes sense."

"I think so."

Joey beeps his car horn as he drives by us, waving out his window. Reese shifts me so he can open my door. "Come on. They're going to be waiting for us."

I slide into my seat and start my car. The time on my dash catches my eye. "This time tomorrow night we'll be married." He ducks down and reaches across my body with my seatbelt, buckling me in. I give him a quirky look. "Really? I'm capable of buckling myself in, you know."

"You were too slow about it." He kisses my temple. "Don't speed this time."

"Yes, Mr. Sparks."

He goes to close my door but the title I've just given him stops him. "Mr. what?"

"Sparks. I like the sound of that. Reese Sparks. Some men take their bride's name."

"I'm not one of them," he says with authority in his tone. One that's saying this is in no way negotiable. He closes my door and walks toward his vehicle. And I could pull away, but I wait because I know he's going to give it to me. Even though I can't see his face, I know he's smiling at what I've just said despite the seriousness in his voice. And as he grabs his door handle, I see the slight shake of his head before he gives me that smile over his shoulder, the smile I'll always wait for. Satisfied, I finally pull away from the Whitmore with a very happy man behind me.

Chapter
TWENTY-THREE

"**J**ESUS. THIS PLACE IS PACKED," I yell over the music as Reese leads me through the crowd of people.

Friday nights at The Tavern do tend to be a bit busier, but I don't think I've ever seen it this mobbed before. I stay close to Reese, my hand in his as he weaves me in and out of the mass of bodies toward one of the tall tables surrounding the dance floor. I spot our friends once we get close enough. Juls is sitting on Ian's lap, Joey is talking intimately with Billy, and Brooke is looking between the two couples, rolling her eyes.

"Why I agreed to show up here dateless is beyond me," she snaps before taking a sip of her drink. Her eyes widen when they focus on Reese and me. "Ahhh! You're here!" She moves past Billy and Joey, wrapping her arms around me. "Thank you for inviting me out tonight. I'm so fucking excited about tomorrow." She glances up at Reese. "Wait until you see your wedding cake. It's unreal."

"I can't wait," he answers, dropping my hand. "You want anything from the bar?"

"Just a water." I turn to Juls once Reese leaves the group. "Is that what you're having?"

She holds up her glass. "Nothing but water for me for the next eight months. I need it tonight anyway after bawling my eyes out at the rehearsal. I can't imagine how emotional this is going to be tomorrow."

"Am I the only one who didn't cry?" Billy asks, reaching up and fixing Joey's collar.

"I didn't," Ian says, glancing over at Juls who shoots him a disbelieving look. "What? I wasn't crying. My allergies were acting up."

"Sure they were," Brooke teases. "Because you didn't shed a few tears during your own wedding, or when you heard your baby's heartbeat. You're practically a chick, Ian. Whereas Reese exudes manliness."

"Easy, hornball," I direct at her. She wiggles her brows at me as a response.

Reese returns to the table carrying a beer and a glass of water for me. Ian points at him. "You think he won't be emotional tomorrow? Are you fucking kidding? I'll bet a hundred bucks he cries before any of us. Including you." He motions toward me and smiles. "Shall we make it interesting?"

"Fuck you. I haven't cried since I was a kid. I'll take that bet," Reese says. He looks down at me as he slides his arm around my waist. "Honeymoon money."

I laugh as Joey slides off his stool. "I'm in."

"Me, too," Billy adds.

"Yup. I say you're going to weep like a baby the minute you see her," Juls says behind her glass, smiling at Reese. "I've seen the dress. Good luck getting any money from us."

"I want in. I don't have a hundred bucks yet cause I'm waiting to get paid," Brooke pauses, shooting me a look which I give right back to her. "But, I'm betting Reese holds his ground. I think Dylan will cry before he does."

Reese presses his lips to my hair. "You want in on this, love?"

Demi Lovato's "Really Don't Care" begins blaring overheard, and I put my glass down and shimmy out of his grasp. "Nope!" I yell over the music, moving toward the dance floor. I connect with him from the other side of the table. "But if I were, I'd be betting against you, handsome." I grab Joey by the shirt and pull Juls off Ian's lap. I wave over Brooke and the four of us move into the crowd of people on the dance floor.

The guys stay at the table, watching, amused as we all twirl around each other and sing at the top of our lungs. I keep meeting Reese's eyes, motioning for him to join me, but he stays put and occasionally shakes his head in disapproval when I begin dancing way more flirtatiously than I did today in the shop. Billy joins us after a few songs and takes turns dancing with all four of us, giving Joey extra attention. The dance floor is mobbed and we get moved farther and farther away from the table when more people try to pack in. Juls motions she needs a drink after a while, and I do, too. I'm sweaty and definitely parched, but I need to use the restroom first.

"I'll be right there!" I yell over the music, seeing all four of them indicate they've heard me as they walk back toward the guys.

I push my way through the crowd toward the back hallway which leads to the bathrooms. There are entirely too many people in the bar tonight. There must be some sort of crowd cap that is definitely being ignored. But as long as there isn't a line for the ladies room, I'm fine with the mob.

I follow a group of girls into the women's room, who luckily only want to check out their makeup situation, leaving me an empty stall. Once I'm finished, I wash my hands and clean up my face a bit, forgetting all about the tears I shed earlier and what it ended up doing to my eye makeup. But luckily, it's so dark in the bar I doubt anyone noticed. Once I'm satisfied with my appearance and so thirsty I contemplate drinking straight from the tap, I exit the bathroom.

I'm stopped by a hand on my upper arm, big enough to wrap around my bicep. It tightens and pulls me out of the bathroom doorway while another hand grabs my hip, pinning me against the wall. Everything happens so quickly, I don't have time to register any of it. The hard body is pressing against me, preventing me from moving and keeping me boxed in. I look up at a man invading my space and meet those eerie yellow eyes I never thought I'd see again.

"Get the hell..."

My words are cut off when his hand covers my mouth, He moves closer, flattening his body against mine. I clench every muscle as I try to squirm from his hold. I know the hallway is packed with people, but the way Bryce is pressing against me and given his size compared to mine and his ability to shield me completely, it probably looks like two people making out. I try to shake my head to remove his hand but he stays with me. He pins my arms together in front of me when I try to push him away. Panic sets in. Blood fills my ears and I want to scream, but I can't.

And then he leans in and I squeeze my eyes shut. I don't know what he's about to do. I don't know if he's just going to run his mouth like usual. Given the fact he probably knows he's going to prison, I'm thinking he isn't going to hold anything back.

"Hey, baby. Miss me?"

I gag at the alcohol and cigarette cocktail filling my nasal cavity with each word he spews. It's nauseating, as is everything about this guy. I feel his nose rub against my forehead and hear him inhale.

"Your bastard boyfriend messed with the wrong guy. And he was really fucking stupid to let you out of his sight."

"I didn't."

Reese's voice and the closeness of it has me shooting my eyes open. He's over Bryce's shoulder, grabbing him and pulling him off me before he slams him against the other wall. Bryce protests with flailing limbs and some incoherent words which are broken apart when Reese punches him in the jaw. Repeatedly. His arm flies back, fist clenched, and he delivers blow after blow while his other hand pins Bryce in place. Blood starts pouring from Bryce's nose and mouth, and that creepy grin of his is nowhere in sight.

"Fight!" someone yells.

I'm glued to the wall, unable to move as I watch the crowd form around us, which includes our group of friends. Juls and Brooke both gasp, covering their mouths as they watch Reese pummel this loser, while the guys all react differently.

Billy pulls his phone out of his pocket and quickly dials what I assume to be the police.

Ian pushes his way back toward the bar, yelling over the commotion for someone to get security.

And Joey comes straight over to me. "Are you okay?" he asks, alarm in his voice.

I nod my response, keeping my eyes on Reese. No one stops him and I know someone has to. He could kill this prick.

He should kill him.

Just when I'm about to open my mouth, Reese grabs Bryce by his shirt and drags him off the wall, moving across the hallway to where I'm standing. Juls and Brooke both dart out of the way and Joey flanks my side. Bryce looks like shit run over. His nose has to be broken by the looks of it, his left eye is swollen shut, and he seems to be having trouble standing.

Aww. Poor baby.

Reese holds him up in front of me. "You see her? Do you?" Bryce moans. "Fucking look at her, you piece of shit!" Bryce peeks his good eye open while the blood pours from his nose. "Get a good fucking look, because this is the last one you're ever going to get. If you so much as think about her again, I will hunt your ass down and fucking kill you. Do you hear me?" Bryce moans again as Ian comes rushing back over to the group.

"All right. Cops are here. I don't know where the fuck security is, but it looks like you don't need them." He looks at Juls and then at me. "You okay?"

"Yes," we both answer.

"Dylan," Reese says, gaining my attention. "If you want to hit him, you better do it now."

He holds Bryce by his shirt in front of me and I step closer, tilting my head down so his one eye focuses on me. "I've been wanting to do this for a really long time." I bring my hand back and strike him hard across the face, the loud cracking sound filling the hallway.

"Damn!" someone yells through a laugh.

I smile at the crowd. I don't think I've ever felt this satisfied with slapping someone before.

Brooke steps up next to me. "Ooo! Can we all take turns? I want a go at him."

Just then, Billy pushes through the crowd, signaling for the police to follow him. "Oh, damn it," Brooke utters, moving back and falling in next to Joey. One officer grabs Bryce from Reese and moves him away from the group while the other walks over to us.

"Someone want to tell me what happened here?" the officer asks, looking at each of us.

I give him the rundown of the situation, making sure to point out that this isn't the first time Bryce put his hands on me. I tell the cop about the time in the elevator and mention he's kind of been stalking me, using the flower on my van as an example. When I get a stern look from Reese, I realize I forgot to tell him about that and mouth "I'm sorry", seeing his face soften instantly. Reese tells the officer about the investigation on Bryce and how he thought he should've been arrested by now. The officer tells us they have been looking for him, but he hasn't been at his condo and also hasn't shown up to work for the past two days. But now that they have him, he'll be in custody until his trial. After everyone gives their statements about what they saw happen, we are told we can leave.

"Well, this has been interesting to say the least. I'll see you crazy kids tomorrow," Brooke says as we all walk outside. She heads down the sidewalk, glancing over her shoulder. "And I got dibs on every single guy there!" she yells.

"All right, boys. Say your goodbyes," Juls says. Ian grabs her and kisses her sweetly while Billy and Joey share their own private moment a few feet away on the sidewalk.

I glance up at Reese. "Hi."

His eyes meet mine after scanning my face. "I don't want to say goodbye."

I predicted this, especially after what just happened. But it's over now. Reese has nothing to be worried about.

I wrap my arms around him and tilt my head up, pressing my chin against his chest. "I tell you what. I'll text you as soon as I get home, and then every fifteen minutes until I fall asleep."

"Every five minutes," he counters, pressing his lips to my forehead. His arms envelop me and hold me against him.

I'm about to argue but let it go and agree to it. "Okay. Every five minutes. How is your hand?"

"Fine."

"Let me see it."

"It's fine, Dylan."

"Reese."

He sighs heavily and lets go of me, holding up his right hand for me to examine.

"Fine, my ass. See how banged-up it looks?" I run my fingers over his fourth and fifth knuckle where most of the damage seems to be. The skin is cut up and a bit swollen, and he flinches at my touch. "You might need an x-ray, Reese. It could be broken."

He flexes it several times before grabbing my hip with his other hand and pulling me against his chest. "It's not broken. I'll ice it when I get to Ian's."

As if he hears his name, Ian comes up to us and slaps Reese on the back. "Come on, man. She'll be all yours tomorrow."

Reese looks at him and then back down at me. He tilts my chin up. "Every five minutes."

I press my lips against his. "You got it."

Juls and Joey flank my side and we watch our men walk toward their vehicles. They both grab one of my hands.

"You ready for your last sleepover as a single woman?" Juls asks.

I smile at Reese as he looks back at me one last time before getting into his car.

Yup. Absolutely. "I'm so fucking ready."

❧

WHEN WE GET BACK TO the bakery, Juls and I help Joey carry the dresses inside and up the stairs to my practically empty loft. After changing into our pajamas, I hang my dress up and unzip the bag, smiling as the white lace slowly comes into view. I run my hand over the material while Juls and Joey laugh on the bed behind me.

"It's been five minutes, cupcake," Joey reminds me.

I zip up the bag and grab my phone before falling back onto the bed between the two of them.

"Thank God all this shit with Bryce is over," Juls says as I type my message to Reese. "I can't believe Ian didn't tell me the real reason for working with him."

I press send and look over at her. "They couldn't. You know Ian wouldn't keep anything from you unless he absolutely had to."

"Fo' reals. I'm sure he'd tell you the nuclear codes if he had them," Joey jokes. "I'm actually surprised he didn't spill it. That man likes to gossip more than me."

Juls reaches over me and slaps his arm. "No one likes to gossip more than you."

My phone beeps as I laugh at the two of them. I hold it above my head and quickly scan Reese's message.

REESE: *I told you. My hand is fine.*

"So, are you ready to move out of here permanently, sweets?" Juls asks.

I look down my body and around the empty space surrounding my bed, tucking my hands behind my head after placing my phone on my chest. All the sadness I felt just last week at the very thought of moving is absent. The boxes stacked against the wall and on the kitchen counter no longer depress me. This is my last night in my loft, and although I once never imagined leaving it, I can no longer picture myself living here. The majority of the memories I have of this space are missing one vital element. And I want all my memories to include him.

I look over at her and smile. "What's your favorite memory of being here?"

"Hmm. I don't know. We've had so many good ones," she replies, grabbing the pillows and handing them out to us. She takes one for herself and places it under her head. "You?"

I open my mouth to tell her I have no idea when Joey cuts me off.

"Well, I'll tell you what mine wasn't. Fucking tequila drinking games." Juls and I both make noises of agreement as Joey rolls on his side facing us. He smiles that winning smile of his. "You're getting married tomorrow, cupcake. And I think you need to let everyone on this fucking block know."

I glance between the two of them before quickly scrambling to my feet on the bed, placing a hand on either side of my mouth, and yelling at the top of my lungs, "I'M GETTING MARRIED TOMORROW!"

Juls and Joey both hoot and holler at me as I drop to my knees and fall back between them. And we don't move from our spots for the rest of the night.

There's laughing and talking more about the wedding, a few more text messages between Reese and myself, and a ton of discussion revolving around Juls' pregnancy. It's my last night in my loft, and it's one of the best ones I've ever had.

With two of the most important people in my life.

Chapter
TWENTY-FOUR

TODAY, I MARRY MY WEDDING *hookup*.

Not that I'm an expert on this sort of thing, but I'm pretty sure most people never see their flings again after sharing that one moment together. That's the whole point of wedding sex, isn't it? You're watching two people vow to love each other for the rest of their lives while you wallow in your own single self-misery. Then you see an opportunity in the form of another hopefully-not-married wedding guest and proceed to get it on to help ease your loneliness. Or I suppose in my case, experience something you never have that your overly-knowledgeable best friend brags about. Either way, I'm certain in most cases of slutty wedding sex, no one expects to fall in love with the guy who romantically takes you against a bathroom sink at your ex-boyfriend's wedding reception. It's supposed to be a one-and-done deal. A shake of hands and saying how nice it was to make each other come before walking away. You're not supposed to continually think about that person after you've gone your separate ways. You're not supposed to lose sleep and briefly contemplate pursuing anything further with a man who you've been told is married. And you're definitely not supposed to begin a casually-monogamous relationship with that same man, especially when you're incapable of not falling in love with him.

But like I said, I'm not an expert at this sort of thing. And it's a good thing, too; otherwise, I probably wouldn't be standing in front of my mirror while my mother and fabulous wedding planner/best friend button me into my wedding gown. Without any difficulty, I might add.

"I knew you could do it, sweetheart. This dress fits you perfectly now," my mother says behind me.

It does fit perfectly, thanks to the diet I'll never be adhering to again. My low-carb days are way the hell behind me.

"Yeah, well, I plan on tearing into that wedding cake later, so I better have plenty of room." I connect with Juls in the mirror, smiling at the sight of her in the floor-length, pale-gray bridesmaid dress she looks amazing in. "What time are you heading over?"

She looks over at the stove and quickly spins around, grabbing her stuff. "Shit. Right now. I'll have your bridal suite set up for you, so go straight there when you get to the Whitmore. And use the side entrance. If Reese sees you beforehand, I'll kill him."

I laugh and hear my mom's agreeing noise behind me as Juls walks to the door. It swings open just as she gets to it, Joey emerging from the stairs and decked out in his tux.

"Wow. Look at you," he says to Juls, earning himself a kiss on the cheek.

"Right back atcha. I'll see you guys there." She disappears down the stairs as Joey comes to stand beside me.

"Everything go okay?" I ask as my mother steps back, seemingly done with her task. I spin around and face Joey, seeing his awestruck expression.

His eyes twinkle with adoration as he takes in the sight of me. "You look fucking fabulous."

"Joseph," my mother scolds.

He glances over at her. "Well, she does! Seriously, I don't think anyone has looked this good in a wedding gown before. Aside from Juls." He shakes his head with an exhaustive sigh. "Single gal, party of one over here."

I smack his shoulder. "Whatever. No problems with the cake?"

He steps up to the mirror, straightening his tie. "Of course not. I gave it the Joey treatment. It's waiting for you at the Whitmore, as is your anxious groom."

"You saw him?" I grab his shoulder and spin him around. "How does he look?"

His eyebrows raise. "Like he might pass out if he doesn't see you soon."

I frown. "Really?"

He nods before the crease in his brow sets in. "Billy, on the other hand, is acting all weird. It's like he purposely avoided me while I was there. And let me tell you, if this is how it's going to be today, Brooke might have some competition on her hands. I don't need this shit from a guy who obviously has zero plans of one day giving me the wedding of my dreams."

"Dylan, sweetheart, we need to get going," my mother says as she grabs the stuff I'll be taking with me to the bridal suite.

I grab Joey's chin and lower it, narrowing my eyes at him. "Don't count Billy out just yet."

His eyes widen. "What does that mean? Do you know something?"

I put on my best poker face and loop my arm through his. "I *know* he loves you. Now stop making this day all about you. I seem to be the one in the fancy dress."

He gives me a smile as we collect the rest of my things. Standing at the door, I look around my loft one final time. The movers will be coming sometime during the ceremony and taking everything out for me. The next time I come to work, my loft will be an empty space above my bakery. And I'm okay with that.

"Let's go, cupcake."

I take one last mental shot before heading down the stairs behind Joey. I beam at the beautiful white lilies sitting in the center of the worktop, a gift from the other bride. I assumed someone else in the wedding party was going to stop in this morning to pick up her cake, but she wanted to personally thank me for fitting her in on such short notice. And she also wanted to give me the flowers herself.

Joey holds the front door open for me as my mom walks close behind, holding my train off the ground. Cool air lifts my hair off my shoulder. The driver smiles and opens the back door of the limo, allowing the three of us to file inside. The excitement I feel rushing through me as we make our way to the Whitmore is unlike anything I've ever felt. But I know it won't top the moment I see Reese.

୧ୠ

WE'RE ALL HUDDLED IN THE bridal suite as I check my hair and makeup in the mirror for the thousandth time in the past half hour. I twirl a few curls of my hair around my fingers before fluffing the waves falling past my shoulders. My makeup is looking better than it ever has; elegant yet simple. One of the girls from Chicago Bridal worked her magic on me early this morning while her partner styled my hair. Juls has been in and out of the room, keeping everyone in line while Joey slipped out minutes ago to take care of something he wouldn't elaborate on. My mother has been trying to keep herself from crying, but every time I make eye contact with her, she loses it. And then there's my dad. The calmest of the bunch without a doubt. He's sitting in a high-back leather chair, looking out the window between stealing a few glances at me I've caught in the mirror. He really is the yin to my mother's yang. Complete opposites, the two of them. She's barely holding herself together while he looks like it's just another Saturday. Nothing major happening today or anything.

The door to the suite swings open and Joey darts through, slamming it shut behind him. "He's trying to see you! Is he nuts? That's bad luck!"

I step off my pedestal, letting my dress fall out around me. "What? Who is?"

"Reese!"

My heart flutters at the sound of his name. I move closer to the door just as the knob begins to rattle.

"Dylan?"

Joey spins around and presses his mouth to the door. "You are out of your mind if you think I'm letting you in here."

"Joey, it's okay."

"It most certainly is not," my mother adds. "Dylan, you can't see each other before the ceremony. This isn't like *not* having a rehearsal dinner." She moves between me and the door, pulling Joey off it. "Reese Carroll. You are not allowed in here."

"I don't need to come in. I just want to hear her."

Joey looks back at me and then his eyes lose focus. "Goddamn it, Billy."

I chuckle, stepping up next to my mom. She looks over at me and sighs before waving her hand and giving me the go-ahead. I move up to the door and flatten my hand against it.

"Reese?"

A soft thump knocks against my hand. "Please, tell me you're almost ready. I'm fucking dying."

I giggle. "I'm ready. I've been ready. I'm just waiting for Juls."

I hear a faint growl. "Go get your wife and tell her we're starting. Now." The sound of footsteps leading away from the door makes me smile as I picture Ian as a man on a mission. "Love, can I... I don't know, can you just give me something? Crack the door open a little?"

I glance over my shoulder, seeing my mother and father in quiet conversation. Joey hears the request and immediately spins around and blocks my parents' view of me. I turn the doorknob and pull, opening the door a few inches and peering around, making sure to keep my body completely hidden. His eyes meet mine, and I see the desperation in them.

I keep all focus on his face, not letting my eyes wander down his body. I want to save that for the ceremony. I smile behind the door. "You okay now?" I whisper, not wanting to alert my mother.

He leans his head against the doorframe, blinking heavily. "I'm not spending another night away from you. I barely got any sleep last night."

"What, is Ian not a good snuggle buddy? I've heard otherwise."

He smirks. "You're hilarious. Give me a kiss."

"No way."

"Why?"

"Because the next time I kiss you will be when you're officially my husband."

I hear the clicking sound of heels as Reese argues my reasoning with a scowl. Juls grabs his shoulder. "Get the hell out of here! Are you insane?"

"You're the one who's making us wait. She's ready. I'm ready. Let's fucking go."

Juls shoves him in the direction of The Great Hall. "Go. We'll be there in a minute."

He looks past her, connecting with me. "If you make me wait, I'll be hauling you down that aisle over my shoulder."

"I'm right behind you," I reply as Juls pushes her way into the room.

My mother walks over to us, disapproval stamped on her features. "I'm not saying a word."

I shrug before turning to Juls. "Can I *please* get married now?"

Juls waves my dad over who has remained in his chair. "Are you ready to give your daughter away, Mr. Sparks?"

He looks at her then at me before standing and tugging at his suit jacket. Reserved and poised, he walks over and takes my hand, looping it through his arm. He tilts his head down, giving me an endearing look. "I will never be ready to give my daughter away. But if I had to pick one man to take care of her in my place, it would be Reese."

I blink rapidly, trying to stop the tears from forming. Juls sniffs and wipes underneath my eyes, keeping my makeup intact while Joey fans his face and my mom pulls out a handkerchief, blowing her nose into it.

My dad leads me toward the door. "Come on. You heard the man. He isn't going to wait much longer for you."

We walk down the side hallway which dumps into the main room of the Whitmore. It's empty, all the guests already inside The Great Hall. I hear the soft music playing behind the closed giant double doors. My mother comes up to me and kisses my cheek before doing the same to my father. Joey moves me to the side, shielding me while Juls opens the door and allows my mother to enter the room and take her seat.

"Okay," Juls says in a soft voice. "Let's line up." She walks over to the side table and grabs my bouquet, handing it to me and taking hers. Joey stands at the front of the line, Juls right behind him. He grabs the door handles, glancing back over his shoulder.

"Ready, cupcake?"

Juls gives me a quick wink and I nod, shifting my weight on my feet. *God, yes. Come on already.*

The doors open and the music becomes noticeably louder. I move forward once Joey begins his walk, gripping my bouquet tightly. As Juls makes her way between the rows of chairs, my father takes a few more steps with me. I look around the room, smiling at the familiar faces of family and friends who have joined us today. And then I can't stand it any longer. I give into the biggest temptation of my life and let my eyes find Reese.

I see his reaction to me immediately. And even though I know this ceremony is being videoed, I won't need any help remembering the look on his face right now. I know without a doubt I will never forget this moment and the mix of emotion in his eyes.

My dad turns me toward him. "Are you sure I can't walk you down the aisle, sweetheart? It's my only job today."

I smile and look back up at Reese, because it physically pains me to not look at him at this point. "No," I reply, letting go of his arm. "He'll come get me."

My father makes his way down the aisle alone, gaining muffled reactions from the guests. No one knows why I'm standing back here by myself. No one but Reese. And as my father takes his seat next to my mom, Reese begins his walk toward me.

Actually, it's more like a sprint.

I hear the familiar laughs of our friends from the front of the room as Reese gets to me in record timing. He cradles my face in his hands and drops his forehead to touch mine.

"Thanks for coming to get me," I whisper for his ears only.

"I'll always come to get you, you know that." He leans back and looks down my body. "You have never looked this beautiful, and you always stun me, Dylan. This dress…"

"Wait 'til you see what's under it." My tease gets the reaction I was hoping for out of him. I'm quickly being escorted down the aisle, almost at the same pace with which he reached me moments ago with. The hall becomes filled with everyone's laughter as they take in my flustered fiancé. Once we reach the front of the room, I hand my bouquet to Juls who can't seem to stop giggling. Reese positions me across from him, steadying me with his hands on my upper arms before releasing me.

He looks up at the preacher. "Hurry up."

We run through the majority of the ceremony without any glitches. When it comes to our vow exchange, I turn around and grab a few tissues from Juls. If last night was any indication to how I'm going to react to this, and given the fact Reese has never looked sexier than he does right this moment, I'm going to need these.

I go first, with the steadiest voice I can muster, repeating after the preacher. I only shed a few tears but quickly wipe them away before my makeup is affected. Reese keeps his eyes on me the entire time, giving me the sweetest smile I've ever seen as I promise to love him forever.

And then I prepare myself for his turn.

The preacher doesn't ask him to repeat anything. In fact, he doesn't say anything after I finish reciting mine. I look up at him and then to Reese with what I can only assume to be my most perplexed expression. Reese reaches into his inner jacket pocket and pulls out the familiar brown card he's always sending me notes on.

I crush the tissues in my hand as my breath lodges in my throat.

He steps closer to me, holding it out for me to take. "Did you really think I'd ever use someone else's words on you?"

"Oh, my God," Juls chokes out behind me.

I hear Joey's annoyed reaction, too, but can't respond to it. I have to put all my focus into taking the card from him. It's a difficult task. My hands are shaking so bad I'm not sure I'll be able to stop them enough to read the card. I go to unfold it when his hands cover mine.

"No, love. That's for you to never forget the words I'm about to say. Right now, just listen."

I bring the card against my chest, holding it there while he barely leaves an inch of space between us.

"Dylan, until today, the day you fell into my lap, the day you came back to me, the day I knew I was going to marry you, those were the best days of my life. I promise to always look at you this way. To give you every part of me, and to cherish every second I share with you. Because you have always been mine, ever since I first saw you in this room. And I will spend the rest of my life being yours." He looks down, breaking our contact briefly as I wipe underneath my eyes. "I feel like I've been waiting for this day forever. I still can't believe I'm the one who gets to marry you." He finally lifts his eyes and I see the tears in them. "I want you in every way, Dylan. I want the woman who fell into my lap, and the one who's slapped me across the face more times than I care to remember."

I laugh through a cry, hearing everyone's chuckles around me.

Reese's lips curls into a smile. "I want the woman who dances around her bakery every Friday, and the one who lets me watch her from across the room and acts like she doesn't know I'm doing it." His hand tucks my hair behind my ear, and my throat suddenly feels too dry to swallow as he holds my face. "I want the woman who protected her heart when she had to. The one who gave it to me when she was ready. And the one who is now giving me the best day of my life."

I can't control myself now, nor can any other woman in the room, I'm sure. Even Joey is blubbering behind me as I reach up and wipe the tear that's trickled down Reese's cheek.

"I promise to always love you. To send you deliveries when I want or when I think you need them. Even if it's every day. To hold your hand and your hair when you're hung-over. And to let you take care of me when I'm at my worst. I promise to give you every day of my life. To always protect you, even if it means breaking my hand in the process."

My eyes widen. "What?"

He gives me a half smile. "Yeah, I... it might be broken."

"Oh, my God," I grab his hand and hold it out in front of me. I barely glance at it before he puts it back on my hip. "I wasn't finished."

"Neither am I." He pulls my body against his, wrapping his arms completely around me. "I promise to laugh with you and comfort you. To love you when life is easy and when it's hard. And to be the man you deserve." He sighs, his face breaking into a smile. "Okay. I'm finished."

"That was the best note you've ever given me." Instinctively, I tilt my head up to kiss him but am stopped when the preacher clears his throat. Reese and I both turn our heads.

"Not at that part yet, folks. We still need to exchange rings."

"Oh! The rings!" I spin around and hold out the card for Juls to take, swapping it for the ring. Turning back, I look over at the preacher. "All right, start talking. I need to kiss him."

The bridal party and congregation all share a laugh before the preacher instructs us to slip the rings on the other person's finger. I study the way the platinum band stands out on Reese's skin.

My man looks good wearing a wedding band.

And then finally, after what feels like an eternity, we get to the best part.

"And now, by the power invested in me by the State of Illinois, I now pronounce you husband and wife." He looks at Reese and I follow suit, bouncing up and down on my feet. I'm so ready for this fucking kiss, I might just burst before I get it. "You may now finally kiss your bride."

"About time," Reese grunts before pressing his lips against mine. This kiss wipes my memory of anything besides him, leaving me breathless as he cradles my face. I hear everyone clapping and cheering around us, but Reese doesn't pull back. Not until he's ready. "You're mine, Mrs. Carroll," he says against my lips, finally ending our kiss.

"Always have been," I reply.

We walk down the aisle, my hand in his while everyone claps around us. Once we get through the doorway, Reese leads me to the room where the bridal party has to wait until it's time to be announced upstairs. He pushes the door open and immediately pins me against the wall, his lips crashing against mine.

"Reese." His name comes out as a plea. To stop because the bridal party will be in here any minute. To keep going because I'm dying to be with my husband this way.

"I need to get you out of this dress." He kisses down my neck, nipping at my skin. His hands roam my body like he hasn't touched me in years. There's an urgency to it, a drive to touch every part of me. He grips my waist and spins me so I'm facing the wall. "How the fuck do I take this off?"

I flatten my palms against the wall as his fingers pop the buttons of my dress. I should be telling him we don't have time for this, and we're definitely about to be interrupted, but all words have escaped me.

"What the hell... Jesus Christ, Dylan. What are you wearing?"

The door swings open just as I'm about to answer and Reese quickly spins me around, closing in on me and shielding me with his body. I glance over his shoulder and see our friends walk in, all wearing the familiar 'busted' look on their faces.

"Mmm hmm," Joey teases, pointing a finger at us. "You may have won the crying bet, but we just all won one hundred bucks from both of you for trying to stick it in before the reception."

"I never agreed to that," Reese scowls over his shoulder. "And will you all give us a fucking minute?" His fingers are trying to secure my dress blindly as I laugh against him, dropping my head against his chest. And then I feel him relax into me, his laugh echoing around us as we both enjoy the humor of this situation. The fact that we can't make it through a few-hours-long reception before we need to have each other.

"You have two minutes before we need to line up," Juls voice fills my ears as I keep myself completely submerged against Reese. Embedded almost. And then the sound of the door closing and the fading voices in the hallway are the only thing I hear besides our breathing

I glance up and take him in. All of him. Maybe I didn't get a good look when we were standing in front of the congregation. Maybe I was too distracted by the heaviness of the situation and his vows to me, so honest and real, so Reese in every word. Because now as he looms over me, hands stilled on my back, I take my first real look at the man I've just given my life to.

Hair that's been pulled by my fingers. Eyes wide and wild. Lips parted to speak, or ready to clamp down on my skin. His tongue teases the slit in his lip, and I know he *knows* exactly what he's doing. I'd be doing the same thing if I didn't think Juls would drag me from this room by my hair. But we don't have time to tease or touch. Not yet.

I drop my head back as his finger runs along my jaw. "You need to button me up, husband."

He stops all movement at the sentiment. All breathing ceases as he closes his eyes. I watch his neck roll with a heavy swallow. "Say that again."

God, I love him. I love how he needs to hear me call him that. Not only to be mine, but to own the title.

"Husband," I repeat before turning around. "I need some help."

I feel his lips form to my shoulder. My neck. The shell of my ear. And now I'm the one closing my eyes and silently begging to hear him speak. To say the word he hasn't spoken yet. "Wife," he says against my ear. The material of my dress shifts as he buttons me up. "Can you please explain to me what you're wearing under this? It looks like a torture device."

I blush at my naughty secret. "It's a corset. I figured I'd up my game a little for my wedding night. It's uncomfortable as hell, so you're welcome."

He grabs my waist and spins me. "I better not have any trouble getting that off you. It looks complicated."

"You can always rip it."

His eyes turn feverish as he contemplates that solution while he leads me to the door. "Done. Let's get this over with. I need my wife alone."

I smile, feeling my body spark with anticipation, and can't agree more.

Chapter
TWENTY-FIVE

ALL THE GUESTS ARE WAITING for us inside the reception area while Reese and I stand at the back of the bridal party line in front of the double doors. Juls and Ian are directly in front of us, stealing kisses every few seconds while Ian doesn't try to keep his hands off her belly. And Joey and Billy are in front of them. I hear a few words of their not-so-lovey conversation over the music pumping underneath the door. Straining to hear more, I lean to the side and see Joey shove Billy before storming back toward Reese and me.

"Joey!" Billy yells.

My fuming assistant stops next to me, connecting with Billy over Juls' head. "I'm not walking in with you. Why should I? You've barely spoken to me all goddamn day! Fuck you. Walk in by yourself."

I grab his arm and yank him forcefully. "What the hell is going on?"

He opens his mouth to answer me when the doors are opened and the voice of the DJ spills out into the hallway.

"The wedding party is ready to make their grand entrance! And starting us off, we have Groomsman Billy McDermott and Man of Honor, Joey Holt!"

"Joey, get up here," Billy harshly orders over the cheers of the guests.

Joey crosses his arms, firmly holding his ground next to me. "Fuck.

You."

Juls tries to pull him in the direction of the room. "What are you doing? Are you not going to walk in?"

"Not with him I'm not."

We all look over at Billy who gives his forehead a quick rub. "Fine. Whatever." He walks into the room by himself, disappearing into the crowd.

I smack Joey on the arm. "That was really mean. Now who the hell are you going to walk in with?"

He thinks silently for a moment before pulling out his phone.

I ignore him and turn to Reese. "Do you know what's going on with them?"

He looks at me, shaking his head impassively. "Why the hell would I know what's going on?"

Before I can answer him, the DJ interrupts me.

"And now please give a warm welcome to our Best Man, Ian Thomas, and his beautiful wife, Matron of Honor, Julianna Thomas!"

Reese and I step forward as Juls and Ian enter the room. Brooke slides past them and waves at us.

"Hey. I told the DJ. Now what?" she asks, pulling down the hem of her dress. She looks from Joey to Reese and me. "That ceremony was so beautiful. I cried my eyes out. Well played, Reese."

Joey grabs her arm and slips it through his. "Come here. You're being introduced with me."

"What? But I'm not in the bridal party." She tries to pull her hand from his grasp but doesn't get anywhere. "No way! I'm not being introduced!" The DJ's voice comes overhead again.

"And now our Man of Honor is ready to grace us with his presence. Everyone please show him some love. Mr. Joey Holt!"

"Joey!" Brooke protests as Joey moves her with him into the room.

"Billy wasn't acting weird or anything when you were with him earlier?" I ask Reese as we step up to the entrance. "Joey said he was avoiding him or something."

He places his hand over mine. "Dylan, Billy and Ian could've been fucking each other in front of me and I wouldn't have noticed. I was too busy pacing the room."

Billy and Ian? Shit. I'd pay to see that.

I give him a cheeky grin. "Oh, man. You just gave me the hottest image. Would you ever watch gay porn with me?"

Not that I have, but let's be real here. I've read some crazy hot M/M books recently, and I'd be lying if I said I haven't gotten heated over Logan and Tate's sex scenes. In fact, Reese has benefited greatly from my extracurricular reading habits.

He glares down at me as the DJ's voice comes booming out into the entryway.

"All right, folks. The moment you've all been waiting for. Everyone please go crazy for the couple of the hour, MR. AND MRS. REESE CARROLL!"

"Ready?" he asks, but he doesn't give me time to answer before he bends down and hauls me over his shoulder.

"Reese!"

I wrap my arms around his waist as he carries me into the reception hall. A mixture of cheers, laughs, and whistles greet us and I lift my head, smiling at everyone the best I can as my hair falls into my face. Once Reese stops walking, he slides me down the front of his body, depositing me on my feet. I look around and see we're in the middle of the dance floor, the crowd fanning out around us.

I smile up at him, watching as he lifts his gaze off my face and connects with something or someone over my shoulder. His lips part slightly, and a look of admiration washes over him as he studies whatever or whoever it is with deep concentration. I turn, looking through a gap in the crowd and instantly narrow in on what he's looking at.

Our cake.

He takes my hand, moving me with him across the dance floor. He holds a finger up to the DJ before we slip through the mass of people and step in front of the dessert table. He leans down and studies my creation with great interest as he tightens his grip on my hand.

"Do you like it?" I ask, expecting him to glance over at me. But he doesn't. He doesn't take his eyes off our cake.

"It looks like your dress," he says, moving around to the side and back to the front, making sure he takes it all in.

"And it's all mint chocolate. The icing. The filling. Pretty much the whole cake."

That makes him straighten up and turn to me. He brings our conjoined hands up to his mouth and kisses the back of mine. "The perfect union of flavors."

I nod, motioning with my head toward the center of the room. "Dance with me, handsome."

After he escorts me out into the middle of the dance floor, he wraps one arm around my waist, taking my hand and holding it against his chest. "'Look After You'" begins playing overhead and I smile up at him as we share our first dance, letting him lead me all around the floor. When we get close to the bridal party, I notice Joey standing as far away from Billy as possible. And I also notice Billy's anxious eyes and the fact that they are glued to his heated boyfriend. As the song comes to an end, I steal a kiss from Reese before we're instructed to take our seats at the bridal table.

I snap my fingers at Joey, gaining his attention once he sits two seats down from me. "What the hell is wrong with you?"

He leans back, seemingly insulted by my question. "Me? Nothing. I'm not the one acting like I want nothing to do with my boyfriend. I'm so sick of this shit."

I look over my shoulder at Billy who is seated at the opposite end of the table next to Ian. He seems to be lost in thought, fidgeting nervously with his napkin and tearing it into tiny pieces.

Shit. My mother better not see that. It'll be the cloth-napkin debacle all over again.

The sound of a woman's throat clearing overhead gets my attention and I turn back around, seeing Juls standing behind me and holding a microphone. She smiles at me before looking out over the crowd.

"Can I have everyone's attention for a moment, please?" The sound of shushing fills the room before the silence. "I don't think there's a person in this room who knows Dylan better than I do. Well, except for Joey." She places a hand on his shoulder and he smiles up at her. "We've been best friends for as long as I can remember, and I have seen every side of her. Her pissed-off, slap-happy side. Her tipsy, nickname-giving side. Even her focused, career-driven side. I've seen every emotion. Every personality trait. Except one." She focuses on me. "I've never seen my best friend in love. Not until she met Reese."

His hand squeezes mine and I look over at him, smiling before Juls continues.

"She fought it. She was scared, but there was no denying what that man did to her. Or what she did to him. And I loved watching it. I loved seeing them completely blissed out on each other. I also loved seeing them both lose their shit over the other person."

"Julianna," my mother scolds from her seat. She shakes her head disapprovingly, glaring at me like I'm the one who just used profanity.

Juls laughs into the microphone, and we all join in. "Sorry." She clears her throat, dropping all humor. "Anyway, I love you both very much and I couldn't be happier for you. To the bride and groom."

Everyone cheers as I stand and wrap Juls in a hug. She kisses Reese on the cheek as I take my seat again.

"And now, the Man of Honor has a few words," she says, handing the microphone over to Joey as he stands out of his seat.

"Actually, the Man of Honor isn't saying anything." He looks over at me as he walks off the platform. "I, uh, put together a little video instead. I hope that's okay, cupcake."

I nod, bracing myself for what I'm hoping isn't some slideshow of my awkward years. I was at a wedding once where the Maid of Honor did that to the bride. But I'm sure Joey knows better. I'm not afraid to use any of the utensils in front of me if a picture of me with braces pops up. And he knows that.

He steps in front of the DJ booth, leaning close and exchanging some words with the man. Everyone turns in their seats as the video is cued up, projecting on one of the walls. Soft music begins playing and I glance over at Reese who is watching intently, completely focused. And then I see a baffled expression set into his profile and look up at the wall, following his gaze.

Pictures of Joey and Billy begin filtering onto the wall. Selfie shots of the two of them together, and others of just Joey when he isn't looking at the camera. I glance over at the DJ booth and see the puzzled expression on my Man of Honor's face.

"Uh, this isn't… what the hell?" He turns around and begins talking to the DJ, motioning over his shoulder at the wall. "Where's the video I gave you? Where did you get this?"

I turn to look back at the strange collage when Billy begins walking off the platform and over toward Joey. I squeeze Reese's hand as tightly as I can, remembering Billy's words to me before my rehearsal last night. *"This is the grandest gesture I can think of."*

Oh, shit.

Billy steps up next to Joey and takes the microphone, moving into the center of the dance floor. Joey remains glued to his spot, mouth gaped open and eyes full of panic and curiosity.

Billy brings the microphone up to his mouth while his eyes scan the room. "Umm, so this obviously isn't the video Joey put together for Reese and Dylan. I watched him put that video together and it's really sweet, and I guess he kind of inspired me. I don't know. I'm not really good at this sort of thing. I'm really private, and I'm kind of freaking out right now." He rubs the back of his neck with his free hand before looking up at the wall. "Reese isn't the only guy who met the love of his life at a wedding. I did, too. But unlike Reese, I'm not the kind of guy who sends deliveries or writes his own wedding vows." He looks up at the platform, connecting with my husband. "Seriously. You kind of make us all look bad." He ignores the laughs he's just earned and turns around, focusing on Joey. "I know I've been a complete shit today, and I'm sorry. I've just been really nervous about this, but not because I'm not sure about what I want. I am. I'm very sure." He pauses in thought briefly before continuing. "I'm sorry I'm not the kind of guy who does these romantic, grand gestures like Reese. I might not ever be. But I am the kind of guy who will risk a major rejection in front of hundreds of people if you don't agree to marry me."

My free hand slaps over my mouth as I gasp, hearing Juls' dramatic reaction next to me. I glance down at movement on my lap and see Reese's other hand, holding out a bunch of tissues for the two of us.

I look at him. "Did you know about this?"

He simply smiles his response as Juls and I both take the tissues, readying them for use.

"Joey," Billy says, his voice much softer now but somehow steadier. "Can you come over here, please?"

Everyone's eyes are on my dear assistant as he falls apart, head down, shoulders shaking with his cries. I want to get up and console him, but I know these are happy tears. So I stay put next to my severely emotional, pregnant, best friend, and my husband who apparently knew about this all along.

Joey makes it to the center of the dance floor, slowly, but he gets there. And when he does, Billy drops to his knee in front of him. I'm a mess. Makeup be damned; there is no stopping my tears right now. Billy holds the microphone to his mouth, ready to ask the most important question of his life. Until suddenly, he brings it down and sets it next to him on the floor. He reaches into his jacket pocket and pulls out a ring box, holding it open for Joey as his lips begin to move. Juls and I lean in, wanting to hear Billy's words, until we both realize this moment is for the two of them. His words are only for Joey. And we must sense it at the same time because we both sit back together.

Billy's face breaks into the biggest smile I've ever seen him have before he stands up and grabs Joey's face, kissing him passionately in front of everyone. I stand, along with everyone else, and cheer for them at the top of my lungs. Once they break away from each other, which seriously takes a good several minutes, we all join them on the dance floor to congratulate them.

"Oh, my God! I'm so happy for you!" I scream, wrapping my arms around Joey. Juls does the same and when she pulls back, he holds his left hand out for us to see.

"Look how good my baby did!" he squeals. A platinum band with diamonds set into it adorns his finger, and we marvel over the beauty of it. "God, I'm so fucking happy right now. I'm engaged!"

"And now we can plan your bachelorette party. Naked men galore!" I yell, earning a curious expression from Ian who is congratulating Billy. Juls and Joey both laugh as the man who surprised us all walks over to us.

"Thank you for giving me that moment, Dylan. I can stop the slideshow and play your video now," Billy says into my hair as I hug him.

I lean back. "No. Leave yours on. It's the sweetest thing." I reach up and ruffle his hair. "I'm so excited for you."

"Holy shit! This wedding is insane," Brooke declares with her drink in her hand as she comes up to the group. She motions with her free hand toward the rest of the crowd that are all mingling and dancing. "Side note. There is zero play for me at this shindig. You all seriously need to find some more single friends." She winks before grabbing Joey and Billy, congratulating them. Juls and Ian begin dancing and I look around for my groom, only scanning half the room before I feel him behind me.

His lips press against my hair as his arms wrap around my waist. "I love you, Mrs. Carroll."

I spin around and link my fingers behind his neck. "I love you. Feel like taking a bathroom break? I've heard the amenities here are prime for fucking."

He shakes his head, laughing at me. I think he's going to respond with some filthy comment, but he kisses me instead. And when that happens, I no longer hear the hysterical excitement of our friends. I no longer hear the song playing overhead or the noises of the crowd around us. I'm purely focused on Reese and the way he kisses me.

The way my husband kisses me.

And nothing could pull me out of this moment with him. Not even a vacant men's bathroom.

⊘

"WHY ARE WE STOPPING AT the bakery?" I ask as the limo pulls in front of my shop and comes to a stop. Reese and I left The Whitmore underneath a cloud of bubbles before getting into our getaway vehicle. It was supposed to drive us straight to his condo. Or so I thought.

I don't get an answer from my groom before he opens the door and steps out, offering me his hand. I take it and exit the limo, looking up at him.

"Umm, did you not get enough of that cake? Is that why we're here? For treats? Because I thought I saw you eat, like, four pieces."

He opens the shop door, keeping my hand in his as he enters the alarm code. "That was the best cake I've ever had. And I meant what I said about you making that every year on our anniversary."

"Not to scale, I hope," I reply with a smile.

He pulls me through the back and toward the stairs. I stop him, firmly holding my place by the worktop.

"Wait. What are you doing?"

Did he completely forget that all of my stuff was moved out today?

He smiles sweetly. "Come upstairs with me."

I can feel the wrinkles setting into my skin as I put on my most baffled expression. Before I have time to ask any more questions, he steps into me, lifting me off the floor and cradling me in his arms. I hold onto his neck as he carries me up the stairs, swings the door open, and steps out into my old loft.

Because that's what it is.

What I'm looking at now is definitely not the loft I'm familiar with.

Some of my stuff is here, but it's been moved around. Blended with his. A perfect mix of his furniture and mine. The screen that separates the bedroom area from the living room space is now moved to the far corner of the room, separating a smaller area from everything else. The arrangement is different, making the space seem bigger somehow. My bed has been moved against the wall, leaving more room around it. After taking in my surroundings, I turn my head to meet his anxious eyes.

"I'm confused."

He smiles, setting me down on my feet and taking my hand in his. His other hand works at loosening his tie. "Why are you confused? This is your wedding present." He pulls me toward the bed and spins me around to face it while he stays at my back. I feel his fingers tug at the buttons on my dress. "Dylan, I don't need things. I don't need a big condo, or extra room, or all this shit I've accumulated over the years. This place is tiny, but we can make it work. I had the rest of our stuff put into storage until we figure out what to do with it."

"But what about when we have a baby? We agreed we'd be cramped in here."

His finger points over my shoulder, and I follow it to the decorative screen. "The baby can be right there. That way he's right next to us."

"He?" I ask, biting back my smile. I feel his fingers unsnap the clasp behind my neck holding my halter up and seconds later, my dress drops to the floor. Turning around, I watch his gaze slowly move up my body, taking in my wedding present to him. His chest rises with a deep inhale as his eyes seems to lose focus somewhere between my stomach and my neck. I let him look for a few more seconds before I coax an answer from him. "Reese?"

"Hmm?"

"You said 'he'. We're not having any daughters?"

With that question, his eyes quickly meet mine as he grabs my waist and tosses me onto the bed. He lowers himself onto me. Blanketing me. "I don't know if I can handle more than one of you. I'm shooting for all boys." I throw my head back and laugh as he straddles my waist. "Now, what the fuck am I supposed to do with this thing?"

I look down my body, seeing his hands physically tremble as they hover over my corset. "There's ties in the back that...ahh!" I'm quickly flipped over on my stomach as his knees brace him on either side of my body. I feel the strings being loosened as I rest my head on my cheek, looking out at our loft.

Our loft. No longer mine. Every memory I make here will now contain my husband and the family we create.

"Thank you for what you did. I really love my wedding present."

His lips press between my shoulder blades. Then lower, as my corset is loosened completely. Once my back is completely exposed, I'm flipped over so I can see him. He sits back on his knees between my legs, taking in the sight of me, and I see his chest shudder with his inhale. As if it's the first breath he's taken in hours.

"Are you okay?"

"It'll always be like this with you." His eyes hold mine with a gentleness I don't remember ever seeing from him. And I want to ask him what he means, but I wait, because I know he's going to give it to me. I see his throat roll with a swallow, his lips parting slightly as his eyes commit me to memory with the most profound look he's ever given me. "After 323 days, I should know the effect you have on me. But I don't. I'm never prepared for it. Every time I see you, it's like I'm at that wedding all over again."

The air leaves my lungs in a trembling rush, and I'm suddenly not concerned with breathing at all. Nothing gets to me like the words he chooses for me. And I know nothing ever will.

"How do you do that? How do you make me love you more than I ever dreamed possible?" I ask as the tears pool in my eyes. I reach my hand out, needing to feel him. Needing that constant contact now more than ever.

His hand touches mine and he laces our fingers together. "I should ask you that."

I blink, sending the tears down the side of my face. He releases my hand and grabs my foot, resting my heel against his chest. One shoe is removed then the other. I watch him run his fingers up the inside of my leg along my stocking until he reaches the metal clips of my garter. And after his declaration to me seconds ago, I think this is going to be gentle. I think his next moves with be unhurried and tender.

Until I see the tremor in his hand as he brings it up to rake through his hair.

He pushes off the bed and starts ripping his clothes off, not giving a shit about buttons or zippers. He's frantic, like a man deprived, watching me frozen on the bed.

Hungry.

Greedy.

He's normally so controlled, so calculated with everything he does. Especially sex. His movements are precise. Well-orchestrated. Practiced. And I love that side of him. But when he's chaotic like this, when he can't seem to settle himself enough to remove clothing properly, when he appears human, faulted like the rest of us, this is the side of Reese which drives me insane.

"I don't think I've ever needed to be inside you so badly before. I'm fucking shaking," he pants as he drags his rigid cock up my leg. He puts a hand on each of my thighs, digs his fingers into my skin, and shreds my stockings away from my body. My garter and panties are removed, tossed off the bed and disregarded like everything else that isn't him and me in this moment. His hands anchor into the skin of my hips as he lifts them off the mattress and, in the same motion, drives into me.

"Reese," I cry out, digging my nails into his shoulders.

He pushes my knees against my chest, lunging so hard into me my teeth chatter. "You're finally mine. I've waited so long for this."

I nod through a moan, closing my eyes and silently chanting. *Yes. Yes. Yes.*

His hands massage my breasts as his thrusts become frenzied. Fingers pinch my nipples and my eyes flash open when I feel the slide of his tongue over one hardened peak.

I thread my fingers into his hair, fisting it when he bites down. "Oh, God," I cry as he buries his face between my breasts.

"Say it, Dylan." He lifts his head, capturing my mouth and stealing the words from me. "Beg me like you do."

I don't hesitate. I never will. "Please, Reese," I say against his lips, hearing him react with a soft moan. "I need you. Please."

His arms brace himself on either side of me, flexed and fully extended as he begins thrusting forward in a slow, steady rhythm. We keep our eyes on each other, never breaking contact. He runs his hands over every inch of me. His lips follow. Then his tongue. He drags his cock on my skin each time he pulls out, the heaviness of it slicked with my desire for him. He gives me his words, sweet and filthy, as he moves in me. He's wild one minute and tender the next, sliding between my tits while he tells me how hot my tight, little pussy is and then whispering against my ear how he'll need me forever while he finger-fucks me. I'm clawing at his skin, wanting to somehow embed myself beneath his surface as he brings me to orgasm over and over, denying himself his own release to focus on me. He grinds into me from behind, his deft fingers rooting themselves into my hip bones as he bottoms out with punishing thrusts. My body breaks, bowing in submission as a wave of pleasure surges through me. He tastes the skin of my neck. My breasts. Between my legs. My fingers tangle in his mess of hair as my body arches off the bed into another rolling climax. I don't think I can take anymore as he crawls up my body, chin and lips wet, prowling over me like a lion.

I grab his face, making our foreheads touch as he slides his cock between my legs.

He enters me, brushes against my mouth with his, and says, "Mine."

"Yes."

"My wife." He lunges forward, then back.

"Yes." My response is softer, barely above a whisper, and I feel his body tense against mine. Ready to break.

"Dylan." My name escapes his lips the moment he loses all control. Sweat drips from his forehead to my chest before he collapses on top of me, sealing our bodies together.

And we stay like that, long after our breathing steadies.

Long after the dull ache of his hipbone against mine becomes familiar.

Reese gives me the contact we both need. The intimacy we both crave.

His life.

His love.

He gives me everything.

And I know he always will.

Epilogue

Reese

I CAN'T CONCENTRATE.

I haven't been able to concentrate for over a week.

I know I'm supposed to be contributing to this meeting, but all my attention is on the phone weighing down my pocket. And the conference room doors. Any second now, any fucking second I could get the call.

Papers shuffle. Ian's voice fills the room again, followed by collective murmurs. All distractions I need right now, but don't give in to. I can't. But it's been like this. I've been a walking zombie, present in the office but not functioning at the level I'm used to. Or that my colleagues are used to seeing from me.

It's pathetic, really. I haven't felt this unhinged since I first met Dylan.

I twist the band around my finger as my eyes lose focus.

I've been told this kind of anxiety is normal for this situation, but constant? Is it possible to have a coronary at thirty-three? The problem is I have zero control over this situation. None. And I need fucking control.

The conference door swings open, grabbing my attention immediately, and I'm on my feet before I even register who steps through because there are two things I know for sure right now.

Everyone who is supposed to be in this meeting is here.

And no one's stupid enough to barge into this room without

knocking first. Unless the reason behind the intrusion is too important for pleasantries, such as knocking.

Dave sees me walking straight at him. "Mr. Carroll, it's time. You need to go."

My hand is in my pocket, pulling out my phone. "Why didn't she call me?" But before he can answer my irritated question, I see the missed calls. One from the bakery number and one from Joey. "Fucking piece of shit phone." I look around at the stunned faces of my colleagues, giving them an apologetic nod.

Ian's at my back, hand halting me on my shoulder. He pulls me into a hug. "This is it, man. You ready?"

"Yeah. Yeah, I…" I stammer on my words, suddenly not feeling prepared for the moment I've been more than prepared for.

He slaps me on the back, ending our hug. "You're ready. You'll be fine."

I think I say goodbye to him, to Dave, to every person I pass in the hallway. It's all a blur of distractions. Fucking distractions I no longer want to be aware of. I go over what I'm supposed to do, replaying my role over and over again in my head. The classes, the books I've read, marking pages, highlighting shit that freaked me the fuck out. Internet searches and YouTube videos I ignored the warnings of.

"Don't watch those. It won't be like that," she said to me.

But I did. I watched them all. Trying to somehow retain enough knowledge of every possible scenario that could play out when the time came. Needing to know more information than the damn doctors who have studied this for years. I've smothered her with my overbearing, overprotective side that's way the hell surpassed anything she's ever seen from me. And anything I've ever felt. I will always be possessive over my wife, but the domineering drive which took over my body two hundred and eighty seven days ago is borderline psychotic. Luckily, she seemed to have been expecting my behavior.

I don't know where to go, so I stop at the information desk. The young woman looks up at me, expectantly waiting for me to speak with raised eyebrows. *Speak. Speak, asshole!*

"Dylan Carroll."

Her fingers press the keys like a fucking child would, one at a time. I close my hands into fists, clamping my eyes shut because I can't watch her do this to me right now. Twelve keys. That's all she needs to press. Twelve. *Come fucking on.*

"Take the elevators to the second floor. She's in room two fifteen."

I see the line of people waiting in front of the row of elevators. Too many people. I opt for the stairs, taking them two, three at a time and exploding onto the second floor.

Two fifteen. Two fifteen.

I push the door open, stepping into the room filled with people in turquoise-colored scrubs. Joey and Juls are standing on either side of the large hospital bed, each of them holding a delicate hand. My delicate hand. I think I hear the doctor say something to me but can't comprehend it as I step up and connect with who I'm here for.

Dylan lifts her eyes to me, those big brown eyes that dilate every time she sees me. Her hair is sticking to the side of her face, cheeks flushed bright red, and lips pursed as she squeezes her eyes shut and lets out a sound that has me shoving Joey nearly clear across the room to get to her.

"Jesus Christ, Reese!"

I give him the quickest once-over, making sure I haven't drawn blood, and then all my attention is on her.

I can concentrate on this.

"We'll be out in the waiting room. I'll let your parents know you're here," Juls says, letting go of Dylan's hand. I hear the door close and the movement of the nurses, but I don't look up.

I touch her cheek and she leans into it as the contraction lessens. When she rolls her head back onto the bed, I flatten my hand on her extended belly. "Can I do anything?" I ask, feeling the jabs against my palm I've become addicted to ever since I first felt them. Before she can answer, I press my lips to her hospital gown, just above my hand. "Don't hurt your Mommy."

She laughs but it's short-lived as her hands grip the rails of the bed. "Fuuuckkkking shit!" Her body arches, head thrown back as her belly begins to jerk against me.

"Mrs. Carroll, I need to check you," the doctor says, sliding his hand into a glove.

I know what that means and I can't watch him. Him. Why the fuck Dylan insisted on a male doctor is beyond me. The only reason why I agreed to it was because he's apparently the best in the state. But that doesn't ease the throbbing tension which sets into my body whenever he's examined her.

Especially now.

I brush her slick hair off her forehead as she moans in discomfort. Eyes clamped tight, face contorted in pain.

I hate this.

"You look so beautiful right now."

Her eyes flash open, and the magnitude of her stare and what it does to me is profound. I'd do crazy shit for that stare.

"Reese, shut up."

Especially when it's paired with that mouth.

"You do," I affirm, kissing her sticky forehead.

She frowns. "I'm massive, sweaty, and will seriously injure someone if I'm not told I can push in five seconds." Her eyes narrow in on the doctor between her legs. "Well?"

He reaches into a compartment on either side of the bed and removes two metal arms with brown straps on the end. "You're ready. Baby's head is down and in position. Put your feet in these and scoot all the way down."

I feel my body surge with panic as Dylan slides down the bed. Legs in the air, spread wide. Body flattened out on the bed. She grabs my shirt and tugs me down. "Hey, look at me."

I do. I can't not look at her. If Dylan is anywhere within my line of sight, she has my full attention. And for six hundred and sixteen days, my eyes have strained to stay on her because nothing else matters to me.

I hear her breathing quicken as she breaks our contact to look down her body. "When do I push?"

"As soon as you feel the next contraction. Push for ten full seconds, Dylan. Don't stop until you get to ten."

"Love, please, I…" I feel my legs shake underneath me. The strength in my body seems to evaporate as I lean over her. Everything I've read.

Every pamphlet, book, internet site. Every instruction from our labor and delivery coach, everything leaves me. My mind draws a blank as I stare down at my wife, looking up at me for support. For me to do my job. For help through this. "Fuck... what do I do?"

She grabs my hand and squeezes it as she takes in quick, short breaths. "You're doing it."

Everything clicks, and it's just her and I in that room. Doing this together.

Ten seconds. Come on, love. You're almost there. Push. Push. Good. Okay, take a breath. You're doing so well. I love you. I love you so much. Look at you. Look how amazing you're doing. Here comes another one. Don't stop, Dylan. Push. Six. Seven. Eight. Squeeze my hand. You want to meet our daughter. Come on, you're almost there.

"Arrggghhhhhhhh!"

Everyone has moments in their lives, which are superior to others. They become an obsession, your reason for living, and all my moments involve Dylan. The moment I saw her, standing at the end of my row next to Ian. Our wedding day, when she officially became mine. And now this.

She's so tiny in my arms. I've held babies before. My nieces and nephews. Even Juls' and Ian's son. But none of them seemed this delicate. I've counted her fingers and toes several times. I've memorized the feel of her skin and every detail of her face. She looks like Dylan, except her hair is darker and apparently resembles mine after I've run my hands through it, whatever the hell that means. She waited forty-one weeks to meet us, but she still seems so small. I've been told seven pounds is a very healthy weight, but that information isn't comforting me. I was a nervous wreck before she arrived and now, maybe I'm worse off.

"You're going to stress me out like your mother, aren't you?"

She coos against me, a reaction I've picked up on since I started whispering softly to her.

I never want to put her down. Ever. That crib I spent hours putting together weeks ago isn't going to be used any time soon. I hold her closer to me, running my nose along her cheek, when I feel a hand in my hair.

I look up and meet my wife's sleepy eyes. "Hi, handsome."

Standing from my chair, I carry our daughter over to her. "Do you want to hold her?" *Please, say no. Let me keep her for a few more hours.*

She shakes her head slowly. "She'll want me when she wakes up hungry." She slides away from me, patting the bed. "Come here."

I climb into bed, cradling Ryan against my chest. Dylan leans over and kisses the top of her head.

"Mmm. She might have you beat on smell." She reaches for the birth certificate on the tray next to her and grabs a pen. "I thought of a middle name."

I pull my eyes off the only other girl who commands my attention and look over at my wife. "Yeah?"

She looks at Ryan, then at me. "Love. Ryan Love Carroll. Whatcha think?"

I smile and her face lights up before she begins filling out the blank box on the birth certificate. We picked Ryan months ago, something I threw out as an idea. But we couldn't settle on a middle name. And Dylan refused to pass hers down.

She caps the pen and pushes the tray away, just as her phone beeps on her lap. Grabbing it, she looks at the screen before smiling over at me. "They want to meet her."

I pull Ryan away from my chest when she begins to stir. Her body goes rigid in my arms as her lips part with a yawn. I relax when she stills, looking over at Dylan. "Five more minutes?"

"You can't keep them out forever. Your mother is probably going crazy." She rolls onto her side and runs her hand over Ryan's head. "This hair," she says with snarky disapproval.

"She's perfect." I look up. "She's just like you. She's already hit me in the face twice with her tiny fists."

We both laugh as I shift onto my right hip, turning my body toward her and lying on my side. I hold Ryan between us as Dylan drapes her arm over my body.

"Do you have everything you want?" she asks through a yawn, her eyes struggling to stay open.

"Not yet."

My answer puzzles her. I smile at her confusion and lean in, pressing my lips against hers. "I want to do this again."

She leans back. "You know we have to wait six weeks before we do *anything* again, right?"

"What?"

She laughs, lying her head on her pillow. "No sex for six weeks, handsome. Doctor's orders."

I feel my jaw twitch as my hand pulls her hip so she's closer to me. She's never close enough. I could crawl inside her skin and bury myself there and I'd still need more.

"I'll be speaking to him about that."

Nobody gives me the go-ahead to touch my wife. I'm certain rules can be stretched. In fact, I think I read it somewhere. *As long as she's comfortable. Shit. What did that article say?*

"You're thinking very loudly over there."

Her voice cuts into my thoughts, bringing my attention back to her. I press my lips to Ryan's head, inhaling the second-best thing I've ever smelled. "Thank you for giving me this."

She smiles, closing her eyes and humming softly. My eyes drift from her face to the one who fiercely entered this world with a scream, which rivaled a damn war cry.

I do have everything I want. Everything I never imagined wanting, but now, I'd do anything for.

Dylan Sparks came into my life, grabbed onto me, and rooted herself so deep she practically became a part of my genetic makeup. She challenges me, she pushes every button I have, and she loves me more than I could ever deserve. I vowed to give her my entire life, but I didn't need to. She took it the moment she fell into my lap.

I'm a better man for knowing her.

A father because of her.

And I have everything I will ever need as long as I have her.

The End

Acknowledgements

SWEET JESUS! I DON'T EVEN know where to begin with these Thank yous. So many people have helped me on this journey. Family, friends, bloggers, authors, readers… the list is endless. But first and foremost, I'm going to start off by thanking my main man. The man I fell in love with when I was eighteen years old. The man I married a year later. And the one who will always be my favorite person in the entire world. I love you hard, Mr. Daniels, and I always will.

My beautiful bloggers!!! Oh, I just want to squeeze every single one of you. My girls over at Give Me Books, thank you so much for all you have done for me. Kylie McDermott, I'm tackling you in Vegas. You've been warned. Thank you to A Book Whore's Obsession, BestSellers & BestStellars, Dirty Girl Romance, Romance Room, Blushing Reader Michelle, and all the other blogs I know I'm forgetting for helping me reach more readers.

To my lovely betas! Beth Cranford, Erin Thompson, Lisa Jayne and Heather Peiffer. You girls rock! Thank you for reading Sweet Possession when it still had massive typos and strange word usages. You made it better. You make me better. And I heart all four of you.

And, lastly, to my readers. Thank you all so much for waiting for this story. Reese and Dylan will always be my favorite couple, and it makes me so happy to see your enthusiasm over them, not to mention all the Juls, Ian, Joey, Billy, and Brooke love. You all have embraced them and me, and I can't thank you enough for that. Goddamn it, Billy.

Thank you all again,

J

Books by
J DANIELS

SWEET ADDICTION SERIES
Sweet Addiction

Sweet Possession

Sweet Obsession

Sweet Love (Coming Soon)

ALABAMA SUMMER SERIES
Where I Belong

All I Want

When I Fall

Where We Belong

What I Need

So Much More (Halloween Novella)

All We Want

Say I'm Yours (Coming Soon)

DIRTY DEEDS SERIES
Four Letter Word

Hit the Spot

Bad for You

Down too Deep (Coming Soon)

About the Author

J DANIELS IS THE NEW YORK Times and USA Today Bestselling author of the Sweet Addiction series and the Alabama Summer series.

She loves curling up with a good book, drinking a ridiculous amount of coffee, and writing stories her children will never read. J grew up in Baltimore and resides in Maryland with her family.

www.authorjdaniels.com

Facebook
www.facebook.com/jdanielsauthor

Twitter
@JDanielsbooks

Instagram
authorjdaniels

Lightning Source UK Ltd.
Milton Keynes UK
UKHW011846270621
386250UK00001B/189